"Perhaps now that you have captivated the famous Lord Byron, Mr. Canby's irritation will be soothed."

"Well, you need not sound as if I had set a trap for him," Susan protested. "We merely had a talk—about books!"

"I should dearly like to have been a fly on the library wall," Lord Everly said meditatively.

"Should you? It was not very interesting. Indeed, I cannot understand what was said that would make him take so much trouble on my behalf, when he has many other friends in London."

Lord Everly gave a cynical little laugh. "Can you not? It's the hunter's instincts, my dear. The prey that shows no interest is the one you must have!"

Susan choked. "Surely you don't think that I—"

"I do not care whether you did it on purpose or not. My sister will tell you that the results of your little flirtation will have set you on the path to success, although I daresay it may get you more attention than you bargained for!"

In fact, Susan *was* getting more than she bargained for—not just the attentions of the infamous Lord Byron but the knowledge that she was falling in love with a rake who would gladly give her his name but not his heart . . .

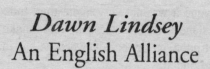

ROGUE'S DELIGHT

by

Elizabeth Jackson

A SIGNET BOOK

SIGNET
Published by the Penguin Group
Penguin Books USA Inc., 375 Hudson Street,
New York, New York 10014, U.S.A.
Penguin Books Ltd, 27 Wrights Lane,
London W8 5TZ, England
Penguin Books Australia Ltd, Ringwood,
Victoria, Australia
Penguin Books Canada Ltd, 10 Alcorn Avenue,
Toronto, Ontario, Canada M4V 3B2
Penguin Books (N.Z.) Ltd, 182–190 Wairau Road,
Auckland 10, New Zealand

Penguin Books Ltd, Registered Offices:
Harmondsworth, Middlesex, England

First published by Signet, an imprint of Dutton Signet,
a division of Penguin Books USA Inc.

First Printing, July, 1995
10 9 8 7 6 5 4 3 2 1

Ⓓ REGISTERED TRADEMARK—MARCA REGISTRADA

Printed in the United States of America

I want a hero: an uncommon want,
When every year and month sets forth a new one.
Till, after cloying the gazettes with cant,
The age discovers he is not the true one.

— George Gordon, Lord Byron
Don Juan, Canto I

Chapter 1

The monstrous accommodation coach lurched and dipped its way along the rutted roads, tumbling the unlucky passengers confined within its capacious maw like so many pieces of gravel in a streambed. As at least one of the passengers was rather large, and another was of a disposition that could not be called happy, such enforced contact could only be declared uncomfortable by even the most determined optimist.

The youngest among them, Miss Susan Winston, though generally of a cheerful turn of mind, was resigned to a journey of appalling discomfort at the very best, the tedium broken only by the random discourse of Miss Pennyfeather, her companion, whose conversation contained rather more volubility than content. That there might be danger as well she discounted; traveling in France was perfectly safe, she had heard, so long as one claimed to be an American (however treasonable that claim might be at present) if stopped by the authorities or an errant band of the Emperor's troops. She had not met many Americans, but she imagined that they were rather less strict in their manners than the English, and she was sure she could imitate one if the need arose. In fact, it would be far easier than imitating an English girl of birth and breeding, which in truth she was. Her many years on the Continent traveling from one military posting to another in her father's wake, with only Penny's stories for guidance, had, it must be admitted, given her a rather less confined and more unconventional upbringing than most.

The thought of her father caused her heart to constrict suddenly, and she drew in a sharp breath. It had been over a year since General John Winston's death, and his frequent absences had made him more of a stranger than either of them would have preferred, but she still missed him dreadfully. The past year had been spent in the spirited company of the colonel and his wife and four children, and she had repaid their many kindnesses to her by acting as a sort of honorary older sister to their lively brood, but she was lately turned eighteen and must now make her own way in the world. Unfortunately, her father's generosity to others had often exceeded his means, and his untimely demise had left her only just provided for. When she received an offer from her Great Aunt Harrington (written by her ladyship's son William, as she was, he said, temporarily too indisposed to write herself) offering her a home and shelter in return for the light duties of a companion, she had overborn the colonel's objections and insisted on setting forth at once.

Despite her youth, the probable disadvantages of her prospective situation had already occurred to her, but she was determined not to be downhearted. She was the daughter of a soldier, and a famous hero at that, and she would do what she had to do without complaint. She caught Penny looking at her with concern, the certain prelude to a loquacious outbreak of sympathy, and smiled and shook her head. Just then the coach gave another hideous lurch, and the large man seated next to her dropped apologetically onto her reticule and slid sideways onto a covered object wedged into a corner under her feet. The object, which hitherto had not spoken, responded with a series of noises not usually generated by inanimate parcels, an event which caused the fat man's rather disagreeable spouse to regard it, like so much else, with frank suspicion.

"Miss—er, Miss—" began that personage in an aggrieved tone.

"Hush, my dear," said the fat man, and leaned over to whisper something into his wife's ear.

His words, whatever they might have been, did not appear to mollify her. "Well, I cannot see what that may signify," she said, addressing one and all in apparent appeal. "For my mother was related to the Whitelaws, and though the kinship was rather remote, I hope I may claim to be as much a member of the Quality as the next person and need not fear to speak my mind to *anyone.*" As she spoke she looked meaningfully at the young lady, who unfortunately was not attending. "What—"

"Perhaps we should introduce ourselves, since the journey is such a long one," said the fat man quickly, in an attempt to hold off his determined spouse. "I am Oswald Lorry, and this good lady is my wife. I am a wine merchant," he added with satisfaction.

A rather prim man seated at the window opposite, who had

every appearance of being a clerk of some sort, sniffed audibly and said nothing.

Mrs. Lorry, a woman of forceful and decisive character, would not easily be diverted. "What I should like to know," she continued accusingly, "is *whether there is an animal of some sort in that basket.* Excuse me, miss," she added with exasperation, when her inquiry did not receive an immediate reply, "I am addressing you. Miss—, Miss—"

"Miss Winston," replied the young lady calmly, roused from her reverie of far happier times. "I am sorry. What did you ask me?"

The frank and artless gaze of two very lovely gray eyes only momentarily checked her inquisitor, who drew herself up in preparation for imparting the superior wisdom she was quite sure she possessed. "I wish to know," she articulated in frigid accents, "what is in the basket on the floor."

"That basket?" inquired Miss Winston with a pang of dread.

Miss Pennyfeather, who had awakened from a rather stentorian nap first to find her beloved Miss Susan not only in low spirits but under apparent attack, had had quite enough. "I am quite sure," she said blightingly, "that it is no one's business what may be in anyone else's *personal* effects."

"My good woman," said the other, sizing her up at once as a governess or, at best, a poor relation and therefore fair game, "surely you will admit that if someone has admitted *vermin* or something of a dangerous nature to the interior of this compartment, we have every right to be concerned. If there is some such thing in that basket, I demand that it be put out *at once.*"

"It seems to me," replied Miss Pennyfeather, her thin bosom heaving with indignation, "that those who take it upon themselves to go poking into what clearly does not concern them—"

"It's all right, Penny," said Miss Winston in a clear voice. "Naturally, I did not wish to speak of it before, but I am quite certain I can trust everyone her with the secret," she said confidingly.

Miss Pennyfeather crossed her arms and attempted to give her companion a quelling look, but she was not heeded. Miss Susan Winston had not been her father's daughter for more than sixteen years without learning the value of a strategic offense.

Mr. Lorry said jovially that he hoped she might trust them all, and as for himself, he added with a wink, he might carry discretion to the grave. The clerk looked sour but nonetheless nodded his assent.

"Well?" demanded Mrs. Lorry.

Miss Winston lowered her voice. "The French must not hear of it," she began. She touched the cover of the basket with a trim little foot. "It is a . . . a . . . Malaga eagle," she said in tones of grave seriousness, which caused Miss Pennyfeather to moan a little and cover her eyes with one bony hand. "It is quite rare. It is a symbol of . . . of the monarchy in Spain, and Napoleon has vowed to exterminate every one he can find. My father gave it to me," she added, for once with perfect truth, "and I hope to take it to safety in England."

The clerkish-looking man regarded her through narrowed eyes. "*I* have spent a considerable time in Spain," he said, "and I have never heard of any such symbol, or animal."

"I did say it was quite rare," Susan assured him, "and of course, the Royal Society of Malaga Eagles is rather select."

The clerk, who did not know quite how to interpret this, muttered that in that case he would certainly like a look at it.

"Just so," added Mrs. Lorry, with a skeptical tone that made Miss Pennyfeather bristle, despite the promptings of her conscience.

"Certainly," said Miss Winston mildly, and made to bend over the basket. "Are your gloves of a heavy material?"

"Naturally they are not," retorted Mrs. Lorry in an outraged voice.

"Then I should nevertheless advise you to put your hands in front of your face," said Susan earnestly, "just in case, you understand. There is the matter of the talons . . . "

"Talons?"

"Oh yes, and the beak, too. They are very great hunters, you know, and one can never be sure what they will consider prey. I have tried to train him not to attack so readily, but he is rather moody, you see," she added with apparent regret. She removed the cloth from the basket, and it began to rock slowly from side to side.

Mrs. Lorry remarked hastily that after all she felt sure that one of the Whitelaws had had a Malaga eagle as a pet long before they were in fashion in Spain, and she quite remembered now that it was a hideous brute. She yawned ostentatiously. "In that case, you know, there is no need for me to see it. I'm afraid I'm beginning to find the subject a bit tedious. In fact," she added querulously, "this entire journey is becoming tedious. I wonder how long it will take to reach Bordeaux?"

"Some hours yet," replied her husband, grateful to turn the subject. "And that is the best possible case. If we are stopped . . . "

"*Pray* do not suggest such a thing," said his wife with a visible shudder. "For I do not know what I shall do if we are questioned. My nerves are quite unequal to such an event, I assure you."

"My dear," replied Mr. Lorry patiently, "we have rehearsed this, you know. And in any event, I do not believe anyone will think we are spies or clap us in prison. We have only to say that this was the only possible route to catching our ship, which is no more than the truth after all."

"It is perfectly natural that you should disregard my feelings, as you have done so on more than one occasion," said she. "However, some of these wandering soldiers are said to be *animals*, and you cannot convince me that no mishap will befall us should we chance to encounter any of *them*."

An audible sign escaped Miss Pennyfeather's lips and she gathered her shawl more tightly around her shoulders. The clerk looked out the window, drumming his fingers in time on his knee. Miss Susan Winston found herself unaccountably alert and restless.

"Well, I am quite sure there is nothing to worry about," said Mr. Lorry in a rather faltering tone. "Ten to one we shall not be stopped at all until we reach the port."

Mr. Lorry's abilities as a seer, however, were shortly to be called into question. Before the coach had lumbered its way down too many more tedious miles there was a shout, and the sound of pounding hooves, and the vehicle came to a sudden stop. As this was naturally not accomplished without a great deal of lurching and skidding, it was some moments before any of the passengers were collected enough to inquire what was happening.

The coach had stopped short of a small crossroad, and after craning his neck cautiously out the window, the clerk announced in rather breathless accents that the way appeared to be blocked by a very large figure on a horse.

Mrs. Lorry shoved her reticule under her voluminous skirts. "A soldier! What did I tell you?"

Susan found Miss Pennyfeather's hand clutching hers in a death grip.

"Let's not be hasty," said Mr. Lorry quietly. "Stay calm, everyone."

The driver, who was Spanish, could be heard arguing volubly with the stranger.

"We shall all be killed," moaned Miss Pennyfeather, momentarily losing control.

"Or worse," muttered Mrs. Lorry darkly.

"My dear," said Mr. Lorry, giving his wife's hand a reassuring squeeze, "let us but consider that if the stranger meant us violence he would surely not be *arguing* with the driver. That is to say—"

"Oh, do be quiet, Oswald," said his beloved. "Why do you not get down and see what is the matter?"

Mr. Lorry gave a little choke. "I do not think . . . " He cleared his throat. "I have my pistol at the ready, if need be. I am sure that I can best protect you from inside the coach."

"You are quite right," said Mrs. Lorry with majestic condescension. She cast a scornful eye on the clerk. "It is for *him* to go."

The clerk turned to her with a look of positive dislike, but before he could utter an acid rejoinder the door was thrust open, and a voice said in perfect English: "I beg you will forgive this interruption, but I'm afraid I must ask your assistance."

The speaker was a tall gentleman of about five-and-thirty, well dressed in a voluminous cloak, but rather harried-looking.

Mr. Lorry, recovering his aplomb, said stiffly, "What is the matter?"

The stranger lowered his voice. "The coachman tells me that you are . . . Americans, traveling to Bordeaux. I must beg you to take on my friend as a passenger. He is ill, and it is of the utmost importance that he return to England at once. There is a ship leaving Bordeaux at midnight. If you will but see him to the port, someone will meet him there."

"Ill?" inquired Mrs. Lorry with a sniff.

"Madam, I assure you with all my heart that it is not catching."

"But," suggested Mr. Lorry helpfully, "should he not see a doctor first?"

The stranger ran a hand through his hair. "Sir, I am sure I do not have to tell you that there is some danger. Like you, it is not altogether *comfortable* for him to stay in France."

"But a *doctor* would not . . . "

"I can only repeat that he must sail for England at once."

"I'm afraid I do not see . . ."

"Sir, if you will not help my friend, he may die. Someone must see that he catches the ship."

"Then why don't you do it?" asked the clerk, not unreasonably.

"I am not at liberty to explain," replied the stranger miserably.

"Of *course* we will take him," interjected Susan suddenly. "My friend and I are taking that ship ourselves, and we will see that he gets on it."

The others looked at her with varying degrees of surprise and dismay. "Well!" harrumphed Mrs. Lorry when she had recovered her poise. "You are but a child, and a fanciful one at that. *You* can have no notion of what is involved in nursing a sick person. Besides, it would not be proper."

"Fiddlesticks!" said Miss Pennyfeather, unexpectedly entering the lists. "I don't know of a better nurse than Miss Susan. She tended her father often enough. If Miss Susan says we take him, then we do. Besides *I* shall be here, and that is proper enough for anyone."

Susan smiled at her gratefully and turned to the stranger. "You must bring your friend then, as quickly as possible. We will only attract attention if we stand here much longer."

The man snatched up her hand and kissed it. "A very brave child," he murmured. "I thank you."

"Well I never!" began Mrs. Lorry when he had turned away. "The presumption of it, to speak for us all."

"I am sure I beg your pardon, ma'am," said Susan unrepentantly, "but was it not our duty to help?"

"Hoity-toity! I shall not wonder at it if we are all murdered unawares."

"Unawares?" asked Susan innocently. "Only the first, perhaps. After that . . ."

"You are impertinent, miss," said Mrs. Lorry with stern disapproval. "Well, I wash my hands of it. *I* am setting sail on that ship, and I am sure I am a more appropriate person to take charge of the sickroom than a miss barely out of the schoolroom. However, it is no matter. Oswald, you are my witness. I wash my hands of it."

Miss Pennyfeather looked at her with reproach, and Susan inwardly cursed her unbridled tongue for making a confirmed enemy of Mrs. Lorry when later she might have good cause to value her help. "Beg pardon, ma'am," she said meekly, but her apology went unheard in the distraction caused by the arrival of the stranger's friend.

The new passenger looked far more than ill. In fact, he was scarcely conscious, and his pallor, in contrast to his tousled black hair, gave him the appearance of one who might, as her father's batman used to say in unguarded moments, stick his spoon in the wall at any moment. When his friend had settled him stiffly on the seat he managed to open his eyes and murmur "Thank you," before he relapsed into a dreamlike state again.

"And just what," demanded the formidable Mrs. Lorry in a somewhat ominous tone, "are we to do with him if he does not survive until Bordeaux?"

"Hush, my love,' said her husband in a whisper. "He will hear you! Surely there is no question of such a thing."

"He is quite unconscious," she replied with admirable—if inaccurate—certainty. "I would not be surprised if he does not last the night. And if he does not, I repeat: *what* are we to do with him, pray tell? Moreover, before I travel another step with him in this coach, I demand to be informed of the exact nature of his illness."

She turned an inquiring look toward the stranger, but her gaze fell upon empty space. "Now where has that man got to?"

"There," said the clerk somewhat enviously, pointing out the window to where the stranger, mounted, was wheeling his horse to ride away. "He's loping off!"

"Well!" ejaculated Mrs. Lorry, outflanked. "This *is* infamous! His friend may have typhus or some such thing, and we will all be carried off in our sickbeds. And *then*, miss," she added, rounding on Susan, "I hope you will be satisfied with what your misdirected charity has led to."

"If you please, ma'am," said Susan, who had been observing the way the new passenger was holding his arm, even in his semiconscious state, "I think you will find that he is not ill, but wounded."

Mr. Lorry leaned over to make an inspection just as the coach lurched forward again, and almost toppled onto the new passenger, who moaned a little in his delirium. "Egad. Bless me if it don't look as though you are right, my child. Shot, I believe. You can see the bandages under his shirt. Now, we can only wonder how it happened. I must say, he does not look like a highwayman, nor did his friend."

"You are too trusting, Oswald. I have always said so. I will admit that he is dressed as a gentleman," she said with reluctant approval, "but what is that to anything? This is *France!*"

In the face of this irrefutable argument, Mr. Lorry could only concede defeat. "Perhaps we should examine his documents," he said apologetically to the clerk, to whom these items had been entrusted.

The clerk shrugged. "You may do so if you wish, but they are doubtless forgeries. I have some experience in these matters, from my employment as secretary to Lord Foppington," he said with a superior glance at Mrs. Lorry, "and it is my opinion that the gentleman has been wounded in a duel."

"A duel!" sighed Miss Pennyfeather wistfully.

"I believe that is the most logical explanation. He is clearly a gentleman, and as he is not a soldier and very likely *not* a highwayman"—he raised a haughty eyebrow at Mrs. Lorry, who sniffed in return—"I think that may answer. In all events, his papers identify him as Mr. Desmond Smith, if that is what you wished to know. Though I should stake my reputation that that is no more his name than what is in that basket is a Malaga eagle."

"A duel," interposed Mr. Lorry hastily. "I daresay you may be right. I don't hold with it much myself—it seems like a lot of foolishness over nothing—but the gentry do seem to go in for it."

"Like as not he has been trifling with the affections of some silly female," observed Mrs. Lorry censoriously, "and got what he deserved."

Susan, who had a wide acquaintance with diplomats and military men but almost none at all with duelists, looked thoughtful but held her tongue. Mrs. Lorry having had, on this occasion as on so many others, the last word, the passengers rode along in somnolent acceptance of the status quo for a number of miles.

It was growing dark, and some among the company were feeling the need of refreshment, though it had been agreed at the outset that they could not risk stopping at an inn for any longer than was required to change the horses. Mr. Lorry, who had been coming to the Continent to purchase wine for his business for long enough to have sustained a great fondness for French cuisine, whatever his wife might say about its deleterious effects on the digestion, could only lament that the current state of affairs between England and France must make such caution necessary.

In all events, they had been forewarned, and all except Mr. Smith, who did not appear to be in a position to relish any sustenance, had come provided with baskets of provisions. These were brought out now, and Mr. Lorry handsomely offered to share around a bit of meat pie and a bottle of that wine which, with any luck, would soon be stocking the cellars of his most valued clients. The ladies refused, but the clerk, rendered more affable by the sight of an excellent claret, accepted with reasonable grace. These satisfactory rituals apparently occupied the entire company to such an extent that they did not comment when Miss Winston opened her packet, removed a napkin rolled about what appeared to be a bit of raw meat, and stealthily placed the contents into the basket with the Malaga eagle. This creature, still generally unseen, was becoming restive, and she had now and then to place her foot on top of its basket to keep it from toppling over.

The potential antics of the Malaga eagle were momentarily eclipsed by another ominous shout in the darkness, however, followed by the all-too-familiar attempts of the coach to come to a precipitous stop. The clerk, whose pride had been injured by the aspersions Mrs. Lorry had cast on his bravery, leaned out the window with alacrity, and just as quickly drew in his head again. "Soldiers," he said in an intense whisper.

The coach's occupants were suspended in a frozen silence, scarcely daring to breathe.

"What do they want?" asked Mrs. Lorry, whose accomplishments did not number a familiarity with any language but her own.

"I cannot tell. I'm not quite sure . . . " began the clerk, straining to catch the words.

"They are looking for a wounded man," said Susan, whose French and hearing were superior to those of her fellow passengers. "We must act quickly! Please, Mr. Lorry," she said, in a low, urgent tone, "will you pass me that bottle of wine?"

"Well!" hissed Mrs. Lorry. "If they are looking for *Mr. Smith* I believe we should not hesitate to give him up. For my part, I find I am heartily sick of his presence. And I *really* do not believe that young ladies scarcely out of the schoolroom should be drinking wine on such an occasion, whatever the provocation may be. It seems altogether unfitting, whatever *some* persons may have to say about it."

"Was that meant for *me*?" inquired Miss Pennyfeather, momentarily forgetting her fear of French soldiers in the face of Mrs. Lorry's odious hints. "I scarcely think—"

"*Will* you pass me the bottle," interrupted Susan through gritted teeth. "It is not for *me*, I promise you!"

Mr. Lorry passed her the wine without comment, despite an audible sigh of disgust from his esteemed spouse. Susan grasped the bottle firmly and proceeded to pour some of the fine claret down Mr. Smith's shirt front. Then she emptied the remainder into a glass, which she eased up to the wounded man's lips. "Please," she implored, "try to sip a little if you can."

Mr. Smith had apparently retained enough of his senses to attempt to obey her instructions, and she was able to get a little of the wine down his throat.

"Miss Winston," said Mrs. Lorry with frigid disapproval, "I'll have you know that that wine you have just spilled down the front of a *perfect stranger* cost a pretty penny."

"Be quiet, Aurelia," said her husband with sudden authority. "I see what the young lady is about. Leave her alone!"

"*Really,* Oswald, this is the outside of enough! I—"

Her fellow passengers never got to hear what form Mrs. Lorry's protestations would eventually take, because at that moment this enlightening discourse was interrupted by the silkiest request, delivered in quite passable English, that they surrender their travel documents at once. The clerk, seated on the side of the coach next to the French officer—who stood erect and formidable on the coach's step—passed him these objects without comment. As it was very dark, he could only study them with some difficulty in the torchlight, and at length he said, "Messieurs, mesdames, and—" he glanced admiringly at Susan—"mademoiselle, I regret that I must interrupt your journey to inquire whether you have taken on any passengers in the last few miles. We are looking for a man who may be wounded and dangerous, and it will go very ill for anyone who renders him any aid." There was a pause, while his eyes swept the passengers one by one.

They came to rest, not unnaturally, on Mr. Smith, who was reclining back against the cushions with his eyes closed. He thumbed through the papers in his hands and looked up again. "Who is that man?" he demanded.

"He is—" began Mrs. Lorry, oblivious to a pinch from her husband.

"He is my brother," said Susan quickly.

"Son nom? Ah, pardon! His name?"

"Desmond Smith," she replied, praying that she had got it right.

"What is the matter with him? Is he ill?"

Susan looked down into her lap.

Mr. Lorry leaned over to the Frenchman and said confidentially, "You can see what the trouble is. He hasn't been off the bottle since we boarded the coach. No need to distress his sister further," he muttered.

"Je regrette, mademoiselle, but I must inquire—you are saying the gentleman is—how do you say it?—drunk?"

Susan lifted wide eyes to the officer's face. "Mama would have it that his constitution is very delicate, so that he cannot tolerate spirits of any sort, though he *would* drink wine for medicinal purposes, or at least that is what he said," she added thoughtfully.

The soldier gave another glance at the prostrate passenger. "Mademoiselle, your defense is more suited to a boy than to a man who must be—if I judge correctly—more than thirty years old."

"Well, but Papa always said he *acts* like a boy, when one considers the gambling, and the wild sprees, and"—she lowered her voice—"the women."

Beside her Miss Pennyfeather gave a little gasp and Mrs. Lorry snorted audibly. Susan stole a glance at her "brother" and thought she saw, just for a moment, the gleam of his eye from beneath his lid. A moment later she was sure she had imagined it. "I'm afraid," she added in a tone of maidenly regret, "that he has turned out rather badly, like our Uncle Lucius. They say he—"

"Very well, mademoiselle," interrupted the soldier with a touch of impatience. He consulted his papers again. "Your name is also Smith?"

Susan consulted her lap again. "No."

He leaned farther into the coach, peering at her. "Yet you say he is your brother?"

Susan nodded. "I did say so."

"Really, sir," interjected Mr. Lorry, attempting a rescue, "it is not at all uncommon. Perhaps her mother married again, and he is her half-brother."

The officer eyed him narrowly. "And you, sir, do you vouch for this man?"

Mr. Lorry sank back against the cushions. "How can I?" he muttered. "I never laid eyes on him before today."

This information seemed to provide the officer some satisfaction. "In that case, I must—" His eye was caught by the basket, which had begun its rocking motion again. "To whom does that basket belong?" he demanded.

There was silence in the coach.

"Is it yours?" he inquired of Mr. Lorry.

"It is *hers*," replied Mrs. Lorry, pointing at Susan in a manner brooking no misinterpretation, and ignoring the blackest of looks from Miss Pennyfeather.

"Yes, it's mine," said Susan calmly. "Do you wish me to open it?"

"No, mademoiselle," said the officer triumphantly, "I wish your brother to tell me what is inside!"

Susan frowned. "I doubt very much whether he could tell you his name at this moment."

"Nevertheless, he must try." He reached over and prodded the apparently insensate Mr. Smith on the arm. Susan had to will herself not to wince. "You, sir! Wake up now. Tell me what is in your sister's basket."

Mr. Smith barely opened his heavily lidded eyes and gazed at his questioner with disapproval. "Foxed," he said distinctly, and closed them again.

"*Renard?*" questioned the Frenchman in disbelief. "Does he say there is a fox inside?"

"Vermin!" huffed Mrs. Lorry. "I knew it."

"Aurelia, *will you be silent*!" thundered Mr. Lorry, surprising himself and the others.

The officer gave him a brief nod of approval. "Now then, let us see whether it is indeed a fox in the basket."

"Not fox, foxed," corrected Mr. Smith, rousing himself to make this correction. "Told you already."

Despite her anxiety, Susan could barely suppress a giggle. "I believe, sir, that it is an expression gentlemen use to indicate that they have had too much to drink," she said innocently.

The officer turned to the clerk. "This is true?"

"In some circles," said that person sourly.

"Going to shoot the cat," added Mr. Smith helpfully.

"Good God!" cried Mr. Lorry.

The officer, on whom this conversation was beginning to have a discernibly negative effect, wiped his brow on his sleeve. "Is it that, then? And why would he wish to shoot the cat of mademoiselle?"

Mr. Smith hiccupped, and the clerk edged away from him toward the door. "Blast it, man," said Mr. Lorry, "this is no time to be sick." He turned plaintively toward the officer and spoke very slowly. "The gentleman says he is going to throw up."

"He must not do that," cried the Frenchman in a last-ditch attempt to marshal his authority, "until he has told me what is in that basket!" He looked as if he might burst into tears at any moment.

Mr. Smith opened his eyes again. He smiled at the officer in a friendly way. "I have the greatest dislike of being told what to do," he said conversationally.

"And I have the greatest dislike of elbow crookers!" cried Susan in a distressed voice. "Oh . . . Desmond, how could you be . . . *disguised* at a time like this?"

"Quite easily," said Mr. Smith, smiling again.

"Disguised?" inquired the Frenchman.

"Foxed," instructed Mr. Smith, who seemed to have taken over the role of translator momentarily. "And I shall be worse than that if this vehicle does not start moving soon," he added with the over-careful enunciation of one very far gone in his cups. He patted Susan's hand clumsily. "Sorry, my dear. Hate to disappoint you. Didn't want to turn out like Uncle Lucius, but there it is."

"I am waiting," said the officer, who seemed to have been forgotten during this conversation, "for mademoiselle's brother—*if* he is her brother—to prove his identity by telling me what I have asked. I am losing patience," he added unnecessarily. "And if I do not receive a satisfactory answer *at once*, I shall require that you all accompany me to appear before the *commandant*!"

The threat of this august personage appeared to exert a powerful influence over the officer, if not his opponent, who said in a bored voice, "Oh, bother the man's obsession with that ridiculous basket." He closed his eyes again and said languidly, "I fear you will find that it is a common screech owl."

Susan started, but Mrs. Lorry, whose anxiety had reached a fever pitch during these proceedings, lost control all together. "No it is not! It is a—a *Mallorca beagle*, and she is trying to spirit it out of the country, and this is *all her fault!*"

The passengers observed a shocked silence in the face of

this treachery, but the officer, who had suffered enough at the hands of these insolent foreigners, turned red in the face. "*Un chien?* So it is a dog now?" He turned a leering countenance to Mr. Smith. "And just what do you have to say to that, monsieur?"

Mr. Smith remained upright in a stiff posture that might have conveyed a quelling hauteur if only he had succeeded in not slurring his words. "I have already told you that it is an animal of the feathered race," he insisted.

"Perhaps you feel you can make a fool of me," said the Frenchman, confident that he had unmasked something amiss through the cleverness of his interrogation. "Well, we will have the basket here, and we will open it to find the little lap dog, yes? And then we will see who is the fool after all!"

He took the basket confidently and lifted its lid, peering into the interior.

Two baleful yellow eyes glared back at him.

"Who?" inquired the owl. "Who?"

Chapter 2

Miss Winston was unable to satisfy her curiosity immediately as to how Mr. Smith had correctly divined the contents of her basket, but she was grateful to discover that the French officer was a man of his word. Indeed he seemed as eager to be rid of the coach and its passengers as they were to resume their journey, and if his look condemned them all to perdition and his words were not perfectly civil, at least he had fulfilled his obligation as an officer and a gentleman. However, it was some minutes after he had finally waved them on their way before anyone spoke. Those who had become, against their will, rather better acquainted with Mrs. Lorry than they might have wished could only hope that the status quo might continue for some time, but they could not depend overmuch on the influence of a guilty conscience in shaming her into silence for very long.

In fact, it was the wounded passenger, to every appearance seriously drained by the ordeal of his interrogation, who spoke first. He roused himself to say in a voice that was very weak but in no way affected by drink: "My thanks, child! That was quite a performance."

Susan looked up to find his dark eyes shadowed with pain but nonetheless filled with amusement. "You are welcome, sir," she told him, "though I think that *your* performance was a great deal better than mine. But how did you—"

Mrs. Lorry, too long excluded from a conversation that did not acknowledge her, chose this moment to interrupt with the comment that was foremost in her mind. *"That man,"* she said with a loathing hitherto reserved for her rival for preeminence in the small circle of families with which they dined, "said that you were *dangerous*," she informed Mr. Smith.

Mr. Smith acknowledged this with a stiff nod.

"Are you dangerous?" she demanded.

"Not at present," he said, turning very white.

"I wonder how you came to be wounded," she suggested.

"I thought," he said in a rather faint voice, "that you had established that amongst yourselves."

"A duel? That seems to be exceptionally foolish. I cannot credit it! How is it—"

"Madame," said Mr. Smith, overriding her, "I know you will forgive me if I fail to satisfy your curiosity in all things, but circumstances compel . . . " His face drained of its remaining color and he slumped over against the seat.

"He's swooned off," said the clerk with some degree of satisfaction. "That's one way out!" He leaned over and loosened Mr. Smith's neckcloth but made no further effort to revive him.

"Oswald, did you hear what this man has said to me?" she demanded of her hapless mate. "I fear," she added, giving the offender a chance to withdraw, "that I must have misunderstood you, sir, for you cannot have meant that he has fainted in order to avoid my conversation."

No withdrawal was apparently forthcoming. "It is the outside of enough!" she murmured sotto voce to her spouse. "First I must travel with a repellent animal carrying who knows what sort of disease—however much *some* people might pretend it is exotic, or royal, or some such thing—and then I must take on a wounded man who has clearly been involved in some sort of unpleasant scandal, and now I must put up with hints of an odious nature from a *clerk*."

In this fashion Mrs. Lorry, who had already betrayed the confidence of one person and nearly accomplished the far more serious betrayal of another, amused herself by abusing her fellow passengers until at length even she subsided into exhaustion. Susan, who had busied herself with keeping Miss Pennyfeather from expostulating in kind, felt that no torment she would ever endure could possibly rival this excruciating, protracted journey. She kept her foot firmly on the owl's basket, lest it draw Mrs. Lorry's notice again. She, like the clerk, could only regard Mr. Smith with some envy, and felt that attempts to bring him back to consciousness might only do him harm. Mr. Lorry, who was looking quite red-faced and cowed now that his momentary mastery was at an end, she could not but regard with profound pity.

It was far into the night when the passengers disembarked in Bordeaux, with scarcely an hour to spare before their sailing.

The ship was of foreign registry, and not until they were safely aboard could they feel completely free from pursuit of further obstacles to their progress. Susan stepped out of the coach behind Miss Pennyfeather, and then turned to assist the clerk, who was helping to support the unconscious Mr. Smith. Susan prepared to shore up his left side, handing her reticule and the owl's basket to Miss Pennyfeather, when she was brushed aside by a large man in a sweeping cloak. "Des!" this person cried in a strangled voice. "Good God! What's happened?" He slipped a powerful arm around the unconscious man's shoulders and peered into his face. Then he turned and said to a very rigid man standing behind him, his face a mask of concern, "We've got to get him aboard at once! Quickly now!"

The other man stepped forward. "Is his lordship—"

"Not now, Marston," said the big man in a warning tone.

"Are you his friend, sir?" asked Susan. "The man who brought him did say he would be met."

The big man seemed to notice her for the first time. "I have been waiting since afternoon. Were you with him, child? Do you know what happened?"

She shook her head and told him about the unexpected stop on the road.

"He appears to have been wounded in a duel," added the clerk as he proffered the traveling papers.

The big man laughed shortly and appeared to be on the brink of some comment when he looked at Susan again. "No doubt," he said vaguely. He bowed. "You will excuse us, I know, but we must get him aboard. There is a doctor on the ship who will attend to him immediately. He must have expert care!"

"Well, I like that!" said Miss Pennyfeather when the three men had disappeared into the darkness. "Expert care, indeed! If he was so concerned, why wasn't *he* the one propping him up and chafing his wrists and spinning Banbury tales to the French instead of you? The man owes his life to you, and not one word of thanks did you get!"

"Well, he was hardly in a position to thank me himself, and his friend knows nothing about it," said Susan reasonably. "Besides, it was a splendid adventure, don't you think?" She shrugged her shoulders. "I wonder who he really was?"

"Someone it is far better for you not to know," said Miss Pennyfeather with a sniff. "Dueling ! Ha!"

"Do you think so?" asked Susan with interest. "Did you not

hear . . . well, never mind. Very likely we will never find out the truth. Let us go on board now! I could sleep for a week."

A week's sleep, in the event, did not prove necessary to restore her health and spirits, and she awoke in her berth the next morning feeling very much refreshed and even looking forward to her arrival in England. It was very much otherwise with Miss Pennyfeather, however. Her constitution did not thrive on the pitch and roll of an ocean-going vessel, and she declared that she would not leave her bed until her removal to dry land could be accomplished with appropriate haste. She urged Miss Winston to keep to her room likewise, but other than to wave away the offer of some dry toast and a bit of tea with milk, she made no other effort to direct her behavior.

Susan was fond of her old governess, but Penny's company was occasionally oppressive and her mood censorious, so that Susan could not but relish a few hours on her own. When they reached Yorkshire, Penny would be going to keep house for a bachelor brother, and the imminence of their parting had caused her to redouble all her efforts to mold Miss Winston into a pretty-behaved young girl. Which, thought Susan with a sigh, was probably a task beyond even the most strenuous exertion. Her father, lacking a son, had always treated her with an easy camaraderie more suited to a boy, indulging her scrapes and athletic antics with a certain pride and scorning any airs he might deem "missish." As a result, Susan was quite certain she was deficient in the appropriate sensibilities of a delicately nurtured female: very little shocked her, and she had never once felt the need to resort to such restoratives as a vinaigrette. She knew that her behavior and her tendency toward rather imaginative stories—the Malaga eagle for example—were a severe trial to Miss Pennyfeather, and she was sincerely sorry, but as her only imaginable future was as a companion to an infirm elderly relative, she could not but believe that the airs and graces of a fashionable lady would be rather more of an encumbrance than otherwise.

Meanwhile, the day was fresh and cool, and a few precious hours of freedom lay ahead of her. She put on a warm traveling dress of navy blue, wrapped in a mantle about her shoulders, and went out on deck.

The breeze was blowing steadily and whisked her bonnet from her head before she had secured it. She picked it up in one hand and stood facing into the wind, enjoying the sensation of it on her face, despite the havoc it wreaked on her chestnut curls. She presented an altogether lovely picture, but the first person who happened upon her was not in the mood to appreciate it.

"Good morning, Miss Winston," said Mrs. Lorry in frigid tones. "I did not see you at breakfast. I am glad to learn you are not ill."

Susan dropped her a curtsy, hiding her dismay at encountering the person she least wanted to meet again. "Thank you, ma'am. I am quite well. Miss Pennyfeather is a little under the weather this morning, so I took a tray in my cabin."

"*I* am seldom ill," commented Mrs. Lorry. "I feel that if one's character is strong, one should be able to overcome any trifling indispositions. With Oswald, however, it is quite otherwise. His constitution cannot support the rocking of the boat, and he is confined to bed."

Susan murmured that she was sorry to hear it.

"It is of no consequence," said Mrs. Lorry majestically. "I am pleased to have met you so speedily, for there is something I particularly wish to say to you!"

"To me, ma'am?" asked Susan with foreboding.

"You may well wonder," said Mrs. Lorry. "I cannot pretend that I approve of your unbecoming levity yesterday, or of your assumption of a responsibility well beyond the capability of your years. However, Oswald tells me that you are an orphan, and if you have only that gabble-grinder for company, it is no wonder that you need further guidance."

Susan, digging her fingernails into her palms in an effort to keep her temper, assured her that she need not put herself out on her behalf.

"You need not thank me," replied Mrs. Lorry. "But I am older and wiser than you, and when I have imparted the information I speak of, you will more clearly understand why I have chosen to undertake a mission clearly repugnant to every natural feeling."

Susan resigned herself to another disagreeable conversation with Mrs. Lorry. Indeed, she wondered what information of such import she could have gleaned overnight, in the company of strangers, that might be of interest to herself or Miss Pennyfeather. "Yes, ma'am?" she asked, suppressing a sigh.

"It is about *Mr. Smith*," Mrs. Lorry said in a tone more suited to the theater than ordinary discourse. "I have found out his *true identity!*"

"Indeed?"

"Yes! He is Viscount Everly! The porter told Oswald so last night!"

"Viscount Everly?" Susan asked, confused. The name meant nothing to her.

"*I* do not move in such circles, but I believe it is generally known that he is a notorious rake. Naturally I would not wish to gossip, but the *on-dit* is that he had no sooner embarked on a diplomatic career than he fell top over tail for the Season's toast. Everyone expected they would make a match of it, but in the end she accepted a regular Midas, a man, admittedly, somewhat older than herself but *full of juice*! That is to say, very well off," she amended. "At the time Everly was merely a younger son, so of course there was no contest! Since then his older brother has died, I believe, and he has inherited. But he has not settled down! Quite the contrary, I understand. In fact, he seems determined to avenge himself on the entire female sex. His reputation . . . well, I need not go into that. In all events, you see why I felt it my duty to inform you as soon as may be."

Susan had been listening to this recitation with apparent interest, but now she frowned. "I'm not sure . . . that is, I don't quite see what it is to do with *me*?" she inquired.

"Very probably nothing," admitted Mrs. Lorry, "since you are so young. But as you are without protection, I must warn you that this is not a fit person for you to know. Should he make any push to further the acquaintance—which it would be the shabbiest thing in the world for him to do—you must take care to avoid him at all costs. Indeed, it would be as well for you to keep to your cabin until we are safely docked."

Susan had to suppress a giggle at the thought of Mr. Smith—no, Lord Everly, she reminded herself—whom she had last seen bandaged and unconscious, lurking about the ship in pursuit of her virtue.

Mrs. Lorry, who did not approve of levity in young women, sniffed. "You may smile, but I trust you are not such a ram-shackle female as to court the attentions of a rake. However it may be, I have discharged my duty, and I wash my hands of it!"

Recalled to *her* sense of duty, Susan thanked her with as much gravity as she could muster. "And you know, ma'am," she added, "it is very likely that he will remember nothing of yesterday in any case. I believe it is often so with wounded men."

"I must bow to your superior knowledge," said Mrs. Lorry. "Naturally *I* have little experience of such things! I bid you good morning. I must see how Oswald gets on."

"Insufferable woman!" thought Susan when Mrs. Lorry had swept away. "Her passion for interference is inexhaustible, and in this case it is absurd as well." She resolved to think no more about it, although she had to admit her curiosity was piqued. She had never met a rake, and none of her admittedly limited experience with men had led her to believe that their hearts could be so wounded by a jilt that they would scuttle a career or alter the course of their lives. It seemed quite romantic and rather foolish, like a story in books.

In the event, scarcely twenty minutes had passed before she was granted the opportunity to discover more on the subject that had engaged her curiosity. She had finished her stroll around the deck without encountering any further mishaps, and she was retracing her steps slowly, postponing her descent to her cabin as long as possible, when a person accosted her.

"Beg pardon, miss," said one of the men she recognized from the previous evening's embarkation, "are you not the young lady from the accommodation coach?"

The man was quite respectable-looking in the daylight, and now she could see, as she had not noticed before, that he looked to be in all probability an upper servant, and a rather distinguished one at that. She nodded.

"My master—Mr. Smith—would like a word with you, if you would be so good as to accompany me," he told her. He looked about him. "Are you out here alone?"

"My companion is ill," Susan replied in a rather scared voice. In spite of herself, Mrs. Lorry's dire warnings resounded in her head.

The servant, taking this in, unbent enough to say kindly, "I am Marston, valet to . . . er, Mr. Smith. My master is confined to bed, but he wishes to thank you himself for what you did for him. No harm will come to you, my child, I assure you.

"Oh," said Susan, relieved. "If that is all, of course I will come. But he need not thank me, I'm sure!"

Desmond Wyndham, Viscount Everly, lay back against the pillows of his bed and tried to put the sequence of yesterday's events together in his mind. He had at best a mercifully dim recollection of that nightmare journey; pain had clouded his wits and memory, and a phantasmagoria of strange faces and bizarre events floated through his consciousness in random sequence. His one certainty was that someone—a girl, he thought, though he could not recall her face or age—had helped him, possibly even saved his life, and honor required that he fulfill what was owing in such circumstances, however much his doctor might have advised him that total rest and isolation would profit him the most. He closed his eyes to summon the strength for what he hoped would be the briefest of interviews with the child and her voluble duenna—that much he *did* remember—and when he opened them again Marston was announcing "Miss Winston."

Lord Everly was a veteran of many encounters with the female sex, and since he was rich, titled, and handsome, despite his reputation, he was accustomed to being greeted with a certain guarded degree of approbation. He was not prepared, however, for Miss Winston's frank, appraising gaze, with no hint of consciousness or censure in her very large and trustful gray eyes. He studied the feathery chestnut curls for a moment. Of course, he told himself, she is scarcely more than a child. And, he thought, with a hint of bitterness, she doesn't know who I am.

"How do you do?" cried Miss Winston, coming forward a little shyly. "You look much better!"

"Thank you," said Lord Everly with a smile. "I did not consult my mirror last night, but from what Marston tells me I should have found it difficult to look a great deal worse. Won't you sit down?"

The valet pulled out a chair for her facing the bedside. "I don't expect you're feeling quite the thing yet," she told him sympathetically. "When one has been shot, it takes such a long time to heal."

"Does it?" he asked in an interested tone. "Yes, I suppose it must. You sound as if you have acquired some expertise in the subject. For me it is an entirely novel experience."

She smiled in return, showing a pair of dimples. "I'm glad to hear it," she said, thinking of Mrs. Lorry.

"And have you?" he prompted her.

"Have I what?"

"An expertise in gunshot wounds?"

The smile faded. "Well, my father was a soldier."

He searched his memory. "Winston, did you say? Was your father *General* Winston?"

She nodded.

"Oh, my poor child. I am so sorry. He is greatly missed."

"Thank you," she said simply.

Marston cleared his throat. "Forgive me," said his lordship, obedient to this hint, "I have not introduced myself. I have been traveling under the name of Smith, but I know you will keep my confidence if I tell you my real name. I am Desmond Wyndham."

"Lord Everly?" inquired Miss Winston without apparent surprise.

"You've heard of me?" asked the viscount with a hint of bitterness.

"Well, no," admitted Susan. "That is, I hadn't, until this morning. I think it is only fair to warn you that if you are traveling incognito or some such thing, it is too late to keep the secret. One of the coach passengers—Mrs. Lorry, do you remember her?—has recognized you."

"My memories of that dreadful coach are somewhat unreliable, I fear. Let me see—was she masterful, unpleasant, and determined to hand my corpse over to the French?"

She giggled. "You *do* remember."

"Unfortunately, yes. It's of no consequence, however. I had only thought to protect a lady's reputation . . . My own, I can tell by your look, has already been ripped to shreds."

Susan raised her candid eyes to his. "I confess she did not give you a very good character," she said calmly.

"You don't seem very shocked," suggested his lordship, rather taken aback.

"I thought that is what you wished. Haven't you gone out of your way to convince everyone you were wounded in a duel?"

Behind her, Marston gave a little gasp. "And you don't believe it?" asked his lordship, somewhat stupidly.

" No, I do not believe it," Susan said with conviction. "However, it is not my concern, and I certainly would not presume to contradict you if that is what you wish people to think."

"And what do you think?" he could not forbear asking.

"I think," she said, her eyes shining, "that you have been on a secret diplomatic mission!"

"Romantic nonsense," he scoffed. "I regret to inform you

that the character the redoubtable Mrs. Lorry has given me is far too accurate!"

"I won't doubt it if you say so, but no one would credit it, I assure you. But that reminds me," she said as a sudden distressing memory intruded itself, "if you really do remember a great deal about yesterday, I feel I should apologize for my part in blackening your reputation."

"No! Did you?" he asked, a smile lurking around his mouth.

"Yes. I said you were drunk, and . . . a womanizer and . . . had not turned out well!" she said uncertainly.

He laughed out loud, which caused him to clutch his right side in pain. "Like Uncle Lucius," he said when he had recovered. "Now I remember."

"Yes, and it was not fair to Uncle Lucius either, for he was the model of sobriety, and as far as I know was not a *skirt chaser* either," she said pensively.

"Do *not*, I beg you, make me laugh again," said Lord Everly with some urgency. "You probably saved my life, you abominable child! If you had not spun that Banbury tale to the French about my being your dissipated brother—"

"I was afraid you might not like it," she said anxiously, "but it was all I could think of at the time."

"—I might be rotting in some French prison, or dead, for that matter," he concluded frankly.

"Yes, the French are remarkably hard on duelists," she remarked with asperity.

He winced. "Touché. You will understand, I think, if I do not confide in you further. In any event, I asked you to come here so I could thank you from the bottom of my heart."

"It is not necessary, I promise you! Indeed if you had not been so very ill I might have said that it was quite an adventure."

"Ha! I regret that I must sound very poor-spirited, but it is an adventure I have no desire to repeat!"

"Well, I am not the one who got shot," offered Miss Winston charitably.

"Very true," his lordship agreed gravely. "If it would not seem impertinent in me to ask, how old are you?"

"I am turned eighteen," she told him.

"Ah. That would make me your much older dissipated brother. I am five-and-thirty."

"Are you?" she asked, surprised. "The French officer said as much, but I thought it was only because you were pretty well knocked up." She surveyed him critically. He was very pale, and his eyes were shadowed, but his appearance was youthful despite a heavy-lidded countenance which made him look rather cynically bored. "Except for a certain look in your eye, no one would think you are as much."

He gave another shout of laughter, whose unfortunate after-effects caused Marston to rush solicitously to his side.

"Oh, I've hurt you," cried Susan remorsefully. "I am so sorry! I have overtired you too. I must be going."

"No! Wait!" he said, gasping. "Stay a little longer. Tell me, do you always say exactly what you are thinking?"

"Of course not," she said indignantly. "It might seem so to you, and with my father I had got into the habit of expressing myself a little more freely than customary, but you would not have believed the restraint I was forced to exercise with Mrs. Lorry."

"My memory is agreeably dim on the subject, but I am not inclined to doubt you. I hope you will not feel the need to put a curb on your tongue for *my* benefit, however."

"Oh no," Susan agreed.

"Excellent," said his lordship with a smile. "I detest chits who blush and bridle! Do you go to family in England?"

"Yes, I am going to be a companion to my Great Aunt Harrington in Yorkshire."

"Amanda Harrington?" he asked, surprised. "She is eighty if she's a day."

"That is why she needs a companion," confirmed Susan placidly. "I think she cannot be in very good health, because her son William has written that at present she does not have the strength to quit the house."

"My poor child, that is no life for you! Is there no one else you could go to?"

She shook her head. "There was my stepmama. My father married her six months before he died, but afterward she went home to her family. She is Spanish, and while she was kind enough in her way, it did not suit either of us to remain too long under one roof. I did live with the colonel's family for a year, but I could not subsist on their charity forever. I am sure I shall not mind taking care of an invalid. I nursed my father when he was ill, you know!" She rose from her chair. "And now I really must leave you to rest," she said firmly. "I am pleased to see you so much better."

"Will you oblige me in one thing before you leave?" he asked her.

"Of course, if I can," she said, turning back to face him.

"Put to rest my gravest fear, that this accursed wound has addled my wits. I cannot seem to shake the impression that an *owl* was amongst the passenger on the accommodation coach, and I feel sure that cannot have been the case!"

Her lips twitched. "Well, Minnie was not a *passenger*, precisely."

"Minnie?"

She blushed. "Minerva. It is very trite, I know, but how *do* you come up with a suitable name for an owl?"

"I confess I am at a loss to answer you. The owl—Minnie—I take it, was yours?"

"My father gave her to me. One of her wings is injured, and she doesn't fly very well. She catches mice sometimes, but I fear she would have starved to death if we didn't feed her. The thing is," she continued in a wondering tone, "some people do not quite like owls or are superstitious about them or some such thing, so I was *obliged* to make up the most outrageous story about what was really in the basket! Minnie was hungry, you see, so she started rocking."

"I don't see, precisely," he said shakily, "but I will take your word for it."

"That reminds me," she said suddenly, "how did you know what was in the basket? I thought we were at *point non plus*!"

"I should like to satisfy your curiosity, but my recollection is rather vague. Could you have removed the lid at some point?"

She paused, remembering. "Yes I did, when I gave her a bit of meat from my supper. I didn't think anyone was watching."

"No doubt that accounts for it. Doubtless it accounts for what I believed were my hallucinations as well. Where is this animal now?"

"She was sitting on the cupboard in my cabin when I left," Susan told him.

"I regret exceedingly that that is a sight I shall not be privileged to see," he told her. "My child, thank you for coming. I've enjoyed myself most shamefully. I cannot help suspecting that subsequent encounters with the opposite sex will seem a trifle dull in comparison."

"Oh. You mean that I do not behave as a delicately brought-up female should?"

"That is one way of putting it. But I find it delightful."

"Thank you," she said, a little wistfully. "I was afraid that must be so. I had a rather lamentable upbringing, but when one is happy such things do not seem so very important." She shrugged. "I daresay it will not signify, so long as I can rub along well enough with Great Aunt Harrington. If she is very old, perhaps she will not notice?"

"I trust not," said Lord Everly kindly.

Chapter 3

The delegation admitted to the well-appointed parlor of Summerland Abbey—ancestral home of the Wyndhams since Great Henry had wrested it from the possession of some unlucky monks in the sixteenth century, and country seat of the current viscount—consisted of Lord Everly's sister Almeria and her husband Lord Wibberly. Their errand was plainly making his lordship uncomfortable: a large man, he could not forbear wiping his brow with his handkerchief at intervals more frequent than the heat of the day would seem to require, and he intermittently cast glances of appeal at his spouse, who ignored him.

Her ladyship, though of a fragile and exquisite appearance, was made of sterner stuff than her husband and did not quail in the face of expected opposition. She did not rate her task an easy one, but she could not but put her trust in the power of reason and her own rather formidable persuasive abilities. When the butler had departed to carry the news of their arrival up to her brother, she threw her husband a look of fond contempt and said indulgently, "Really, Wibberly! Anyone would think you were afraid of Des!"

"Stuff and nonsense!" he replied. "It is only that at five-and-thirty your brother will very likely take snuff at our interference in his personal affairs, and I for one am sure that I do not blame him!"

"However that may be," Lady Wibberly said with determination, "it has been three months now since he provoked yet another scandal and came home with a duelist's bullet in his shoulder, and—"

"Now, Almeria, we do not *know* for certain that he was in a duel," protested his lordship. "I am sure he has never said so, however much you teased him on the subject."

"That is *precisely* the reason I believe it. If there were any other explanation, be sure he would have offered it to hush the wagging tongues. Moreover, you know very well it is just the sort of thing he would do."

Her spouse was obliged to admit that his brother-in-law did seem to display a lamentable tendency toward wildness.

"And *that*," she concluded triumphantly, "is why he must be brought to do his duty without further delay! It was one thing to lead such a ramshackle existence when Kit was alive, but now he is head of the family! Moreover—"

Her expostulations were cut short at that moment by the arrival of the object of her disapproval himself. Lord Everly stood in the doorway, cynically regarding his relatives. Three months had had a considerable restorative effect upon his health and appearance; he was, perhaps, a trifle thinner than formerly, but his coat of dandy gray russet fit him to a perfection Mr. Brummel might have envied, and there was no hint of stiffness in his afflicted shoulder and arm. He had lost his pallor and the shadows about his eyes; only the mocking smile and the look of weary disillusionment remained. "Almeria, Tom!" he said, observing his brother-in-law's discomfort with amusement. "What an unexpected pleasure!"

"I hope we need not stand on ceremony *here*," said his sister calmly, offering him her scented cheek to kiss. "We've come to see how you get on, haven't we, Wibberly?"

"No!" replied his lordship unexpectedly. "That is of course we have but—"

Lord Everly, perfectly perceiving his guest's predicament, said helpfully, "Shall I ring for some refreshment? A glass of Madeira might be just the thing."

"No thank you," said Lady Wibberly, ignoring her husband's look of entreaty. "We have driven over from Dower House and cannot stay above an hour."

"And how did you leave Mama?" asked the viscount, turning away from her slightly.

His sister shrugged. "The same as always, I should say. I am not sure she recognized me in the end, and poor Tom could not awaken any sense in her at all. But, Des, Trimble tells me they knew nothing of your . . . accident. That you have not been to see her these three months!"

His mouth twisted. "What would you have me do? Would you have had me send such news? You surprise me. Besides," he added in a quiet voice, "you know my presence upsets her. Ever since Kit died she can scarcely bear the sight of me. It seemed the greatest kindness to stay away."

"I must own I thought it most unreasonable for her to blame you for Kit's accident," she told him. "How could *you* be responsible for his breaking his neck in that fall? Whatever mama might have believed about him, you know he had a wicked temper, and he crammed his horse at the fence!"

"He was riding my horse," said Lord Everly in a flat tone.

"What does that signify? You know he always envied your seat, and set out to prove he could ride any animal of yours, however restive. You warned him more than once that the horse wasn't properly broken in."

He smiled bleakly. "Don't look so dismayed, Almeria. Your compassion is quite unnecessary, I promise you. I blame neither myself, nor, as you seem to believe, our mother for persisting in her belief that the fault lay at my doorstep. Nothing short of a landslide could stop Kit from doing what he wanted, and I was just his younger brother! I have not stayed away from Mama out of pique, but out of what seemed to make her the most comfortable."

"There is a kindness you could do for her," suggested his sister in an altered voice.

"Aha!" said the viscount.

"You need not use that tone," said her ladyship, annoyed that her subterfuge had been detected. "I daresay you have been wondering why we have called."

"I thought you came to inquire after my health?" said Lord Everly meekly.

Tom guffawed, which earned him a look of disapprobation from his spouse.

"As to that," replied her ladyship, undaunted, "I can see for myself that you look quite recovered. If I did not know it to be the case, I should say that no one would ever believe that you were recently brought to bed of a bullet wound!"

Her brother bowed. "As a matter of fact, I am feeling much better, thank you! So much so that I leave this week for Yorkshire, to look at the farm properties. I shall be gone some time, so if there is any commission you wish me to undertake on behalf of Mama, you should let me know at once."

"You are going to visit . . . the *farms*?" cried his sister, taken aback.

His lordship smiled. "Well, you are forever urging me to take more interest in my properties, are you not?"

"Yes, and if you are doing so at last I cannot but believe that getting shot—in however reprehensible a manner—has done you a world of good," she said firmly. "Will you return before the Season begins?"

"I see you have been listening to gossip, Almeria." He shrugged. "I cannot say just when I shall return. Why do you ask?"

"May I speak frankly?"

Lord Everly gave her a genuine smile, one only his intimate acquaintances were privileged to see. "My dear Almeria, I regard it as the highest degree of sisterly sacrifice for you to make such an unusual exertion on my behalf."

She looked up at him, not without affection. "You need not try to charm me. You might as well listen to what Wibberly and I came to say."

His lordship sighed and crossed one buckskin-clad leg over the other. "Very well," he said with resignation.

"When," she said, taking the plunge, "do you mean to marry?"

Lord Everly remained silent for a moment and then said lightly, "Next year perhaps. Or the year after. Perhaps never."

"That is the sort of vague answer you have been returning for these five years and more!" she protested.

Lord Everly removed a pinch of snuff from his enameled snuffbox and studied it with some care. "That is because," he said deliberately, "I have yet to meet a woman who would make me wish to abandon what has become a highly satisfactory way of life."

"You mean the prime articles of virtue you've been flaunting on the town," said his sister with ruthless candor. Her husband made a sound of protest in his throat, but she stifled him with a look. "However much I may deplore your relationships with my sex, and the notorious companions with whom you pursue such ramshackle ways, it is incumbent upon me to point out that marriage does not necessarily *oblige* one to give up one's other amusements, so long as one is discreet."

The cynical look had returned to Lord Everly's eyes. "You speak of a marriage of convenience, I take it?"

His sister sighed. "I suppose so."

"Satisfy my curiosity, Almeria: does it not seem a rather shabby trick to play on a girl of birth and breeding? At least with what you are pleased to call my 'prime articles of virtue' everything is quite straightforward. I open my purse strings, and they . . . "

"It is quite unnecessary to continue," Lady Wibberly told

him sternly. "And you cannot be such a nodcock as to pretend that your fortune and your title are the only things which make you an eligible suitor, when *dozens* of girls have set their caps for you to no avail."

"Yes, you have obligingly cast any number of potential brides my way!" admitted his lordship. "And *you* cannot expect me to believe that, in view of my 'reputation,' which you have just been pleased to remind me of, any other considerations besides my advantages of name and fortune could make me a suitable *parti*, for I am quite sure I do not!"

"I own that your reputation is not quite what one would like," said Lady Wibberly calmly. "Since you have taken such pains to make it so, I do not hesitate in speaking frankly. That is precisely the reason you must marry a lady of respectable birth and fortune, so that you may be reestablished in the eyes of the world. You need not marry a girl who will hang on your sleeve if you do not like it."

"Thank you," said Lord Everly, helping himself to another pinch of snuff.

"I am quite serious, Des!" she cried. "You must think of the future. What if that bullet had found its way an inch or two lower? It is the most appalling prospect! Indeed I could not bear it if—"

"My dear, I am quite touched," interrupted her brother.

"—if Canby were to step into your shoes!" she continued, with the air of one presenting her best argument.

"Almeria, your solicitude unmans me," he said with a shaky laugh.

"I am not funning. You know he is quite the most deplorable toady, in addition to having a penchant for dandyism. It does not bear thinking of to see him established here, which is what will happen if you do not marry and beget an heir."

"Cursed rum touch," agreed Lord Wibberly.

"I suppose it might be counted an advantage to have such an heir as Cosmo," Lord Everly said meditatively, "if only because one's relatives become so very interested in one's continued good health. Though of course, in his case, that would not apply. Indeed, whenever I have a chill it is never more than a few days before he is at my doorstep to discover for himself whether I might be expected to recover, although he does not put it *quite* like that, naturally. When I was wounded, Raskins had to turn him away almost hourly, so great was his solicitude."

"How *can* you jest about such a subject?" asked his sister. "Really, Des, sometimes your odd humors go beyond what is pleasing."

"I am quite sunk in levity," he agreed. "I wonder at your eagerness to foist me off on some innocent female."

She directed her frank gaze at him. "Because if you do not marry, it would be the greatest act of selfishness imaginable," she said seriously.

"Almeria!" protested her husband.

"No, it's all right, Tom," said Lord Everly, surprising them both. "She is quite right. I suppose in the end I must, after all, consider it."

"At least look about you this Season," said her ladyship, following up this unexpected victory without further loss of time. "Lady Kimbolton's daughter Maria is out this year—a lovely, spirited girl, and—"

"Fubsy-faced," interjected her spouse.

"No, that is Alice," she corrected him. "And in any case, while her figure may run just a little to fat, I am sure no one could call her 'fubsy.' Though of course—"

"I am obliged to you," said Lord Everly with a dangerous glint in his eye, "but I most earnestly entreat you *not* to start pitching innocent young females in my direction. It is rare that I meet a female of that class with whom I can sustain an hour's conversation, much less a lifetime."

"No, perhaps you are right," said her ladyship thoughtfully. "Someone of the highest respectability, who has been on the town awhile and would be grateful for the offer of her own establishment, would be less likely to hang on your sleeve."

"I take it you mean someone who has been on the shelf for a few years!" said his lordship. "What a delightful picture you paint, Almeria!"

"Well, you must own that you have no one but yourself to blame. If you had settled comfortably at a decent age instead of wearing the willow for Clarissa Constable all these years, you might have chosen anyone."

He laughed mockingly. "You are far out there, my dear! I admit I did not care for the role of jilted lover in which Clarissa cast me, but she did me the greatest of favors, I assure you. I learned a great deal about the female sex. And there have been . . . compensations, I promise."

"So I have noticed," remarked his sister with asperity. "Quite a number of them. But if you think Clarissa's behavior is typical of our sex, or some such thing, it is you who are sadly mistaken, Des!"

"I honor your sentiments, but experience has taught me otherwise," he told her. "In all events, I have promised to consider what you have said while I am in Yorkshire, and you will have to be content with that."

"Just as you please, Des," said her ladyship, drawing on her gloves.

Chapter 4

Three weeks later, Lord Everly, driving his own curricle, with a pair of remarkably fine matched grays harnessed to it, entered the lane that led to Lady Amanda Harrington's Yorkshire residence, Fenwood Hall. His motive in making such a visit was to call on Miss Susan Winston and assure himself that she was comfortably settled; he still felt under obligation to the amusing child, and once he was reasonably certain of her well-being he might feel discharged of any further responsibility. His brief acquaintance with Lady Harrington, whose lands were not far from his own, gave him all the excuse he needed; his own reputation would have made it inadvisable to call on a girl of scarcely eighteen years without an introduction to the family. Moreover, he was not in the habit of spending more than a few days at a time on his farmlands; however much he might esteem the skills of his bailiff, that worthy gentleman's relentless recitation of crops and fertilizers bored him so thoroughly that even such a dubious amusement as calling at the home of an ancient dowager acquired an undeniable allure.

He had not been to Fenwood Hall for many years, not since he and Kit, as boys, had ridden over with their father to dine with Lord and Lady Harrington. He remembered it as a gloomy, imposing sort of place, with old-fashioned furniture and chairs that bit into his backbone at the dining table. Her ladyship remained in his mind as one who had expressed almost constant disapproval of his appearance, posture, and appetite. He grinned at the memory, admitting to himself that such disapproval was not entirely undeserved. He wondered what the Old Tartar would think of him now.

Even in the face of such memories, his first view of the Hall shocked him so greatly that even he, a notable Corinthian, let the reins go slack in his hands. The box hedges had grown untended into wild, careless shapes, and the trees were so dense he could scarcely glimpse the house beyond. What he could see looked dilapidated and forlorn, as if no repairs had been effected for a generation or more. Such an appearance could only mean that the family had fallen on difficult times, for no one who wished to support a respectable position in society could have so neglected the principal seat.

He drew up in front of the door, wondering if there would be someone to attend to his team. His knock was answered by a person of great age and scant hearing, who, upon finally being made to understand the nature of his errand, announced that her ladyship and Miss Winston might be found in the morning room, if he would care to go in. As no mention was made of a groom or the stables, Lord Everly inquired as gently as he could whether it might be possible to take care of his curricle. The butler, contemplating this for some not inconsiderable period, was at length brought to admit that such a service might indeed be executed, and doddered off, presumably in search of a groom. This left his lordship to find his own way to the morning room and announce himself, but he could not but feel that in a household where so many of the basic civilities were clearly lacking, even such a gaffe as that was not likely to be remarked upon.

In the end he was spared the necessity by the arrival of a footman, almost as geriatric as the butler himself. Lord Everly wondered whether a staff seemingly consisting of those at least fifteen years beyond the normal age of retirement had remained in service out of sentimental loyalty to their employer, or whether some less benign explanation was at work.

The footman ushered him into a room that he remembered from his childhood. In fact, it might be fair to say that very little had been done to alter any of the furnishings in the ensuing years. It was very dark despite the early hour, and there was no fire in the grate, so that the chill penetrated his clothing to such an extent that he wished he had not divested himself of his greatcoat so hastily.

Miss Winston, hearing him enter, looked up in surprise, as if she could not quite credit the footman's announcement. Her hand clutched a book of Edward's *Sermons*, although Lord Everly did not see how anyone could have been reading in such dim light. Behind her, in an overstuffed chair, sat Lady Harrington, her piercing black eyes fixing him with such a stare of reproach that he felt for a moment that she must after all have uncovered the fact that he and Kit had long ago broken a windowpane in the chapel through the misadventures of an errant kite, however much they had tried to muddy the evidence and place the blame on a passing bird. She was greatly aged, but her disapproval, it seemed, was undiminished.

"Oh, it *is* you, sir," said Miss Winston in a wondering voice. "I thought Jenkins must have had it wrong. He does get confused sometimes."

Lord Everly did not doubt it. He smiled at her and crossed the room to Lady Harrington. "How do you do, ma'am? I have called to inquire after your health, and that of Miss Winston." She looked at him but did not respond, so he said more loudly (in case she might be deaf), "Do you remember me? I am Everly. My father brought me here years ago, with my brother."

Her penetrating gaze swept his elegant frame, from his shoulders to the tips of his topboots. She looked away, out the window, and replied in a voice of perfect clarity, "I saw something wicked in the inglenook."

"Indeed, ma'am?" he inquired, taken aback. "What was it?"

Her eyes flickered momentarily, but she made no other response.

"Aunt Harrington," said Susan, approaching her, "Lord Everly has come especially to visit you. Shall I not ring for some refreshment?"

"I saw something *wicked* in the inglenook," Lady Harrington insisted.

His lordship lifted an inquiring eyebrow at Miss Winston, who shrugged slightly. "Lady Harrington," he said solicitously, "if you do not object, I should like to take your companion for a walk in the garden. I have brought her some messages from her friends in London, and I would not wish to tire you with such commonplaces as young girls exchange. Shall I ring for a servant to attend you while we go out?" Without waiting for a reply, he pulled the bell, which he was somewhat surprised to find in working order. The speed with which the butler responded suggested that he had stationed himself somewhere very close to the door as soon as he had directed the stabling of his lordship's horses. "You rang, miss?" said this venerable personage to Miss Winston.

"I did," corrected his lordship.

"Oh, Fribble," said Susan quickly, "could you ask Betty to attend to her ladyship for a few minutes? Lord Everly would like to see the grounds again—it has been many years since he last visited—and her ladyship is too tired for such an exertion. I have just been reading her her book of sermons, and I think she may wish to take a nap now."

"You run along, miss," said Fribble, with the first trace of warmth Everly had heard from anyone in the household. "I'll see to it. Take your time."

The garden was even colder than the house had been, and considerably bleaker, but to Lord Everly it felt so welcoming and unconstricted by comparison that he almost gave way to an audible sigh of relief. Neither of them had spoken since they left the morning room, by a kind of tacit mutual consent; now he turned to Miss Winston and studied her with concern. She was paler and thinner than the blooming child of three months before, and the gown she wore was so plain and unrevealing it would not have been scorned by the most scrupulous Evangelical tractist of an era some fifteen years before the present day. He was appalled at the brief glimpse he had just had of her life here, and he was scarcely prepared for the vehemence of his reaction. Not the most ardent of Lord Everly's admirers would have ever accused him of selflessness, but the specter of such a lively, spirited girl—to whom he was under an admitted obligation—trapped in such circumstances caused him to abandon his habitual languid demeanor. "You look dreadful," he said emphatically, surveying her critically. "Where on earth did you acquire that—that *costume*?"

"I admit it is a trifle *old-fashioned*," Susan said ruefully. She put up her chin. "If you must know, I got it out of a trunk."

"I am scarcely surprised that someone was astute enough to leave it behind," he told her, "but what I don't quite see is why that means that it must be worn at all."

"Well, Cousin William is rather *frugal*," she said thoughtfully, "and he believes in wearing things out. I understand it belonged to one of his old governesses."

"If what I have seen around here is any indication, he must be the biggest pinch-purse who ever lived! Is the age and condition of the staff another instance of his frugality?"

She smiled wryly. "I'm afraid he doesn't believe in pensions, either."

"Good God! Are the family in such straitened circumstances as all that?"

She shrugged. "I'm not sure. Lady Harrington—"

"I've seen Lady Harrington!" he interrupted. "A Bedlamite, is she?"

"A bit eccentric," she admitted, "although sometimes I feel that she is not nearly so addled as she pretends. It annoys William excessively to think that his mother is 'dicked in the nob,' as he puts it, and I can't help but notice that she seems to be considerably worse in his presence."

"Ha! And in mine as well, if today is anything to judge by. Enlighten me if you please: *what* wicked thing did she see in the inglenook?"

Her dimples peeped. "I'm dreadfully afraid that it was Minnie!"

"Minnie?" he asked blankly.

"Yes," she said earnestly. "She escapes sometimes, and once she flew into the inglenook. I expect she was cold," she added judiciously.

"No doubt," said his lordship shakily, recalled to a sense of Minnie's identity. "What happened next?"

"Well you know she's a screech owl," offered Miss Winston.

"Yes," replied Lord Everly with foreboding.

"Aunt Harrington saw her in the inglenook and thought she was a bat or some such thing. She tried to poke her with a stick!" she said indignantly. "And, well . . . Minnie *screeched*."

"I see," said his lordship, maintaining his gravity. "Hardly inappropriate, under the circumstances."

"You wouldn't think so," said Miss Winston, "but Cousin William was most dreadfully put out. He says if Minnie escapes again he will have the gardener *wring her neck*!"

"Do you know, I think I shall have to become acquainted with your Cousin William. I daresay he was away when I was last here, for I feel certain I should have remembered anyone with such a character as you describe."

"Well, you won't like him," said Susan frankly. "He is quite censorious, and he has lips like a carp."

"Nevertheless," he said, guiding her to a bench overlooking what had once been a lovely prospect but was now a weed-choked ruin of a landscape, "I have some things I particularly want to say to him."

She gave him a swift glance. "Well, if it concerns me, I beg you will not! You will only make things worse! Let us talk of something else. You have not told me why you have come, and I am sure I never expected to see you again."

"I came to see how you got on," he told her, and then, more honestly, "and I have farmlands nearby, and I was—"

"Bored?" she asked him with a smile.

"I very nearly said that," he admitted with a grin. "I beg your pardon!"

"I expect it *is* rather boring, after the life you have led," she said calmly.

"My life isn't all that exciting, my dear," he said with a touch of bitterness.

She smiled but said nothing. "Are you quite recovered then?" she asked after a while. "You look very well. Can you move your arm?"

"Yes, I can move my arm! Good God, I very nearly let you divert me! Miss Winston, I must tell you that now that I have seen Fenwood Hall, I am convinced this is no life for you."

She looked away from him, out over the weed-choked lawns. After a moment, she smiled and said lightly, "It is not nearly so bad as all that. I have an abominable tendency to levity—everyone has always said so—and I've no doubt misled you. Really, everyone has been quite kind."

"Is that why I find you looking pale and listless and wearing a dress my horse would scorn to wear as a blanket?"

"Perhaps your horse has more discriminating taste, not to mention more *pin money*," she said, a little stung. "Why are you prosing on about this dress? It is not as if there were anyone else to see it, and it is quite serviceable!"

"Well *I* see it, and I tell you it is execrable!" he thundered. "And I do not *prose on* about anything."

She rose from the bench and pulled her cloak about her shoulders. "I think we should go back to the house."

He remained seated. "No doubt, but I have not finished! We have not settled what is to be done."

She looked at him curiously. "Do you know, I have the strongest feeling that I should not listen to a word you say."

"*That* will teach me a lesson!"

She choked. "I *wish* you would not make me laugh, when I am trying to be perfectly serious. There is not the least need for you to concern yourself, I promise you."

"You mean I haven't the least right to concern myself in your affairs. It is quite true! Have you no other family?"

"Only my stepmama."

"Who lives in Spain and is no doubt on the catch for another husband!"

She laughed. "I never told you that!"

He cocked an amused eye at her. "You did not have to."

"Well, I cannot blame her," she admitted. "She was much younger than Papa, and it cannot have been very comfortable to have been left with a grown stepdaughter on her hands."

"Particularly not one to take the shine out of her," he suggested.

"Oh, no," she said seriously. "She is quite beautiful."

He smiled but did not reply.

"So you see, there is no one else," she told him after a while. "Under the circumstances, it was very kind of the Harringtons to take me in."

"It was nothing of the sort! They have made you the unpaid servant to an old lady who was cantankerous when she was in full possession of her wits, and they have buried you in this"— he looked about him, searching for the right word—"mausoleum. A girl of your age and background should be going to parties and balls at Almack's."

She smiled at him. "I confess I would not mind moving beyond the confines of this estate occasionally, but I hope you are not offended if I tell you that I have always heard that Almack's is overrated, and very dull. Papa would have it that they would not admit the King himself if he were not wearing knee breeches, and you know I can't but believe that it must be a very *silly* place."

He gave a crack of laughter. "I am not in the least offended, I assure you! It is quite true. Alas, one must put up with such things if one wishes to be received into the *ton* and marry well."

"Well then it is of no consequence," she said placidly, "for I have not the least desire to be received into the *ton*, and without a fortune I am very unlikely to marry well in any case."

He was too much a realist to dispute this, but he felt that with the proper sponsorship for a London Season she might very well take. "Besides," he told her, "even if it were a dead bore, you cannot prefer to remain here for the rest of your life!"

She looked down at her hands folded in her lap. "Very probably not," she said calmly, "but I do not see what is to be done."

Something about her acceptance of her fate reminded him of her father, and the debt the country owed to him. "I'll sponsor you," he said suddenly, astonishing himself and her.

She did not look up. "You are laughing at me, and it is not very kind of you," she said quietly.

"I expect to laugh at you very frequently, amusing child! But I am not joking with you now, I am in dead earnest! In fact, it is the most delightful scheme, and I am only sorry I did not think of it earlier. Of course, it would make a devil of a stir if I were to do it myself. My reputation with your sex is such that my sponsorship would do little to establish your credit."

"Are you so disreputable?" she asked curiously.

"Very," he assured her.

"Oh yes," she said thoughtfully, remembering. "Your heart was broken and you went wild. Mrs. Lorry told me."

"My heart—" He gave a shout of laughter.

"It's not true, then?" she inquired.

"Well, if such ancient history interests you, I'm obliged to confess that I found myself in the throes of a most vulgar infatuation, and made a cake of myself," he said with a queer smile. "I am excessively grateful to the lady involved for releasing me before I became a dead bore!"

Susan was not deceived. "She married someone else?"

"Oh yes! A Florentine count, with a handsome face and a fortune to match. Don't look so dismayed! I promise you, your compassion is quite unnecessary. I am grateful to her—one is not often taught so young the importance of laughing at one's own folly. Had my fortune been greater, I might even now be undeceived."

"But you might be happier," she suggested forthrightly. "Still, I am surprised. I know very little of such matters, but I should have thought your name and fortune must be enough to satisfy any woman of birth and breeding."

"There you have hit on it precisely," he said with a sneer. "Desmond, Viscount Everly, is deucedly popular with matchmaking mamas, it seems. There is scarcely an outrage I could commit that would prove an insurmountable obstacle to getting leg-shackled with any of half a dozen of the most *tonnish* females." He looked over the distant prospect as if it were the past itself. "Des Wyndham was another story," he said bleakly. "I was only a younger son, then."

"Your brother died?" she asked quietly.

"Yes, in a riding accident. Shortly after Clarissa—that was her name—married."

"And did you—have you seen her since then?"

He raised an eyebrow quizzically. "Are you casting me as

the hero in some tragic romantic tale? I did not pine for long, I assure you. And no, I have not seen her since. For all I know she has a passel of brats and has grown quite contented."

"No, bilious," suggested Susan. "And probably somewhat corpulent as well. I am quite sure they use a lot of olive oil in their cooking, because we had an Italian cook once, and he *would* use it in everything. Penny—Miss Pennyfeather, you met her—said it made her dyspeptic and made my father send him away, so we could not put it to the test. Still, I think it is quite probable that you were very lucky, even if you could not think so at the time!"

He laughed. "I must confess I had not quite seen it in that light," he admitted.

"People seldom do, when they are in the throes of passion," said Susan thoughtfully.

"Much you know about it, brat!"

"No, and I don't wish to, if it makes you do silly things and regret them afterward." She sighed. "To tell you the truth, I had much rather have a friend."

"And to tell *you* the truth, so would I," he said, rather struck by this idea. "Have you none, then?"

She shook her head, "Not in this country. And certainly not in *London*," she added with a mischievous gleam. "Whatever caused you to say such a thing to Lady Harrington?"

"It was the only thing I could think of at the moment," he said weakly.

"Well, it is quite fortunate that she is sometimes short a sheet," she said seriously, "because you could hardly have expected her to believe such an outrageous faradiddle otherwise."

"Next time I will be sure to mention that a Malaga eagle sent me instead," he said quizzically.

She had the good grace to blush. "Wretch," she said. "Oh, I beg your pardon!" she cried, suddenly aware that she had addressed him like an older brother or a family friend of many years' standing. "I ought not to have said that! It isn't in the least respectful."

"I thought we had agreed on the virtues of plain speaking over flowery commonplaces," he said with a smile. "That is much better—between friends!"

"That is very tactful of you," she told him, "but you must see that I am a hopeless case, and it would be quite useless to bring me out into society. I haven't the least idea of banter, or how to conduct a flirtation, or any of the other skills required for making one's way in the world!"

He grew very still, and the only sound was the tap-tap-tap of a woodpecker looking for nuts in some distant tree. "Why don't you consider, that is to say—"

She looked at him curiously. *"Yes?"*

Those of his lordship's friends who were acquainted with his indifferent air and easy address with women of a certain class would have found this tongue-tied performance remarkable.

"What I wished to say is," he said at last, "is that I feel quite certain that the best solution is for you to marry me."

Chapter 5

Miss Winston was not sure she had heard him correctly. "I beg your pardon?" she asked politely.

"I am certain that it is much the best solution," he suggested.

"Solution? I am sorry. I must be very stupid today."

"On the contrary," he said, "it is I who should apologize. I have handled this so badly. It only just occurred to me, you see."

"Well, I don't see," she told him. "I don't see at all."

"I am asking," he said a trifle impatiently, "that you do me the honor of becoming my wife."

"But *why*?"

"Because," he told her bluntly, "it is the only way I can think of to provide for your future, and——"

"Lord Everly," she interrupted emphatically, "you are not under any obligation whatsoever to provide for my future, I promise you! Whatever small service I might have rendered you in France——"

"Not so small, my dear," he said with a smile.

"Whatever small service I might have rendered you in France," she persisted, "you have already requited through your visit here. There is no need to think of anything else!"

"But I do think of it. No, hear me out, if you please. I am not proposing to sacrifice myself on the altar of matrimony merely to save you from dwindling into someone not unlike Miss Pennyfeather if you stay on here——"

She made a wry face. "I could not!"

"Well, I would not suggest putting it to the test! In any event, I would stand to benefit from the arrangement as much or more than you."

"How?" she asked incredulously.

His lordship drew a breath. "Ever since I was wounded in France, my family has made it their chiefest concern to get me to think of settling down. I don't propose to do that, of course, but the devil of it is that I must marry, if only to stop the hounding."

"How very *uncomfortable* for you!" she said with such an air of sympathy that he looked at her suspiciously.

"Had you been privileged to meet my heir, Cosmo Canby, you would more readily concede their point," he assured her. "In all events, I owe it to my mother and sister to establish at least the appearance of respectability."

"The appearance only?"

He shrugged. "My reputation, as you would know if you were not isolated here in this dungeon, is not of the best. My fortune is substantial enough, but my 'expenditures' have been such as must necessarily attract attention. However, my way of life suits me for the moment, and I cannot promise that I will ever want to change it."

"In short, you want a marriage of convenience," she told him.

He smiled mockingly. "You are wise beyond your years, Miss Winston."

"It is from living so near to France," she said seriously. "But why me?"

His smile became more genuine. "I am no bargain, my dear. My character is sadly unsteady, and I fear that five-and-thirty does not make a very good husband to eighteen. Shall I speak plainly?"

She nodded.

"If you were a girl of large fortune, with prospects to match, I should be taking the most shocking advantage of your innocence if I were to ask you to marry me. Instead of establishing myself in the eyes of the world, I should make myself an outcast, and you! As it is, I have a home to offer you, and a name, and a life much better than you can expect if you remain here. You would be your own mistress—at no one's beck and call—and I should always hold you in respect. It does not seem such a bad bargain. And besides—"

She raised her eyes to his. "Yes?"

Amusement lurked behind his eyes. "We are friends, are we not? I can speak my mind with you. Indeed, I can think of no other female of my acquaintance to whom I could have spoken in such a fashion who would not have fallen into a fit of the strongest hysterics! That is not such a small thing, and very much more comfortable than scenes and tears and all the other accompaniments of an affair of passion, I promise you."

"I suppose it must be," she said thoughtfully.

"It is," he said firmly. "I am sure we will deal famously together. Still, I would like to propose some terms for our arrangement which I hope will put to rest any reservations you might feel."

"Any reservations—?" Susan inquired faintly.

"Well, yes. Naturally, we could not be married at once. It would cause no end of unpleasant speculation and comment, and defeat our purpose. I have been thinking about it, and it seems to me that the best thing is to take you up to London and arrange for my sister to bring you out. No one outside the family need know anything more than that. At the end of the Season, we will announce our betrothal." He folded his arms and looked at her. "Or not. If you do not wish to proceed when we are better acquainted, we will speak no further of it. I will conduct you wherever you wish to go and help you any way I can. Does that seem fair enough?"

"Would your sister agree to that?" she asked, surprised.

His lordship saw no need to divulge the stratagems to which he would resort in order to secure Lady Wibberly's participation. "I believe so," he said with a smile.

"It sounds very fair," Susan admitted. "But, sir, are you quite sure that this is what you wish? It will soon be apparent to your family and friends that my upbringing has been a trifle unusual, and I have not the air of a young lady of fashion!"

"If you had, I should not have suggested our . . . arrangement," he assured her.

"And you would not mind if Minnie were to live with us?" she asked shyly.

His lips twitched, but he said with admirable gravity, "For the present, I think it would be better for Minnie to remain here. I fear that my brother-in-law's London house offers no suitable accommodations for . . . ah . . . a screech owl. However, as soon as we move to Summerland I will undertake to construct an appropriate abode, and in the meantime, I will guarantee her well-being at your cousin William's hands."

"Well, I don't see how you can do that," she said seriously, "because he is quite unreasonable on the subject."

"No doubt you do not, but nevertheless that is what will happen," he assured her.

She seemed satisfied. "In that case, I agree to . . . to what you suggest," she said, suddenly unable to look at him. "And I promise I shall not interfere with you, sir."

He raised her hand, which was rather cold, to his lips. "We should have something to seal our bargain, but in this house I suppose that is quite impossible. You are chilled, I think, from sitting outside so long. It was thoughtless of me."

"Oh no!" she cried vehemently. "I don't wish to go back in!"

He regarded her with amused understanding. "There is not the least need for you to worry, you know. I will handle everything."

"It is only that Cousin William—who may have returned home by now—is rather hot-tempered, and I am afraid it will kick up quite a dust when you break the news. What *shall* you tell him, by the by?"

"Do you really wish me to tell you?"

She laughed suddenly. "No, I do not! As a matter of fact, I don't care a whit!"

Miss Winston might have professed indifference as to what would be said during the course of his lordship's interview with her cousin William, but she could not remain indifferent to its outcome, nor, when the gentlemen retired to the library and closed the door behind them, did she find it within her power to sit still. On the whole, she found this enforced period of reflection decidedly uncomfortable, and not just because of the presence of her great aunt, whose only comment on her behavior was to mutter *hoyden* and *silly chit* at frequent intervals.

She was prey to an army of second thoughts. Indeed, she was almost horrified at the speed of her capitulation, and wondered how she had let herself be persuaded to throw herself upon the protection of a man—a rake!—she had only just met. The misery of her present situation was no excuse: she had guessed how it would be, and if the house was gloomier and her great aunt rather more eccentric than she had been led to believe, she still could not claim that she had been measurably deceived. If only there had been someone to talk to, and if Cousin William had been not quite so disapproving of any expression of liveliness on her part, her situation might have almost been tolerable. The primary difficulty was that she, who had resolved to make the best of whatever circumstances befell her, could not look into the future with any kind of confidence. Her usefulness to her cousin would end with Lady

Harrington's demise, and even the briefest acquaintance with
his character and the fate of his elderly servants (with whom
she was, despite the family connection, rather more akin in
status than otherwise) could not but inspire in her the belief
that he would soon thereafter be rid of her at the least expense
and trouble to himself. However nobly she had vowed to accept her lot after her father's death, she could not regard with
anything but dismay and dread the prospect of living out her
life as a companion to a succession of elderly ladies. Lord
Everly had suggested that she would end up like Miss Pennyfeather if she stayed on here, but at least Penny had been
loved and valued despite her garrulity, and had enjoyed a sta-
ble home for the better part of fifteen years before being pen-
sioned off into honorable retirement.

Lord Everly's proposal had offered an unlooked-for rescue
from the bleakest of futures. She knew herself to be an innocent about such depravity as he professed to have practiced,
but in truth his reputation did not bother her overmuch. His
eyes were cynical and bored, but not cruel. As a soldier's
daughter, she had seen enough cruelty to recognize and shrink
from it, but his lordship did not make her uneasy. In fact, she
suspected that he deliberately blackened his character and his
reputation for deep, painful reasons of his own. He seemed on
the whole a somewhat mysterious figure, who laughed when
she suggested that his heart had been broken, but nonetheless
had turned his back on Society. As for herself, she had never
been in Society long enough to turn her back on it, but she
could not help believing that its pastimes were sadly overrated.
She had now and then thought wistfully of balls and rout parties, but she had never aspired to the portals of Almack's or a
presentation at Court. She could not fully understand his family's apparent obsession with establishing his respectability,
but then, she reminded herself, if she had been born with rank
and fortune she might very well feel otherwise.

Still, it seemed to her that she could quite easily be wrong
about everything and be making a terrible mistake. The warnings of the detestable Mrs. Lorry would not quite evaporate
from her mind, try as she might to make them vanish. As the
minutes lengthened into a half hour and beyond, her apprehen-
sion grew, and it was all she could do not to run into the library to put an end to whatever might be proceeding there.
Only Lord Everly's promise that she need not go through with

it in the end if she did not wish to kept her anchored, however uncomfortably, to her chair.

The library door opened at length, and a moment or two later the gentlemen entered the morning room. Cousin William's expression looked bland but not censorious, so perhaps Lord Everly had not put him out of temper after all. Behind her cousin's back his lordship winked at her, but she was too nervous to make any sign in return. Her Aunt Harrington remained majestically unmoved by anything but her own persistent ill humor and remained silent.

"Well, my dear," said her cousin in tones warmer than she had hitherto heard from him, "it seems you are to leave us. His lordship tells me that your father appointed him your guardian, albeit unofficially, before he died, although he was prevented from assuming these responsibilities immediately by an unfortunate illness. In fact he says it is only by chance that he learned of your coming here. I must say," he said, pursing his lips in the fashion that most reminded her of a hake, or perhaps a flounder, "that had you disclosed this relationship to me earlier, we might have made entirely different arrangements for your visit here."

Although he clearly meant that he was annoyed at having her servile condition exposed to a highborn stranger, he did not seem unduly exorcised, and Susan wondered what inducement he had been offered to accept whatever arrangement his lordship had offered. "I assure you, sir," she told him gravely, "that the relationship comes as much of a surprise to me as it does to you."

The viscount's lips twitched. "I don't believe you were consulted, being quite young at the time," he said. "I owed your father a debt, and naturally I wish to fulfill my obligations. And, as I have said, our agreement was an informal one."

"What sort of a debt?" inquired Lord Harrington.

"I'm afraid I am not at liberty to say," said his lordship in a quelling tone.

"Naturally! I had no wish to presume, that is . . ."

Susan quite enjoyed the novelty of seeing her cousin discomfited, although she felt somewhat guilty in her pleasure. "I am sure I am very grateful to you and Aunt Harrington for taking me in," she told him, by way of penance.

"Of course, it was no more than our duty," he intoned. "The life you go to—for Lady Wibberly is to bring you into Society, you know—is not one I should care for, full of fripperies and nonsense . . . Well, that's as may be. If you do not find it to your taste, I hope you know that you will always have a home here with her ladyship and myself."

"Nodcock!" interjected Lady Harrington.

As it was unclear which of the company she was addressing, no one responded to the remark, and indeed it appeared that no response was expected. Her ladyship made no further attempt to enter the conversation until Lord Everly bent over her hand in preparation for taking his leave. She gave him a steely glance, and signed that he should come closer.

He put his ear close by her lips. "I saw something *wicked* in the inglenook!" she cried with a shriek of laughter.

"Really, Mother, what will his lordship think of you?" said her son in disgusted tones.

"Looby," said her ladyship with a croak.

Chapter 6

Whatever consternation and distress might have attended the news of the impending departure of Miss Winston from Fenwood Hall, the arrival of a missive from Lord Everly to his sister detailing his plans for matrimony and conveying the information that she would be expected to sponsor the girl's entrance into Society occasioned even more anguish, and far more comment. The happy news was brought up to Lady Wibberly on her breakfast tray; a few moments later, a maid, passing by her ladyship's bedroom door with a water jug, was startled to hear such a cry as to make her "jump out of her skin," as she informed the butler later, and allow the pitcher to slip through her hands to the floor. Shortly thereafter an urgent message was dispatched to his lordship to the effect that his wife required his immediate presence in her bedchamber. Unaccustomed to such a summons, his bad angel led him to put the most flattering possible construction upon it, and he delayed his attendance for a few moments while he took extra care over his toilette. The bracing effect of this on his dignity was somewhat mitigated by a near collision with the maid who was cleaning up a puddle outside his wife's door; once admitted, her mood of hysteria—compounded with severe irritation over his tardiness—at once revealed to him the error of his assumptions.

Lord Wibberly was not a coward, but experience had taught him which of his wife's moods it would be preferable to avoid, and when he saw her clutching the letter in her hands as if to twist and work it into submission, her eye darting flames, he felt it would not be inexcusable to absent himself from the room as soon as may be. His attempt to do so, however, caught her ladyship's attention, and she scornfully directed him to be seated and learn what had befallen them. His lordship was so relieved at not being the immediate object of her obvious unhappiness that for a few moments he could not grasp precisely what *was* the subject of it.

"—And I am quite sure," his wife was saying, "that he is the most selfish creature alive. All my plans for the Season are quite overset, and after I was at such pains to invite Lady Drinkwater and her daughter—a quite eligible girl, despite being in her fourth Season, for she is not to blame for the outbreak of measles that sent them all away from town last year, though I must say, it was most ill timed. In all events—Wibberly, are you attending me?"

"My dear?" he inquired guiltily.

"Did you hear me tell you that Desmond is planning to be married?"

"Ah," he said, brightening. "That is excellent news! Who's the gal?"

She closed her eyes momentarily. "It is anything but," she said, pronouncing each word slowly and carefully. "That is what I have been trying to explain to you."

"It's not? Then why did we have to go to Summerland cutting up your brother's peace and demanding that he do his duty and find himself a wife? Thought that was what you wanted."

"It was what I wanted. But Desmond has found a way to circumvent my plans as usual. He has fallen into one of his distempered freaks and asked a nobody—a nobody!—to marry him. And after all my efforts to introduce him to the right sort of girl, I must say it is positively *insulting*."

Lord Wibberly's jaw dropped. "Not a *farm* girl," he suggested.

"Well, no," admitted her ladyship.

A more sinister idea occurred to his lordship. "You don't mean to say that Everly's been caught in the parson's mousetrap by some alluring bit of game inconveniently well provided with male relations! I thought he was too sharp for that!"

"I don't mean anything of the kind," said his wife indignantly. "At least I trust not. He *says* the girl is respectable enough—her father was some sort of general—but she hasn't a feather to fly with. He also writes that he is under some mysterious obligation for a service the general did him, and feels obliged to provide for her future. That's all a hum, to be sure. I hope I am as fond of my brother as any sister, but he is far too frivolous to have dealings with any general, unless the poor man advanced him a sum to pay his debts of honor, which I sincerely doubt, for when was Des ever in need of funds?"

"Do you know, Almeria," said her husband seriously, "I have always believed you give your brother far too little credit."

"It is most unjust of you to say so, Tom, for you know I have always acknowledged that there is no one more charming than Des, when he chooses to exert himself. Even you will admit, however, that except where the family is concerned he can be the most selfish, indifferent person alive. This latest escapade of his only proves it! In fact, I should not be surprised if he did not arrange it all with the sole object of being provoking. He is all too capable of it, I assure you."

Lord Wibberly felt it prudent to refrain from comment on the improbability of getting leg-shackled merely to disoblige one's sister, but he said, "I see what it is, Almeria! You're miffed because Des has gone and done the thing on his own instead of settling for one of those dull-as-dishwater girls you've been pitching at him these five years and more. If you'd found him a cozier armful in the first place, it might have come off as you wished!"

"I should think," she replied with some asperity, "that it is all too obvious that there has been no shortage of what you call 'cozy armfuls' in Des's history, though none of them, thank God, was able to tempt him into matrimony. You wrong me if you think I should make any objection if I were satisfied that this betrothal was perfectly proper and respectable or even a love match! But it appears to be neither, for how could he have fallen in love in such a short period of time, and indeed he makes no such representation in his letter. I fear there is something dreadfully havey-cavey about the whole business, and we shall end up in a scandal."

"Nonsense!" expostulated his lordship. "Des may be a bit wild but he ain't a scoundrel! Ten to one there will be nothing objectionable at all in the match, if you don't count the chit's lack of fortune."

"If you don't count—" said Lady Wibberly faintly, almost deprived of speech.

"You must admit that Des is excessively plump in the pocket," said her husband a trifle enviously. "He's no need to marry an heiress after all."

"It is not a question of fortune merely," intoned her ladyship in grave accents. "You have not yet *heard all*."

Lord Wibberly waited with resignation.

She glanced down at the letter still crumpled in her fist. "He writes that the betrothal is not to be announced immediately, an unexpected piece of good sense on his part, I must say, for I cannot imagine the scandal broth that would be brewing if he were to take it into his head to be wed at once! However, he says it is not to be known outside of the family, because at the end of the Season he wishes to give the girl a chance to *withdraw*. As if there were the least hope of that! No doubt she is a charming schemer who has gulled him into some imaginary sense of obligation—"

"Des ain't as green as all that," protested her husband.

Lady Wibberly snorted derisively but did not take him up on it. "Nevertheless, I do not see what other explanation there can be, for she has apparently persuaded him that she must have a London Season, and he expects me—us—to sponsor her! To take her into our house with our own daughters! To introduce a corrupting influence under our own roof! And not only that," she added, laying down the final blow, "he expects me to procure vouchers to *Almack's*!"

"Well, can't you do it?" inquired her husband with irritating reasonableness. "Aren't you bosom bows with Emily Cowper? Why can't you just ask her to procure the vouchers for you? Won't she do it if she knows you're sponsoring the girl?"

Her ladyship could only shake her head in exasperation over the abysmal ignorance of her husband in particular, and of men in general. "And what if she isn't *suitable*, as I fear may well be the case? I could scarcely ask Lady Cowper, or anyone, to do me such a favor. They would regard it as the greatest imposition, and possibly even *forward*, and I should be quite ruined. That may not matter to you, and I fear it does not matter to Des, but it does to me, I promise you!"

"Now, my dear," said her husband soothingly, "no need to get into such a taking! I am sure you can bring it off. Besides, we do not know that the girl won't be up to every rig and row, do we?"

She sighed. "Even if she is not a *schemer*, which I do not doubt for a moment, there is every chance she is a rustic. I fear that will be the best we can hope for. I can only pray that she is not one of the *demimonde*, or some such thing, for Desmond writes that she was reared on the Continent, and you know what *that* means!"

"If she is a general's daughter, it probably means nothing of the sort," protested her husband.

"Think of it! Army camps! All those soldiers!" She put a hand to her forehead. "Wibberly, if Desmond has foisted someone *improper* on us it will quite break Mama's heart."

"Possibly, but if the girl's a right 'un, it will very likely be the making of him. You know you were just urging Des to find a wife so he could do his duty by the family and your mama."

"I have no hope of such a happy outcome," she replied. "I must abide by Des's wishes for the moment, but if he is attempting to bring someone totally ineligible into the family, I will stop at nothing until the house is rid of her!"

His lordship, perceiving the militant gleam in his wife's eye, could almost find it in his heart to feel sorry for his brother-in-law's betrothed.

Happily unaware of the animosity her very existence had roused in Lady Wibberly's breast, Miss Winston was savoring her first taste of freedom, or at least that measure of it permitted a young girl about to embark on her first Season, in the company of a hastily secured abigail and the man who would become—in a relatively short period of time—her husband. Since contemplation of this prospect only served to make her shy and self-conscious in his presence, she resolved not to think about it, with the result that their earlier, easy friendship reemerged, and she was soon chatting happily about the treats in store for her in London, which Lord Everly bore with a good-natured resignation. He presently discovered that the proposed delights involved visits to bookstores and museums and such *untonnish* sights as the Tower or Westminster Abbey in lieu of more fashionable haunts.

Lord Everly was amused. "If that is how you intend to spend your time in London, I fear you will cast my sister into a fit of the vapors, or whatever it is she chooses to call it when things do not go her way," he told her as they rode along in the elegant carriage bearing his crest on the panel that would convey them to the Wibberlys' town house in London. "She will think you are quite *blue!*"

Susan looked up at him with concern. "Is it not . . . proper to go to such places?"

"Perfectly proper, so long as you are accompanied," he assured her.

"I see. Then it must be that your sister does not care to go to such places herself."

"Well, no," said his lordship with a smile, trying to imagine Lady Wibberly in rapturous contemplation of the Tower menagerie or seriously engaged in examining the Rosetta Stone at the British Museum. "Nor, I fear, would any lady aspiring to a berth in Society admit to any desire to do so. It would be quite *fatal* to one's chances of success!"

"With all due respect to your sister," she said firmly, "I think that is very silly! All my life I have heard about Hatchard's and the picture gallery of Mr. Angerstein—not to mention the other places!—and it would be the shabbiest thing imaginable if I were to miss them just in order to cut a better figure in Society. I warned you that I should not succeed in town, and I wonder if we should not reconsider our scheme. It does seem very unfair of you to foist me off onto your sister when it is abundantly clear she will be highly displeased!"

"On the contrary," he said, an ironic smile hovering about his lips, "did I not read you the charming letter she has written assuring me of her delight in receiving you into her home?"

"Yes, you did," said Susan shortly, feeling that further comment might be disrespectful to his sister. "What sort of amusements does Lady Wibberly prefer?" she asked after a moment.

"Well, she is excessively fond of shopping," said his lordship in a reminiscent manner. "And I am forced to admit that her taste is exquisite, so you would do well to be guided by her."

"I shan't be doing very much shopping," protested Susan mulishly.

"Do you intend to be a recluse?" he asked her in a disinterested tone.

Despite her resolution, she laughed. "Of course I do not."

"Then you will most certainly be doing a great deal of shopping, for you cannot go around London in those clothes," he said blandly.

"What's wrong with this dress?" she cried, surveying her favorite lawn green traveling dress with dismay. "I thought it was quite acceptable!"

He raised his eyebrows eloquently. "There is nothing wrong with it except that it is more than three years out of style and appears to be much worn," he told her.

"Well, it has been!" she replied, a little stung.

"Exactly," said his lordship with maddening calm.

"Besides, I cannot afford a new wardrobe," she told him frankly.

"But I can," he said smoothly.

"You needn't think I would let you frank me, or your sister! I could not ask such a thing of you, and while I may not know a great deal about the *world*, I do know that it would not be considered proper!"

"Do you?" he inquired, with a glint in his eye. "Are you forgetting my obligation to your papa?"

"Your obligation——?? Forgive me, my lord, but you sound as if *you* believe that Banbury tale."

"Perhaps I am coming to," he admitted. "It is so very reasonable, you see. Your cousin William was highly affected by the tale, I promise you."

"He was more likely highly affected by the handsome present you made him to compensate for my stay, though I wish you had not!" she said ruefully.

"Ungrateful brat! Would you rather he kicked up a fuss, and turned—er—Minerva into a taxidermist's exhibit?"

"No," she admitted unhappily. "It is just that I do not like for you to lay out so much money on my behalf."

Lord Everly, whose relatives were only too willing to encourage his generosity to themselves with uncomfortable frequency, rather enjoyed the novelty of having his overtures rebuffed. However, it was clear that if he did not put an end to such discussions at once, Miss Winston would go about London in attire that would announce to the world in general that she was either poor or eccentric, and neither epithet was one he wished to be attached to a young lady his family would be sponsoring upon the *ton*. "You will admit, I think, that I have more experience than you," he said, assuming a manner that more than once had put an upstart in his place.

"Oh, but—"

"Then you must allow me to decide what is to be done about such matters, and to make such arrangements as I see fit. You would not wish to put me to the blush, would you?"

"I didn't know I could," she said in an innocent voice.

He looked at her suspiciously and then burst into laughter, abandoning his hauteur. "Point conceded! Still, you must come off your high ropes and stop coming to cuffs with me over money, or you will make me highly displeased, I promise you."

"In that case, I will do as you say, because I am far too

obliged to you to give you a set-down, my lord!" she said meekly.

The arrival of Lord Everly's carriage at the door of his sister's house in Mount Street caused a flutter both above- and belowstairs, but nothing in the frigidly correct demeanor of her ladyship's butler was indicative of anything but glacial composure. Susan was inclined to view his starched countenance with something akin to terror, but Lord Everly said merely, "Good evening, Jervis. Is her ladyship at home?"

"Yes, my lord," replied this stately personage. "She and his lordship are in the yellow saloon. I'm to take you up at once, if that is convenient."

Susan had only a few moments to take in the classic sweep of the staircase and the elegance of the hangings before being conducted into the saloon, where even her untrained eye confirmed the quality of the Greek Revival furnishings. Passing through the door which Jervis held for her, she favored him with a smile, which caused the gentleman to so far unbend as to later remark to his subordinates in the servants' hall that he knew Quality when he saw it and Miss was Quality, neither fawning or top-lofty! He conveyed these sentiments with a measure of relief, for although they did not know the precise relationship to the family of his lordship's ward, the servants had detected an ill-concealed uneasiness on the part of the master and mistress with regard to the unknown Young Person. She had been assigned the rose bedroom, reserved for formal guests, but it was some distance from those allotted to Miss Eliza and Miss Louisa. The best dishes had been ordered for dinner, but the housekeeper, inquiring as to what supplies might be laid in to tempt a young lady's dainty appetite, had met with a brisk rebuff. Jervis, usually able to interpret a visitor's status with unerring exactitude, found himself somewhat at a loss, a state which he, who bore the responsibility for setting the tone for all the others, did not enjoy.

Meanwhile Susan, happily unaware of the complicated emotions she was arousing in the butler's breast, passed on into the saloon, where Lady Wibberly awaited her on an enormous sofa with winged paw feet. When the visitors were announced, she set aside her embroidery in a rather leisurely fashion and rose in a dignified manner which would not have put a princess to the blush. She was exquisitely gowned in a half dress of rose silk which had the immediate effect of making Susan feel like the veriest dowd. She was not as beautiful as her brother was handsome, but her profile was classic and her style was undeniably au courant. Coming forward to greet her guests, she favored Susan with an appraising look and two fingers extended, which Susan took care to touch lightly before she dropped into a slight curtsy.

"How do you do, ma'am? I have been so anxious to meet you!" she said in as calm a voice as she could command. "Indeed, I wish to thank you for your kindness for lending me your countenance and taking me into your home."

Lady Wibberly, perceiving that her adversary was, despite her worst fears to the contrary, a girl with both pretty manners and a certain air of breeding, thawed infinitesimally, at least as much as was required to present the child to her husband.

His lordship, stepping out from behind the couch, noticed that Miss Winston was quite a pretty girl and greeted her rather more warmly than his spouse, saying that he hoped she would find her stay with them very comfortable and that if there was anything he could do to make it so she was to let him know at once.

Her ladyship, betraying not by the movement of a muscle how irritating she found her husband's instant capitulation, patted the cushion beside her and murmured delicately that Miss Winston must come and sit beside her and tell her all about her family and her life on the Continent.

Lord Everly, who had been left out of the conversation by design, watched with growing amusement as his sister interrogated his intended, artfully extracting every detail of her parentage and upbringing, down to the details of every military encampment she had visited, and the number of soldiers under the general's command. It began to be borne in on him that Miss Winston was supplying rather more colorful particulars than were strictly necessary and indeed painted a picture of an existence not dissimilar to that of a Gypsy, wandering from camp to camp, unsupervised and unrestricted. She made no mention of Miss Pennyfeather or her stepmother, managing to convey without actually saying so that she had grown up entirely without the benefit of female example or attendance. Lord Everly would not have been surprised if she had claimed to have been reared in a tent. His sister's raised eyebrows certainly gave the impression that the news would not have come as a shock to her.

Retaining a precarious hold on his gravity, he intervened to suggest to her ladyship that her guest was tired and might like to change for dinner.

"Yes, certainly," said Lady Wibberly, looking a trifle wan herself. "I'll ring for Mrs. Hopkins to show you to your room."

"I should take myself off as well," said Lord Everly, rising.

"You'll stay to dine with us, of course!" said his sister in some alarm.

He lifted an eyebrow at her. "What, Almeria? Sit down in my dirt?"

"Well, return then!" she said, surveying him critically. "I'll put it back half an hour. You must come, Des! Cosmo is to dine with us!"

"The devil he is!" cried his lordship. "Forgive me, but in that case I most certainly will *not* be here."

"That would be most unfortunate, since I made sure to tell him that you would be."

"You presume a great deal," he told her.

"I know that you wish for all to proceed smoothly, and I fear I would not deal with his inquiries—you know what he is, Des!—just as you would like. But if you insist—"

"I beg pardon, ma'am, but would it not be simpler for me to have a tray in my room?" inquired Susan, who did not have any difficulty in guessing what direction Mr. Canby's inquiries might take.

"It probably would be," admitted her ladyship, "but he is coming especially to make your acquaintance."

"What I should like to know," said her brother in a voice of dangerous calm, "is how he came into possession of, ah, the facts regarding Miss Winston's visit."

"Well I'm sure *I* do not know," said Lady Wibberly in an affronted tone, correctly divining his implication. "For I have certainly told no one, although I must say if we are going to bring you out, Miss Winston, I do not see the purpose of concealing your existence! I daresay Cosmo is merely curious to see your ward, Des, or some such thing. He is always first with family news, you know that. For all I know he may have an informant among the staff!"

"Thing is," said Lord Wibberly in an unhappy voice, "I told him myself!"

His wife looked as if a potted plant had attempted to inject itself into the conversation. "Really, Wibberly! How could you!"

Lord Everly said soothingly, "What did you tell him, Tom?"

"The thing of it is," explained his lordship, "the fellow's so deucedly insinuating. Latches on like a hound after the scent. Caught me walking home from my club the other night."

"Yes?" inquired Lord Everly encouragingly.

"Wanted to know what you were up to in Yorkshire, Des. He said he could not imagine you amusing yourself on the farms! You know that odd little laugh he has! I said you'd written Almeria that you were bringing back a girl you wanted her to sponsor, because of a debt you owed her father. That's all."

"That is more than enough for Cosmo," said his wife. "Ever since . . . since he perceived that there was a chance he might someday step into Everly's shoes, he has spared no pains to make our business his own."

"I own he has often attempted to do so," said Lord Everly calmly, "but he has not often succeeded, at least not with me."

"Well, it is all very well for you to depress his pretensions," said his sister with some acerbity, "but what are we to do when you are not here to gaze down your nose at him in that quelling fashion you have perfected? You know he is likely to make Miss Winston very uncomfortable, and he is the most dreadful gossip, besides having a very acid tongue."

"Very well, Almeria, I will dine with you tonight. But if I am to do so, I must go at once. I pray you ring for Mrs. Hopkins at once. See me out. See me out, my child?" he asked Miss Winston.

She nodded. "If you'll excuse me, ma'am?"

Lady Wibberly bowed slightly. "I'll tell the housekeeper to meet you downstairs," she agreed.

When the door had closed behind her, Susan let out a sigh of relief.

Lord Everly regarded her with amusement, "Fagged, brat?"

She nodded. "Your sister is very grand," she admitted.

"Wait until you meet my cousin," he said wickedly. "He is quite a Pink of the Ton and most impressive."

"Lady Wibberly seems to think he might be dangerous," she said in an inquiring tone.

He laughed. "You are not to worry about that! I am more than a match for Cousin Cosmo, I promise you. Although I must say that you will not make my task any easier if you persist in regaling him with stories of your life following the drum, wandering from camp to camp like some Gypsy brat."

"Your sister believed me."

"Yes." He waited.

She sighed. "I should not have done it. She believed me because she wished to, so I . . . gave her what she wanted."

"Perhaps. Her questions were impertinent, but it is not wise to make a game of my sister."

"I did not *want* to be rag-mannered," she said ruefully. "It is just that her prying questions put me all on end, and I did not think they were respectful of Papa."

"Don't let it trouble your peace. She has no concept of military life, and distrusts what she does not know."

"No, I should learn to hold my tongue," she said seriously, "especially when she is going to bring me out and I am persuaded does not wish to do so. How did you compel her?"

"Compel?" he asked, with a glint in his eye. "How could I?"

"Well, I am sure I do not know," she said frankly, "because it is quite clear she does not wish to please you."

Lord Everly gave a little choke. "Perhaps, but she has an earnest desire to see me wed."

"Yes," said Miss Winston thoughtfully, "but not to me!"

Chapter 7

Miss Winston was not far off in her assessment of Lady Wibberly's feelings. Scarcely was the room empty of her brother and her guest than she remarked with an air of melancholy that she very much feared that Desmond stood within an ames-ace of committing the biggest imprudence of his life.

"Nonsense, my dear!" said her husband encouragingly. "Seems quite a nice girl. Pretty, too!"

She gave him a smile in which affection was mixed with contempt. "I'll admit she is well-looking enough, and that her manners need not put one to the blush. On the whole, it is better than I expected. But, Wibberly! Such an upbringing! Can you imagine such a child mistress of *Summerland Abbey*? She would turn the greenhouses into barracks, or some such thing."

"I expect she was hoaxing you," ventured his lordship.

"Hoaxing me?" responded her ladyship in a tone which suggested that she found such a notion preposterous. "Impossible."

"Not a military man myself," said her husband unnecessarily, "but I shouldn't think a general's family lives any but the most respectable sort of life. Quite high sticklers, most of 'em. Look at Wellington."

"Perhaps, but Lord Wellington's family is of the very best, you know. His brother is a marquess!"

"Well, we don't know this girl's family tree doesn't sport a lord or two either. In fact, we don't know much about her at all."

"That is precisely the point I have been trying to make since we received that infamous letter," she pointed out. "Besides, why should she want to tell me stories about herself that make her look positively *common* if they weren't true?"

Lord Wibberly, unable to formulate an answer to this question that his wife might find acceptable, said nothing.

* * *

Sometime later, when Susan descended to the drawing room before dinner, she was dismayed to discover that the habit of punctuality, doubtless the result of her military upbringing, had brought her downstairs ahead of anyone else. The general's protocol, not unlike that of royalty, had stemmed not only from a natural courtesy but from the knowledge that a late arrival wreaked havoc with the plans of one's underlings, precisely because events could not truly begin without him. Susan had no such excuse, and indeed, the surprised expression of the butler, quickly masked, demonstrated that promptness was not entirely à la mode. She seated herself on the striped sofa, carefully arranging the skirts of her classically cut evening dress of delicate lawn, and vowed that the next evening should find her descending a full fifteen minutes later, at the very least.

She did not have so long to wait, however, before her solitude was broken by the entrance of a rather large gentleman in evening dress. His swallow-tailed, tight-fitting cutaway was not flattering to a figure of such ample girth, and Susan had difficulty removing her eyes from his waist, which was hung all about with fobs and seals. His hair was pomaded and artfully arranged to disguise the fact that formerly there had been a great deal more of it. His face, which bore the slightest resemblance to Lord Everly despite its fullness, might have been called handsome if nature, or experience, had not given it a somewhat peevish expression. Susan surmised that she was in the presence of what she had always heard laughingly referred to as a dandy, and there was no doubt that this was his lordship's dreaded cousin, Cosmo Canby.

He moved toward her with an instant stare, saying with a slight stammer, "How d-do you do? Do I have the pleasure of addressing Miss Winston?"

She rose and curtsied. "Yes, I am Miss Winston. You must be Mr. Canby, I believe."

A smile—not quite sincere—hovered about his slack mouth, but it did not reach his eyes. "Ah, you've heard of me, I see! I am ch-charmed to make your acquaintance. I did not know Lord Everly had a *ward* till now, and such a lovely one besides."

Susan disengaged her hand from his clasp and resumed her seat. He took the chair opposite her, all the time continuing what she could not but feel was a very uncomfortable scrutiny. "It m-makes a connection between us, you see," he said at last.

"What does?" she inquired politely.

"Your relationship with my cousin. Is it of long standing?"

"I am not precisely sure," she said carefully.

"Oh? Forgive me! I do not wish to p-pry. It is m-merely that such arrangements are often made at birth," he said with great affability.

"Are they?" she asked in an interested tone. "Well, Lord Everly is a great deal older than I am, you see, and his relationship was with Papa. And Papa, naturally, did not discuss his affairs with me."

Susan was rather proud of this parry to his thrust, and indeed it silenced him momentarily. However, after a few minutes he again picked up his theme. "And Lady Wibberly is to bring you out, I hear?"

"She has been so kind as to agree to sponsor me," assented Susan.

"I am sure she is quite transported with d-delight at the prospect," he said with a touch of acid.

She could not help blushing and murmured that Lord and Lady Wibberly had been everything that was agreeable, and that she was very grateful.

Mr. Canby saw that he had scored a hit, and stored up this information for future use. "No doubt your other relations will be most envious," he told her. "I have heard it said that nothing can exceed the pleasure of launching a girl upon the *t-ton*, only to see her become the rage. I have no d-doubt you will become the rage, for you are not just in the ordinary style."

"No?"

"Most definitely not. There is a decidedly old-fashioned air to your dress and m-manner which is quite sweet."

Susan, who realized full well that she had just been called a dowd, dug her fingernails into her palms and said dryly, "Thank you."

"Don't mention it," he said, smiling widely and running his eye over her in a manner that made her feel somewhat ill-at-ease. "I've no d-doubt we'll see you well married before the start of next year's Season."

"I am not on the catch for a husband!" she protested, gasping.

"Oh, ha ha!" he said, uttering that irritating little titter that so annoyed Lord Wibberly. "Naturally not, m-my dear. But you'll forgive my speaking frankly, because of your close connection to my family. One need not be 'on the catch' to see how desirable it would be to m-marry a man who can command the elegancies of life! And I have no doubt you can accomplish that, Miss Winston, particularly with Everly and the Wibberlys to back you!"

She wondered whether he truly suspected the nature of her proposed relationship with Lord Everly or whether he was just fishing. In either case, she had begun to conceive quite as much antipathy for him as did his cousins and was never so relieved as when the arrival of the others in the drawing room necessitated an end to their conversation.

Mr. Canby's efforts to uncover more details about her past, present, and probable future, however, were not limited to their interview before dinner. Susan, hidden behind a large epergne which Lady Wibberly felt lent consequence to her table, remained largely silent, despite Lord Wibberly's kind efforts to draw her out. As these generally took the direction of regaling her with stories of his hunting triumphs, she had only to nod occasionally and attempt to keep her heavy lids from closing, for she was very tired.

At length Lady Wibberly gave the signal to withdraw, and the ladies rose from the table. When the gentlemen were left with their port, Mr. Canby, with an air of paternal benevolence, remarked that Miss Winston was quite a taking little puss, and that he would not be at all surprised if she were to score a hit upon the *ton*.

"Just what I told Almeria!" said Lord Wibberly enthusiastically. "Quite a charming girl."

"A beauty, I should say," corrected Mr. Canby. "Wouldn't you, Everly?"

His lordship, arrested in the act of taking a pinch of snuff, looked up. "What is that, Cosmo? I'm afraid I was not attending."

"I was saying," he said with a glittering smile, "that your *ward* is quite a beauty."

"Is she?" he inquired in a bored tone. "Yes, I suppose she must be."

"B-but very young."

"Very," agreed his lordship.

"It must be quite a shock—and so very t-troublesome too—

to find oneself guardian to a grown girl!" suggested Mr. Canby solicitously.

"Oh, it is nowhere near so formal as that," replied Lord Everly casually. "She was commended to my care, merely."

"I wonder what made the general do so? He must have been out of his senses."

"I beg your pardon?" inquired his lordship, narrowing his eyes.

"Oh ha ha!" ejaculated Mr. Canby. "I only m-meant that it is rather odd to consign a pretty young girl t-to the care of an unmarried man, particularly . . . Well, that's of no consequence," he added hastily. "I collect he d-did you a service, or some such thing."

"Or some such thing," agreed Lord Everly.

"I see that you do not wish to t-tell me," he said a trifle stiffly. "It does not matter, but n-naturally you cannot expect me to believe that a general in the army somehow put you under obligation. You have scarcely led the sort of life which would put you on such terms with a m-military man."

"Really, Canby, coming it much too strong!" protested Lord Wibberly.

"It is a matter of the smallest consequence to me what you believe," said Lord Everly indifferently. "The girl is under my family's protection; that is all anyone needs to know."

"Well you m-must own that they will have to know more than that if you are to get her a husband. And you must certainly do that!"

"Must I?" asked his lordship in an interested tone.

"Oh ha ha! Now I know you are joking," tittered Mr. Canby. "How else are you to d-dispose of her, if you do not see her respectably married? It is a p-pity that her fortune is not large, but perhaps a widower with children, or an elderly gentleman, in need of a nurse . . . "

"What a happy fate you prescribe for a lovely young girl, Cosmo," said Lord Everly, fixing him with a look of contempt.

He shrank from it, but added, "It's all very well, but you know the world. A child circumstanced as she is c-could scarcely hope to look *higher*."

Lord Everly smiled. Then he extended one exquisitely shod foot in his cousin's direction. "Do you admire my shoes, Canby?" he inquired.

His cousin surveyed them with critical scrutiny. He looked up. "Certainly. They are m-most elegant."

"How very fortunate. Then I take it it will not pain you to step into them at a moment's notice?"

Lord Wibberly guffawed.

"Step into them?" inquired his cousin. "Oh ha ha! I perceive you are joking. N-naturally I have no such expectation."

"Naturally," said Lord Everly with admirable gravity.

"I assure you," said Mr. Canby hastily, "that your return to health after your unfortunate . . . accident . . . is the greatest source of happiness to me. But what, pray tell," he added shrewdly, "has that to do with anything?"

"Nothing, Canby. Nothing whatsoever," responded his lordship.

Mr. Canby, thus heartened by his talk with Lord Everly, nevertheless felt it incumbent upon himself to take up the matter with his lordship's sister, as soon as he found her in the drawing room. Miss Winston had already gone up to bed, and her ladyship was yawning by the fire. He arranged himself with great ceremony beside her, murmuring such pleasantries as he was sure she would find agreeable, while the others began a game of cards. When they were so far occupied as to be unlikely to overhear any of his conversation, he said cautiously, "You know, Almeria, should you require my services at any time, I assure you you may d-depend on me!"

Lady Wibberly, who had not been attending him closely, looked rather startled. "Thank you, Cosmo," she said frankly, "but I do not imagine any service I might require you to perform, because Wibberly is so very attentive, you know!"

Mr. Canby barely repressed a smile at this description of Lord Wibberly. "N-naturally, cousin! I refer of course to services regarding"—he lowered his voice—"Miss Winston."

Lady Wibberly had little affection for Mr. Canby and began to find his hints irritating. "And pray what service might you perform for Miss Winston?" she asked him.

"For her, none," he said, hiding his impatience at her obtuseness. "For you, d-dear cousin, anything."

She fixed him with a look of exasperation. "Cosmo, if there is something you are trying to suggest, you will have to speak more plainly."

"I m-merely wish to say," he said in a very low voice, "that it *will not do!*"

Lady Wibberly stiffened. "And what am I to understand by that?" she said acidly.

"Come, Almeria, we need not fence. I am quite certain you cannot like the thought of having a schoolroom m-miss—and a nobody at that—for your sister-in-law."

She gasped.

"I am n-not such a fool as you all suppose," he suggested.

She looked at him with dislike. "You are presuming far too much, Cosmo," she told him.

"Perhaps," he said with a superior smile. "But you must own that it is just the sort of thing Desmond would d-do! How he loves to set Society all in a bustle! Eighteen and thirty-five! Of course, there could be no question of such a thing n-not proving acceptable to the young lady, circumstanced as she is. One need not wonder at her m-motives. And I very much fear that in one of his distempered freaks, Desmond is quite capable of anything!"

"Including putting a bullet through your heart at dawn should he hear you utter such a thing," riposted her ladyship.

Mr. Canby, turning a trifle pale at this remark, nonetheless recovered enough to say, "Oh ha ha! I was only funning, of course! But if one cannot b-be outspoken in one's own family . . . Oh ha ha! I assure you I have no wish to *predecease* Cousin Desmond."

"I am quite sure you have not," said Lady Wibberly meaningfully. "You have your own ends to serve, but it was quite improper of you to approach me. Besides, you mistake me: I have often encouraged Des to marry and will continue to do so!"

"But you will not, I b-believe, encourage him to marry Miss Winston."

She closed her lips.

"Precisely," he said with satisfaction. "I knew it m-must be so."

She threw him a look of disdain. "I do not wish to continue this conversation," she told him.

"Then I shall certainly oblige you," he said, rising and executing a small bow. "We all of us desire the same thing, and I d-daresay I am imagining far too much. Upon consideration, however, if you should wish for my assistance in achieving what I feel sure m-must be your very laudable goals, I beg you will send to m-me. I shall always be at home to any m-message of yours."

"I shall not send one," insisted Lady Wibberly.

"My dear cousin," he said with his broadest smile, "that is

entirely up to you. No one will be the more delighted if you can effect your campaign without reinforcements. I have no wish to find myself looking down anyone else's gun b-barrel at some impertinent hour! I must thank you for your hospitality, and for a most *revealing* evening. Everly! Cousin Tom! I m-must be going. Your servant, Almeria!"

"Do you know," said Lord Wibberly when his guest had departed, "try as I might, I just can't tolerate that fellow. Too coming by half!"

Lord Everly looked over his hand of cards with amusement. "You are the best of good fellows, Tom," he said with a smile. "That's the difference between us: I make no effort whatsoever!" He glanced over at his sister, who sat by the fire lost in thought, her hands clenched at her sides. "And what has our dear cousin been saying to put you in such a pucker, Almeria?"

She turned a stricken countenance to him.

"As bad as that?" he said, raising an inquiring eyebrow.

"Oh no!" she said, putting a hand to her forehead. "It is no such thing! I'm afraid I have a headache. You must excuse me!"

"My dear—" said her husband, getting to his feet.

"No, no, Wibberly! It is nothing. I shall be better after a night's sleep, I promise you."

"Shouldn't be surprised at her having the megrims," said Lord Wibberly when his wife had retired upstairs. "That Canby fellow is a regular jaw-me-dead."

"I wonder . . . " said Lord Everly meditatively.

Chapter 8

Despite the misgivings of almost everyone concerned with the project, considerable effort was expended in turning Miss Winston into a young lady of fashion as soon as possible. Lord Everly had acquired, through very improper means, a thorough knowledge of the most à la mode establishments, and his advice invoked in Lady Wibberly, herself undoubtedly au courant, a combination of admiration and annoyance.

"It must be Madame Lachatte," he told his sister, identifying London's premier modiste with irritating precision. "And for hats, Lucille."

"I prefer Renatta for hats," replied her ladyship, asserting her independence.

"You have not the slightest need to inform me of that," said Lord Everly, tempering the effect of this with a smile. "But for a girl in her first Season, Lucille."

Her ladyship was forced to concede the wisdom in this, as well as in his other suggestions. Moreover, though she could muster no enthusiasm over the prospect of Miss Winston's becoming her sister, she was not unmoved at playing Pygmalion to a very lovely Galatea, who would no doubt do credit to all the beautiful and exorbitant creations for which her brother would foot the bill. Accordingly, she was in animated spirits when she conducted her charge through the portals of the most expensive dressmaker in town.

Miss Winston thought that even the Prince Regent, whose taste for the opulent was highly developed, might have approved the French-style showroom of Madame Lachatte, outfitted as it was with gilded chairs, deep carpeting, and a maze of mirrors. The fashions themselves were delectable. There were dresses for any imaginable occasion, and choosing among the crepes and muslins, spider gauze, and silks provided the most satisfactory entertainment for both ladies, under the shrewd eye of Madame. Lady Wibberly was even moved to choose a checkered Caledonian silk for herself, which suited her so well she was in charity with the whole world for the rest of the afternoon.

Susan, surveying herself in an exquisite gown of sea green gauze open down the front over a dress of ivory satin ornamented with pearl rosettes, felt as if she were walking in a dream. She had the uneasy feeling that all this finery—not to mention the scarves, reticules, bonnets, and gloves she had already purchased—must have cost a rather appalling sum, and the consciousness of her indebtedness to Lord Everly cast the only cloud on her state of perfect happiness. When she broached the subject with him, however, he merely laughed and replied that the expenses were but trifles beside the vast outlay he had made for far less deserving females than herself, and to less effect, an utterance that would have thrown Lady Wibberly into a fit of hysterics, had she been privileged to hear it. Susan, however, was beginning to be a little acquainted with his lordship, and had noticed that he rarely failed, in the most cynically amused fashion, to cast himself in a thoroughly disreputable light. She cherished few illusions about his virtue, but she thought he was far from the unreformed rake-shame his stories and comments depicted. That his family and the world in general apparently chose to believe in this image of him was puzzling, but if that was what he wanted, it was not her place to intervene however much she might deplore it. Besides, she had engaged not to interfere with him, and she could not think of any reason to pretend that she was shocked when she was not.

Lady Wibberly was a dutiful hostess and in the course of their progress through town attempted to inculcate into her charge some of the regulations governing the life of a girl in her first Season. She must never be seen walking or riding in St. James's Street, where the men's clubs were; she must not fail to be seen in Hyde Park between the hours of five and six in the afternoon; she must never put herself forward should they chance to meet one of the Patronesses ("for," said her ladyship, "vouchers are by no means *assured*, and it would be quite *fatal* not to display the proper deference—quite as bad as waltzing without permission"); she must not go out unattended by a footman or her maid. By the time these and other strictures had been made plain to her, Susan was convinced that she was unequal to the task of living up to them and very nearly said so, despite her ladyship's kind assurances that she would be there to prompt and correct her should she fall into error.

One pleasure her hostess could not persuade her to abjure, however, were visits to Hatchard's bookstore, which she discovered was agreeably close to the Wibberlys' town house. The shop, with its bow windows filled with the latest literary offerings, delighted her, and she could scarcely refrain from spending her own modest pin money on any number of enchanting-looking publications. In this regard she found the library helpful, and at last was able to read the celebrated *Childe Harold*, whose youthful author had become the talk of every fashionable dinner table in London.

Closeted in her room in the afternoon with the poem, she found herself admiring it despite what seemed an unnecessary breathless quality and a gloomy melancholy. The hero was a debauched young nobleman with a rather full history of love affairs and self-destructive indulgences. He seemed to brood endlessly over his debaucheries without in any way attempting to give them up. Susan, who had been hearing described daily from Lady Wibberly the behavior in both men and women which would render them acceptable to the *ton*, could not believe that anyone in aristocratic London would willingly have invited a real Childe Harold into their midst, yet the poem inspired a sort of combination of infatuation and pity. Susan thought the author of such a work must be very clever to have brought it off. Her curiosity was piqued, and for a while she could not help looking for Byron at Hatchard's, for she knew it was as popular with poets as the general public. She thought she knew just what he would look like—wild curls over a Gypsy face, a silken handkerchief knotted round the neck, and the swashbuckling manner of a corsair. The improbability of encountering such a personage on the streets of London did occur to her, but rumor would not be denied. Lady Wibberly, appalled at her bookishness, was somewhat relieved to discover that her charge had conceived a fashionable interest in Byron, and confided that half the titled ladies in town were said to be swooning over him, and more than one young eligible maiden had set out to ensnare his heart. Susan, laughing, said that she supposed that if he bore any relation to his literary hero he must be considered very poor husband material and that in any case with such treatment he would very likely be spoilt. Her ladyship, surprised, opened her lips to answer but, apparently thinking better of her reply, closed them again on the topic altogether.

It was settled among the interested parties that Miss Winston would make her debut in Society at the ball of the Marquess and Marchioness of Milton, an annual affair early in the Season at which all those hopeful of a place in the sun were compelled by tradition to appear. Not to receive an invitation was not fatal, precisely, but an early indication that one would not, after all, move among the ranks of the most exalted. The Wibberlys were very good *ton* despite Lord Everly's reputation, and every door in London was open to them. Indeed, word of her ladyship's young protégée had already begun to circulate, and the tattletales had even begun to speculate about her birth and fortune. Lady Wibberly's mantle was an impressive one, and her sponsorship would have guaranteed initial entrée to a charwoman, had she chosen to bring one out into the world. After that, the candidate would be pitched to the wolves, standing or falling on her own perceived merits.

Susan, aware of little of this, nevertheless looked forward to her first London party with mixed emotions. Her ball dress of white crepe trimmed with velvet ribbons set off her chestnut curls and large gray eyes to perfection, and her only ornaments, a strand of her mother's fine Majorca pearls and a wreath of yellow roses in her hair, conveyed the perfect impression of elegant innocence. Standing in front of her mirror to survey the results of Lady Wibberly's dresser's efforts on her behalf, she was forced to admit that that formidable personage had achieved the hoped-for effect, and more. She would have been less than human if she had not been pleased and excited at the prospect of turning heads at such a glittering function as a London *ton* party, as Miss Davis had unbent enough to assure her she was certain to do, but she could not help wishing there were someone there with whom she might share the moment and its pleasures. Her mother, her father, her friends, even Penny had left her in one fashion or another, and all that was left to her was the company of strangers and those, like her host and hostess, who suffered her only because Lord Everly had said they must.

Her keenest disappointment was that his lordship would not be attending with her.

"Of all things, it is the sort of event I particularly dislike," he told her with a smile, when she had asked him whether he would be one of the party. "My appearance there would be like a cat among the pigeons, brat, and ruffle too many feathers."

She looked up at him in confusion and he laughed. "I don't expect you to understand, my child! I am quite sure you will enjoy yourself, so do not trouble about me. Besides, I am not the one to set your feet firmly on the social ladder. That is a task for my sister, and much better accomplished without my presence, I promise you! Be guided by Almeria, and you will not go wrong. She is quite *awesomely* tonnish," he added, his eyes full of mischief.

It was on the tip of her tongue to reply that she had very little interest in achieving such a state herself when she remembered that part of her function was to reestablish his respectability in the eyes of the world, and that, moreover, she had promised not to hang on his sleeve or interfere with him in any way. She was disconcerted to discover that the fact of his absence made the prospect of the evening rather flat, and she was chagrined that he would not see her in her finery. She gave herself a little shake, reflecting that the surest way to ruin their friendship would be to make impertinent demands upon his attention, so she said with a cheerful smile that she would try to be guided by her ladyship in all things.

Lady Wibberly was pleased to discover that Miss Winston displayed neither confusion nor lack of poise as she ascended the great carpeted staircase to be presented to her host and hostess, nor did she gaze about her in open-jawed admiration like a rustic at the flower-bedecked ballroom with its rows of mirrors and enormous crystal chandeliers. She had warned her charge that to seem overly impressed was the surest sign that one did not move in the very highest circles, and that if she were asked her opinion of the party she was to remark civilly but coolly on the crush, and refrain from making enthusiastic pronouncements of enjoyment, but Lady Wibberly could place no dependence on the girl's following her advice.

In fact, Susan had been to parties before her father's death, and, since the houses of European nobility had been opened to him because of his victories over the French, she was able to view the splendor of Milton House with unruffled composure. As she was further able to make her curtsy and reply to Lady Milton's greeting without either unwonted forwardness, or tongue-tied awkwardness, Lady Wibberly could not but feel that they had cleared the first hurdle, and her breath came a bit easier in her chest. Susan was perfectly aware of her ladyship's fears with regard to her behavior, but she could not in justice censure her when she had been at some pains to paint a picture of her upbringing such as must give rise to misgivings on her sponsor's part.

Although Lord Everly's reasons for not wishing to attend had previously remained enigmatic, once she had begun to be presented to the other guests Susan understood the import of his reference to a cat among the pigeons. There were perhaps a dozen girls such as herself, newcomers to the social scene intent on establishing their reputations and position. Lord Everly was just the sort of person their mothers would have warned them against, which doubtless would have increased his attractiveness tenfold. Susan had little doubt that a multitude of ingenious stratagems had been employed to ensnare him, and was glad, after all, that she had not importuned him to come.

Lord Everly's reluctance to run the gamut of matchmaking ingenues, however, was apparently not shared by his cousin Mr. Canby. That gentleman, resplendent in a profusion of rings, pins, fobs, chains, and seals, solicited the honor of her hand for the first set almost as soon as he became aware of her presence. Susan was not moved by his attentiveness; she would far rather have sat out the dance with the other girls than been subjected to his unctuous scrutiny. However, she could not refuse him when she had no other partner, so she smiled mechanically and accompanied him down the set. Mr. Canby's attempt at a wasp waist had failed utterly, but he compensated by padding his shoulders to such an extent that the rest of his body was reduced in proportion. Susan could scarcely take her eyes from his waistcoat, which was striped and rather startling.

"Enjoying yourself, M-miss Winston?" he inquired with a knowing smile that set her teeth on edge.

"Very much," she acknowledged politely. "I have already met a number of very agreeable people."

"Excellent," said Mr. Canby. "I knew I should have to m-move quickly, to get a dance with you. Are you engaged for all the sets?"

"Not all," she answered before she had thought.

"Well, if I see you are not dancing I shall certainly rescue you," he said jovially. "You must allow me my cousinly p-privileges, considering your standing in the family."

Susan suspected that he was about to subject her to another of his impertinent inquiries and wished she had had the forethought to disappear from view before he had come to claim her for the dance. She certainly did not mean to give him a second chance. She was spared the ordeal of swallowing the retorts his conversation always provoked in her a wish to utter by the arrival of a party of rather late guests. One of them, a man of swarthy complexion and dark, brooding eyes, arrested her attention at once. His hair was artfully combed into disarray, and his neckcloth was arranged with so much casualness that he might actually have tied it in less than ten minutes. Susan was suddenly sure that this must be the author of *Childe Harold*. There was a suggestion of sneering carelessness about his person that must have inspired his hero's world-weary pain.

"What is it that interests you, my dear?" prompted Mr. Canby. "I do not believe you have b been listening to a word I say."

Susan started guiltily, and Mr. Canby followed the direction of her gaze to where the knot of young men stood greeting their hostess.

Mr. Canby's expression soured perceptibly. "Ah, Byron. I suppose you share with other young ladies a fascination with our famous young poet?"

"Indeed, sir, we have not been introduced," murmured Susan.

"Well *I* shall certainly not do so," he said in an attempt at archness. "I am quite persuaded that Cousin Almeria would not regard him as a fit p-person for you to know!"

"Really?" inquired Susan innocently. "Why not?"

His eyes narrowed, and he looked at her for a long moment. "For many reasons," he said finally. "His popularity is based on affectation and contempt. It is everything deplorable that such a person should play a leading role in Society, however briefly." He gave a bitter little laugh. "It is said that his n-notice can elevate one to the highest rungs, quite as if he were Brummell himself. It is most outrageous." He noticed her regarding him quizzically and, apparently recalled to his surroundings, gave her a forced smile. "It is of n-no consequence," he said. "He cannot last. In twenty years, I daresay no one will even remember his n-name!"

Since the prospect gave him evident satisfaction, Susan did not dispute it. She could not but hope that the music would soon be over so that he could return her to Lady Wibberly, but Mr. Canby was not yet finished.

"I wonder," he said, with an air of affability, "that Desmond did not accompany Cousin Almeria this evening."

Susan, refusing to rise to the bait, remained silent.

"Of course," Mr. Canby continued, undeterred, "it is not the sort of evening he generally prefers." His eyes swept the room. "Innocent buds are n-not just in his style, you know. He generally prefers the company of ladies with what can only be in charity called experience!" He looked down at her with a smile that made her itch to hit him. "Has n-no one warned you that Desmond is a rather desperate character?"

"No, only yourself," replied Susan indignantly, looking him squarely in the eye. "But if I do not mind, why should you?"

"Do not fly up into the boughs!" he said, still smiling. "If you do n-not choose to heed my warning, it is all the same to me, I promise you. It is only that you are very young, and m-may need a friend."

"Thank you," she said, attempting to keep a guard on her tongue, "but there is not the least cause for your concern."

"Your loyalty is very touching," he said with a slight sneer.

"I hope I know what is appropriate," she said angrily.

"Oh, was that m-meant for me? Oh ha ha! You should not fence with me, you know! You are a very charming girl, and I do not wish to see you hurt. It was m-much the same with Clarissa."

"Clarissa?" Susan could not help asking.

He looked down his nose at her. "Clarissa Constable. If you remain on terms of *intimacy* with the family, you will n-no doubt hear that she broke poor Desmond's heart when she m-married a m-man better hosed and shod. A Florentine count! Almeria would have it that being jilted is what drove her brother to his rake-shame ways. The truth is, he drove Clarissa away himself. She was far too well b-bred to abandon convention, and fly in the face of Society's rules."

"Have you no affection for your cousin at all?" Susan asked him curiously.

"Oh ha ha! Of course I do! Des is a capital fellow. It is m-merely that you do not have the protection of rank and fortune, and so m-must be careful not to excite comment. In the eyes of the world, it would be most unwise for you to, say, associate with Viscount Everly in a m-manner that would give rise to speculation and gossip."

"I don't give a fig for the world," declared Susan heatedly.

"Do you not?" he said, raising an eyebrow. "How very interesting. One cannot, however, say the same for the Wibberlys. I assure you they are m-most anxious to see Desmond settled respectably so that he m-might reestablish his credit in the eyes of the world. You understand, the lady would have to be someone of impeccable lineage and reputation."

"Naturally," said Susan carelessly. "But what is it to do with me?"

Mr. Canby smiled enigmatically. "N-nothing, my dear, to be sure."

Susan's most urgent inclination, upon being returned to her chaperone by Mr. Canby, was to flee from the ballroom and his offensive presence and digest his communications in private. She was engaged for the next several sets, however, and she soon pushed the issue to the back of her mind while she enjoyed the company of several agreeable young men her hostess had kindly presented her to. Unfortunately, not every dance was taken, and when the music started up again after her last partner had departed she looked round in panic to discover Mr. Canby bearing down on her from across the room. She remembered his odious words about an attempted rescue and felt that she had endured quite enough of his company for one evening. Hastily murmuring to Lady Wibberly that she must pin up a tear in her hem, she hurried off in search of a hiding place.

Several rooms in the Milton mansion were already occupied by guests desiring a tête-à-tête or a retreat from the stifling ballroom, so that she was a little flushed and embarrassed by the time she found her way to the library.

This, apparently, was unoccupied. She intended to open a window and take a chair nearby, but she was soon distracted by the splendor and immensity of the Miltons' collection of books. Some of these appeared to be rare first editions, and she thumbed through a copy of a book of travels through the Arabian world that threatened to engross her as much as *A Thousand and One Nights*. Enchanted, she carried the book across the room with the idea of delaying her return to the dance until she had had time to study it further. With her eyes on the page, she half backed toward one of the comfortable-looking armchairs facing the casement windows, and she had almost seated herself within in it before she noticed that it was not vacant after all.

Susan jumped back and colored deeply. "I beg your pardon!" she said to the young man who occupied it, a book open on his lap. "I did not know anyone else was here!"

He smiled up at her with expressive eyes set off by a pale, fine complexion. His curly hair and brows were very dark, and the contrasting effect was rather ethereal. "That has been apparent for some time," he said pleasantly. "It is often so when one is lost in a book. What are you reading?"

"It is a travel book about Arabia," she told him.

He reached for it, and she saw that his fingernails were bitten to the quick. He turned it over in his hand. "Yes, I've read this one. The author writes well enough, but he continues to fall into silly scrapes with the residents because he refuses to believe that any culture—and its customs—can be of value but his own." He smiled again and handed it back to her. "It's an English disease."

"My father said the same," she said seriously.

"I dislike England," he said with a sigh. "I should like to travel forever, but when I am away I long to return. I wonder how that can be."

Susan thought that this was a decidedly odd conversation, but it was far from unpleasant. "I do not know. I have only just arrived, and I like it very much, although there are many things I find strange."

He turned his body in the chair the better to look at her. "Do you? I should like to hear what they are, but I pray you will sit down beside me because my neck is most uncomfortable at this angle!"

She laughed and seated herself on the chair beside him.

"You will excuse my rudeness in not getting up," he suggested, "but I have injured my leg."

"Oh, then I am so glad I did not sit on it!" said Susan. "I very nearly did."

He studied her critically. "But not, I believe, on purpose?"

She frowned. "Of course not!"

"Forgive me. It has happened before."

She was perplexed. "Someone has sat on your injured leg before?" she inquired, trying to puzzle out his meaning.

He laughed. "My dear, I should sound the veriest coxcomb if I were to explain it to you! Why do you not tell me instead what it is you have found strange in this country?"

"Oh many things," she said, waving her hand. "The food, the hours, the rules . . ." She cast an appraising look around the library. "Most of all I do not understand how it is that all the great houses have libraries full of books such as this, yet one is not supposed to appear to have read any of them."

He threw back his head and gave a laugh of genuine mirth. "Very true! Though I must say that the stricture applies more to young ladies than to gentlemen."

"Yes, but only consider how Polite Circles have elevated Lord Byron to the pinnacle of Society," she said, warming to her theme.

He looked rather startled but inquired, "You consider it undeserved?"

"I do not know. It is just that one is forever hearing of his scrapes and affectations. It puts one quite out of patience because—"

"Does it?" he interrupted.

"Yes, because no one at all has read his poems! What does it matter if he has burning eyes or a life squandered in dissipation?" She stopped, noting a rather arrested look in his eyes. "I am sorry," she said guiltily. "Is he a friend of yours?"

"I am acquainted with the gentleman, yes," he answered seriously. "However, you are quite safe in expressing your opinion of him to me."

"I do not have an opinion of him," Susan assured him, "for we have never met. I have seen him, however."

"Indeed?"

"Yes, and from the looks of him I am inclined to believe the rumors are true. Still, it does not matter. It is the poems that count!"

"And have *you* read them, Miss—ah?"

"Miss Winston. Yes, some! *Childe Harold* was very good, although perhaps a little melodramatic."

"Melodramatic?" he inquired shakily. "Did you not believe in the hero's suffering then?"

"Well, naturally I am not acquainted with all the sins he has racked up, because I have led a rather sheltered life, you know! But it did occur to me that perhaps he groaned altogether too often, and if he was really so miserable, why didn't he just stop?"

"An excellent question," replied the young man, biting his lip. "Will you tell me how old you are?"

"I am eighteen," she told him.

"Well I would say that your point of view is most appropriate for eighteen."

"You are laughing at me," she said with a smile.

"A little. Mostly I am envious. I am well beyond twenty, and I feel a hundred."

"Because of your injury?" she asked him politely.

He grimaced. "Yes, if you like."

"Well, I hope my conversation has not overtired you, when you must have been wishing to be left alone."

The smile lurked behind his eyes. "On the contrary, I find your conversation quite salutary. Why did you seek refuge in the library, by the by?"

"I was trying to escape dancing with someone particularly odious," she said candidly.

"A suitor?"

"Oh no! I am supposed to be establishing myself on the rungs of the social ladder, and I believe he hopes that I will not succeed," she said thoughtfully.

He smiled. "Odious, indeed! Well, if it is in my poor power to assist you, I shall certainly do so. I regret that I am unable to solicit your hand for a dance, but if I may do myself the honor of calling upon you, we may laugh at the world's absurdities together."

"I reside with Lord and Lady Wibberly, sir, and we shall be glad to receive you."

"Shall you indeed?" he said enigmatically. "I wonder!"

Lady Wibberly was incensed at her protégée's absence, particularly in view of the fact that her efforts had produced a widower in search of a wife who might be the very thing to take Miss Winston off their hands before her brother proceeded further with his misdirected charity (or perverse revenge!) and married her himself. Sir William, however, could only be held by her side for so long before he drifted off, and accordingly, she was in no very good mood when Susan returned at long last to the ballroom.

"I am sure I am very sorry, ma'am," said Susan, attempting to sound contrite, "but it was very hot, and I went to rest for a few moments in the library."

"The *library?*" cried her ladyship in dismay.

"Yes, I know you said I must not seem bookish, but—"

"I should have warned you," said Lady Wibberly judiciously. "The library is off-limits to guests at any party Lord

Byron attends, because he particularly requires a place where he may escape his public. He will not attend otherwise. Thank heaven you did not encounter him there!"

"Oh no," said Susan, relieved but a little disappointed that she had missed the famous poet, "although I did meet a very nice young man. He said he may call on us."

"He may do so, if he is not some penniless lounger," said her ladyship sternly. "Naturally I wish you to make acquaintances of your own age. But now, my dear, there is someone who particularly wishes to be presented to you, if only I can find him." Her eyes scanned the room. "Oh yes, there he is. Sir William Walpole."

"Where, ma'am?"

"There, beside the card table, talking to the marchioness. Perhaps this is not just the time—"

Susan turned a little pale when she saw whom Lady Wibberly meant, the saturnine gentleman she had early remarked upon. "But ma'am, is not that Lord Byron?"

Lady Wibberly smiled. "Certainly not! Byron is only a few years beyond twenty."

"Really?" inquired Susan faintly.

"Oh yes, and most handsome, with dark curls and a pale complexion I would kill for," said her ladyship frankly. "He is quite the dark angel, you know. Ah, there he is now, taking his leave of the hosts. Take care you do not look too obviously at him, because he particularly dislikes being stared at."

Susan, following the direction of her gaze, saw her worst premonition fulfilled. "Good God, is that Lord Byron?" she asked in a stricken whisper.

At that moment, their eyes met across the room, and he bowed. Then he gave her a grin as devilish as anything Childe Harold had ever conceived of, and exited the ball, limping.

Chapter 9

Polite Society was very soon inflamed by the news, circulated no more than twenty-four hours after the event in question, that Almeria Wibberly's young ward had not only enjoyed a tête-à-tête in the library with George Gordon, Lord Byron, but had apparently won his approval as well. Though the couple had not been seen together at the ball, a remark, carelessly dropped into company by his lordship about the girl's wit and charm, and an apt quotation or two about her beauty, apparently sufficed to bring Miss Winston to the notice of the *ton*. Several who were present at the ball were pleased to recall the girl as angelically fair with an original style (which they could not describe) and a brilliant, barbed fund of repartee. More than a dozen young men were quite certain they had danced with her.

Enthusiasm dimmed momentarily when close investigation uncovered the fact that the girl had family but scarcely a feather to fly with, but it swelled again when it was perceived that the sponsorship of the Wibberlys—and through them, Lord Everly—in all probability was indicative of some connection to that very handsome fortune. Those unfortunate victims of fate who were not in very plump currant and must look to marry an heiress were undeniably disappointed, because reliance on Everly's generosity was too risky to be counted upon, but elsewhere, in sitting rooms all over London, mothers were instructing their hopeful sons that they had heard that Miss Winston might be a very eligible match.

Lady Jersey and Lady Sefton, keepers of the gate to the Holiest of Holies, also took note of the rumors and debated the wisdom of sending vouchers to Almack's.

"I confess I cannot recall meeting her," said Sally Jersey, who had been at the Miltons' ball. "But if Byron is taken with her, she must not be in the usual style. I cannot believe how many young girls have made cakes of themselves over him, and he scorns them all. Except—"

"Don't say it! Lady—well, you know whom I mean—is one of my closest friends, and I would not give her pain by spreading tales about her daughter. Besides, Almeria has not even approached us yet," Lady Sefton reminded her.

Lady Jersey laughed. "She will!"

"Well, perhaps you are right. What is this girl's connection to the family, do you know? Why is Almeria bringing her out?"

She shrugged. "I do not know. I heard a story about Lord Everly's obligation to her father, but I do not credit it."

"Nor do I," said Lady Sefton. "Everly's a wastrel, but he's a regular Croesus. I can't imagine him borrowing money from anyone!"

Lady Jersey closed her lips on the first reply that came to her mind, namely that her friend had the soul of a merchant, and said merely, "Not *that* sort of obligation, Maria."

"Oh," An idea seemed to strike Lady Sefton. "You don't suppose it could have anything to do with *Everly*, do you?"

"I have just told you that I do not credit the story," said Lady Jersey impatiently.

"No, I mean, you don't suppose he has conceived a *tendre* for this chit!"

"Good God! He is five-and-thirty!"

"What does that signify, if a man is in love?"

Lady Jersey looked incredulous. "Everly? He is far too fond of the company of the prime articles of virtue he flaunts upon the town to entertain such romantic nonsense. Besides, since Clarissa Constable broke his heart, he is the most hardened flirt in London, and quite cynical."

Lady Sefton looked thoughtful. "I suppose you must be right, for if he had meant to marry and establish his nursery he would have taken care not to establish such an unfortunate reputation. I cannot imagine that a woman of sense—or sensibility—would even consider becoming his wife."

"Oh, there is nothing so attractive as a rake!" Lady Jersey said carelessly. "If he were bent on reestablishing himself in the eyes of the world, I daresay he could find someone. But I do not for a moment believe that a chit just out of the schoolroom would be at all in his style!"

"So, vouchers or not?" inquired Lady Sefton.

Lady Jersey sighed. "Well, Byron is undoubtedly the rage of

the moment, and his opinion must weigh with those who move in the first circles, but when all is said and done he is from *Yorkshire*, you know. He may not be such an excellent judge of what is right for *us* as one would suppose. And at Almack's we reign supreme!"

"Certainly," concurred Lady Sefton.

"Then let us wait and see," suggested Lady Jersey.

Despite the caution displayed by Ladies Jersey and Sefton, it was soon borne in upon Miss Winston and her sponsors that her popularity had increased geometrically, before she had even had her own ball at Wibberly House. Floral tributes began arriving with a regularity that gave satisfaction to any number of London purveyors, as well as to those within the house who delighted in the success of the young lady. These included Miss Eliza and Miss Louisa, the children of the house, who were old enough to be dazzled by and too young to be jealous of Miss Winston's popularity, and followed her around the house in a state of starry-eyed admiration and worship. Susan, who had grown up an only child, was rather touched and enjoyed their company, and was sorry that Lady Wibberly's regimen of childrearing was based on the notion that young girls were best nurtured by keeping them out of sight, in a corner of the house far from that occupied by its more seasoned occupants.

Lady Wibberly was quick to uncover the source of her charge's newfound popularity and take advantage of it. She was surprised that Miss Winston, whose conversation she did not find at all compatible with her notion of what must be pleasing in the highest circles, had apparently captivated—for the moment—Society's literary lion. However inexplicable it might be, she could not but perceive that Susan had done herself a very good turn, and might find the road a bit smoother. When Byron called a few days later, staying half an hour and chattering amusingly about other members of the *ton* who had entertained him, her bosom knew a swell of triumph. When the door had closed on him, she told Miss Winston that she might, at least for the moment, find every door open to her, if only she were not to do something *farouche*, and that she must certainly follow up these marks of preferment by inviting Byron to her own ball, which was to take place the following week.

Amid so much speculation as to the degree and import of

Byron's interest, there was one who seemed decidedly un-moved by her recitation of this conquest. Susan was human enough to hope that the news might excite in Lord Everly the resolution to bestow equal attentions lest he be cut out by a more glamorous rival. She did not dare hope for jealousy, but she was undeniably disappointed when, upon hearing the story, his lordship merely laughed.

"You are quite in Canby's debt, you know!" he told her with a smile. "If you had not been escaping his unwanted so-licitude no doubt you would not have found your way to the li-brary. How very fortunate!"

"Well, it was," agreed Susan. "But I cannot precisely feel grateful to him, because he makes me so excessively uncom-fortable."

"I know just what you mean," said his lordship. "Would you like me to have a word with him?"

"No!" she cried adamantly. "That is, I feel sure that would only make things worse. He suspects, you know."

"Suspects?" inquired his lordship with a glint in his eye.

Susan blushed. "That you . . . that I . . . "

"I see," he said calmly. "Well, I should have been very sur-prised if he did not. Perhaps now that you have captivated the famous Lord Byron his irritation will be soothed."

"You need not sound as if I had set a trap for him," she protested, "for it was no such thing. We merely had a talk—about books!"

"So I understand. I should dearly liked to have been a fly on the library wall," he said meditatively.

"Should you? It was not so very interesting," she recalled. "Indeed, I cannot understand what was said that would make him take so much trouble on my behalf, when he has so many other friends in London."

Lord Everly gave a cynical little laugh. "Can you not? It's the hunter's instinct, my dear. The prey that shows no interest is the one you must have!"

"How perfectly odious," said Susan sincerely.

"Yes, isn't it? But a very effective stratagem, I assure you. I've fallen victim to it myself—briefly—a time or two."

Susan choked. "Surely you don't think that I—"

"Don't fly up into the boughs with me, brat! I do not care whether you did it on purpose or not. My sister will tell you that the results of your little flirtation—don't scowl at me, I am only teasing you—will have set you on the path to success, although I daresay it may get you more attention than you bargained for!"

"What do you mean by that?" asked Susan uncertainly.

"I wonder if I will tell you," he said, helping himself to a pinch of snuff. "No, I think that I shall not. Time, I believe, will make all clear, of that I feel quite certain!"

The day for the Wibberlys' ball to present Miss Winston rolled round at last, and Lady Wibberly had the deep satisfaction of seeing virtually all of her invitations accepted, despite her earlier misgivings. She was a good hostess, and only served refreshments of the highest quality, so she did not expect her parties to be failures, but neither did she expect them to be brilliant social events. That no fewer than three of the patronesses had accepted, along with a glittering assortment of titles and fortunes, she attributed to Byron's good offices, and despite his reputation as dangerous to women she could happily have kissed him.

Susan was considerably cheered by the news that Lord Everly had indicated his intention to attend, and by the arrival of a charming bouquet—without a card, unfortunately—which she nevertheless felt certain must come from him. Lord Byron had written his acceptance as well, so her cup was filled to overflowing.

Descending the stairs on the evening of the party, she also experienced the pleasure of knowing that she was looking her very best. The sea green gauze of her dress seemed to float about her, and the light from myriad candles bathed her face and form in a soft warm glow. Remembering the life she had only recently left behind in Yorkshire, she felt an enormous rush of gratitude to Lord Everly for his rescue, and for providing her the opportunity to so thoroughly indulge her vanity in the most beautiful dress imaginable. She said as much when she met him in the parlor before dinner.

"I don't want your thanks, brat," he said, raising his quizzing glass at her.

"You needn't look down your nose at me in that fashion!" she responded. "I know you do not care to be thanked, but you must realize that I am deeply grateful for what you have done for me."

"A few dresses and a party. It's not so much."

"Oh, but I—"

"You are not under any obligation to me, you know," he said quietly.

"But I am!" she told him. "I—" She stopped, arrested by the look on his face. "Oh yes, I see."

"I am glad that you do," he said, letting his glass fall again. "Gratitude is a dead bore, I promise you! By the by, you are quite becomingly attired this evening. My sister is to be congratulated."

"Thank you," she said, a little provoked at this manner of compliment but refusing to show it.

"Don't mention it. Forgive me for asking—though in conscience I should have done so before—but will it be necessary for me to engage the services of a caper merchant?"

"To teach me to *dance*?" she asked, swelling with indignation. "Certainly not!"

"Excellent," he said. "Marston has a very particular way with my shoes, you know, and I should not like to explain to him how they came to be scuffed."

"My lord, I will not be treading on your feet!" she protested. "That is," she added, suddenly shy, "should we stand up together in the dance."

"Oh, I think it is time, don't you? I should not want to deprive myself of the pleasure of watching the look on Cosmo's face!"

The arrival of the others put an end to their conversation, so that she was left wondering, upon reflection, whether his only motive in dancing with her was his enjoyment of the prospect of spiting his cousin.

Last of all the guests to arrive, when Lady Wibberly had already released Miss Winston from greeting her guests and was herself on the verge of joining the others, was Lord Byron, who climbed the stairs unhurriedly and surveyed his fellow guests with that penetrating stare which had become so famous in polite circles. Since he affected a very dark style of dress, his pallid complexion and deep, mysterious eyes made him seem a very romantic figure, and more than one heart was aflutter at the sight.

Lady Wibberly was far too skillful a hostess to importune her most famous guest with pointless effusions of gratitude or idle chatter, and she suggested, after the briefest of greetings, that he might number some of his friends among the company, and that in all events he might make himself free with the use of the library. "And I venture to reassure you," she said with some emphasis, "that you will find it unoccupied."

He gave her a smile, which, if she had been a decade younger, might have caused her to swoon. Lady Wibberly had little taste for the sort of nonsense Byron represented, and she was convinced that those who labeled him dangerous were most probably correct, but harder hearts than hers had fallen victim to that smile, which could be, when he chose, extraordinarily sweet. "And what of Miss Winston?" he inquired, raising his brows. "Will she favor me with a dance, do you think?"

Lady Wibberly, who knew that Lord Byron never danced, owing to his pronounced limp, could only stare at him openmouthed until she recovered her wits enough to assure him that her protégée would be only too happy to stand up with him.

This was the sort of answer he was used to, and he sauntered off across the room in search of his partner.

Susan was able to view the specter of Lord Byron bearing down on her with rather more calm than her ladyship, although her reaction was not unmixed with a measure of both admiration and dismay. Byron moved through the room rather as if he were breasting waves, unmindful of those around him who would have engaged him in conversation, or merely impeded his path. His regard was so fixedly intense that the crowd parted for him, and he soon reached her side. She had been talking with Lord Wynchwood, a young sprig of fashion, but his lordship was not up to facing the tide of literary *force majeure* and retreated hastily.

Susan was a bit taken aback by this affected entrance, and felt that if this was his public persona she undoubtedly preferred the slightly shy young man who bit his nails that she had met in the library. She happened to glance across the room and saw Lord Everly regarding her with a look of unholy amusement, his arms folded across his chest. She put up her chin at once and turned to greet her guest.

"Miss Winston," said Byron, brushing her hand very lightly with his lips. "I have been so looking forward to meeting you again," he added in an undertone.

Susan did not have to raise her eyes to know that every other pair in the room was fixed on the two of them. She colored a little, but replied in a natural voice. "That is very good of you, particularly when I abused you rather shamefully to your face! I cannot imagine how I could have been so foolish as not to recognize who you are, but I have but lately arrived in London, and do not yet know my way around."

He snatched up her hand again and kissed it, but she could not suppress the feeling that he did so knowing that the world was watching him. "But you were charming!" he protested.

"I was not altogether kind about your poems," she reminded him perversely.

"Well at least you had *read* them," he said, with a genuine laugh. "Not even all of my critics can claim that."

"I suppose not,"

"And when you said that my . . . *persona* . . . had become more important than my work, you were not far out," he told her.

"I did not say that," she protested.

"No, but you meant it. Please, do not apologize! I am seldom honest myself, but I admire candor above all things."

She was silent a moment at that, and then ventured, "I must thank you, you know. Your . . . notice . . . has done me a great deal of good socially."

He bowed. "I am happy to be of service. This"—his eyes swept the room—"is not the life I would have chosen, but if it is what you want . . . "

"I am not at all sure it is what I want," said Susan candidly, "but it is a great deal better than what I had before."

"We must all make what shifts we can. Shall you dance with me?"

"I am promised for the next set," she told him.

He seemed not to hear her and began to lead her gently onto the floor. "I am so sorry," Susan said, somewhat dismayed, "but I have engaged to stand up with Lord Everly."

"I do not usually dance, you know," he told her. "It is quite rare for me to stand up with anyone."

She looked at him with concern. "Because you have injured your leg?"

He gave her an enigmatic smile. "How kind you are, Miss Winston. It is good of you to pretend you did not know I have been crippled since birth."

"But I did not know it!" she protested.

He shrugged. "Well, it is not a subject I wish to dwell on, but I promise you it is of little consequence to me. I box, I play cricket, and occasionally—as now, for instance—I even find myself on the dance floor."

Susan felt herself being swept away against her will by some irresistible tide. She did not enjoy the sensation. "But Lord Everly—" she began.

"Can he not be denied?" he asked softly.

"No, I—" she said, stammering.

"No, he cannot," said Lord Everly's lazy voice behind her. "George, you are *de trop*."

Byron grinned and shrugged boyishly. "He who risks nothing wins less," he said flippantly. He turned to Susan. "Perhaps you will save me a dance later in the evening," he stated. "Since I am not to lead you onto the floor, I am happy to see that you wear my flowers on your wrist."

Susan's hand flew to her face. "Oh, did you send them? There was no card."

Byron bowed. "I had done myself the honor—undeserved, as I now discover—of thinking a card would not be needed. I had hoped my simple tribute would speak for itself."

"Oh, I—" began Susan, caught off guard.

Lord Everly laid a firm hand under elbow. "You may thank him very prettily when it is *his* dance," he said with some amusement. "But now I really must insist . . . "

"My apologies," he said to her when they had taken their places in the set, "but it will do you no harm to deny him a little, you know. Quite the reverse, in fact. Indeed I should not be surprised if he were not even now composing a poem in your honor."

"That is absurd," said Susan, blushing a little.

"It is quite true. Not, perhaps, about the poem, for he seems to prefer the topic of self-destruction," he said meditatively, "but about the effectiveness of resistance as a strategy, most decidedly. Did I not already say so?"

"Yes you did, and it is no less odious now than it was then," she protested. "I keep telling you that I am not out to snare Lord Byron or anyone else."

"That is very fortunate, for you would not succeed."

"Why not?" Susan was goaded into asking, forgetting for the moment what was between them.

He laughed. "George's passions are very intense, but they burn out quickly. He would not last, and you would break your heart." The last was said very seriously, and he was surprised to discover that it mattered to him whether her heart was broken or not. A plague on the absurd child! If she had to conceive a *tendre*, he had hoped it would not be for someone as unsteady as Byron. He judiciously decided not to add that it was also generally known that the Gordons were pretty well done up.

"You do not care for him," Susan deduced.

"He is undoubtedly very talented, and he can be a very amusing companion," he told her.

"Ah," she said, "I thought that I was right."

"His taste in flowers is demonstrably excellent," Lord Everly offered.

She regarded them thoughtfully. "They are beautiful," she admitted, "but I had hoped—" She blushed and broke off in midsentence. She had almost told him that she had hoped that they were from him, and she would far rather not have made such an admission.

He cocked an eyebrow at her. "What? Another admirer already? Miss Winston, you have quite taken the town by storm! In fact, envious darts are being hurled at me from all directions, because I have engaged you in conversation these fifteen minutes. No doubt if it were not generally known that you are my ward, I should be fearful of being called out at any moment."

"Much you would care for that," said Susan, unimpressed. "And in any case, I thought you *wanted* me to be a success."

The smile died out of his eyes. "But of course. And captivating the most talked-about star of the Season is a most auspicious beginning. But—"

"I do not think I have precisely captivated him," she said frankly. "As a matter of fact, there was something *artificial* about his entrance, as if he were overconscious of effect. It was not the same in the library at Milton House."

"He has had a great deal of fame and attention, very young," replied his lordship, not displeased with this speech. "Perhaps he will find his balance again before he is ruined." He smiled down at her. "I don't intend to dictate your friends, brat. Have a caution, that is all. Succeeding in the *ton* requires a neat balance between being ignored and getting oneself talked about too much."

"I think you are trying to tell me something," she said in her straightforward way.

"Merely to put you on your guard. But now is not the time or the place, and the music has ended. Later, perhaps."

"Very well," said Susan, "but I am very disappointed that you did not notice."

"Notice what?" asked Lord Everly, wondering what he might have overlooked.

"That not once did I step on your shoes!" she pointed out triumphantly.

Lord Everly's warning, in the event, was not destined to be delivered in time. The ball was coming to a very satisfactory conclusion, and the last dance before the guests went into supper found Susan taking her place in the set with Byron, to the admiration of some and the envy of not a few. The dance itself was less successful than might generally be supposed, because his lordship's limp was quite pronounced, impeding the steps, but that minor obstacle could not weigh significantly either with those who observed or those who participated. Lady Sefton, who had been observing Miss Winston carefully, was gracious enough to pronounce her a pretty-behaved sort of girl, without the least hint of pretension in her dress or bearing.

"Well, there is very little reason for her to display any pretension," responded Lady Jersey, "for I cannot believe that she has any fortune at all. If she had, Almeria Wibberly would have puffed it up all over town."

"Unless she is trying to preserve her for Everly," suggested Lady Sefton.

"Maria, do you persist in that absurd idea? Everly has scarcely paid her any attention this evening, except to dance with her once. I do not doubt that he is only here because Almeria forced him to do his duty by the girl. These evenings are not at all in his style, you know!"

"I own he is more often to be found at the Great Go or less reputable haunts than in the drawing rooms of polite society," she admitted, "but do you not think he might be taking pains to shield her from gossip?"

"A child of eighteen? He would be bored in a month!"

"I believe it is often the case that hardened bachelors—indeed, in this case, I might even say 'rakes'—are attracted to innocence."

"Nonsense!" said Sally Jersey cynically. "And if he were concerned about shielding her from the *on-dits* of town, he would do better to keep her out of Byron's clutches. He is an amusing scamp, but I would not wish any innocent buds under my protection to become involved with him."

"Very true," agreed Lady Sefton. "And when it gets about that he is flirting with her . . ."

"Exactly," said Lady Jersey. "Still, I have decided that when Almeria requests them, I shall send vouchers. The girl is well enough, and the complications could be very interesting."

Across the room, Lady Wibberly was accepting the congratulations of her husband on the success of the party. His lordship generally preferred the card tables and the company of other gentlemen to dancing, but he could recognize a glittering event when he saw one and took pains to make his wife aware of it. This thoughtfulness toward her ladyship was an aspect of his character not always apparent to outside observers, but it went far toward explaining the success of their otherwise somewhat ill-assorted union.

"Thank you, Wibberly," she said, accepting his tribute calmly. "It does seem to have come off very well, doesn't it? I think we may safely assume that Miss Winston will take, particularly after Byron singled her out by *dancing* with her." She sighed. "I wonder if we shall be glad of it?"

"Of course we shall," responded her husband. "Damned fine gal. Always said so."

"I suppose we may not hope that Byron will take her off our hands, for he is notorious, and anyone can see that he is not in earnest . . . Still . . ."

"Almeria," her husband began.

The footman, who had been urgently signaling for a few moments the apparent arrival of a very late guest, suddenly commanded her full attention. Lady Wibberly was perplexed, for she could not think of anyone still unaccounted for, but among so many there must have been someone overlooked. Moreover, she was grateful for the interruption, because she was not in the mood to debate Miss Winston's virtues, about which she was still far from certain, with her spouse. Tom's adamant championing of the girl only made her more determined than ever to be rid of her, though she could not find as many faults with her as she first hoped. Indeed, watching her move gracefully across the dance floor with the most talked-about man in London, caused her to feel a pang of envy. Lady Wibberly, an honest woman, did not wish to confront at that moment the idea that she might be jealous of Miss Winston, so she signed to the man to make the announcement.

The footman, in an unusually agitated state, complied with fervor. *"Lady Caroline Lamb,"* he articulated, in a voice that carried down the hall with admirable efficiency.

"Good God," said Lord Wibberly in a strangled voice. "You didn't invite her, Almeria, surely!"

"Certainly not," hissed her ladyship in return, putting her hand to her throat.

"Now we are in the basket," said his lordship, so far forgetting himself as to slip into cockfighting cant. "Whatever's to be done?"

Chapter 10

Standing next to Byron as the last chords of music died away, Susan heard the footman's announcement without recognition and was quite surprised when, around her, the name caused an audible murmur, and then, most astonishing of all, amused glances in her direction. Turning to her companion, she was startled to discover in him a contemptuous smile, his mouth falling singularly at the corners, and an expression that was both disdainful and vindictive. Childe Harold, his soul poised over the edge of the abyss, might have worn such a look, and she drew back from him a little. A moment later, however, she had eyes for no one but Lady Caroline Lamb.

Lady Caroline was a slight, nervous-looking woman with a heart-shaped face and intelligent eyes, who must be called lively rather than beautiful. Nevertheless, one glance was sufficient to demonstrate that whatever else she might be, she was far from unremarkable.

Her attire—Susan could scarcely credit this, but her eyes could not be so deceived—was that of a Turk, apparently some sort of harem slave. She wore wide silken pantaloons and a scarlet sash, and her face was artificially darkened. She carried a very large fan, from the look of it entirely constructed of ostrich plumes, and a bracelet of bells at her wrist jingled at every step. In fact, had she not been announced, Susan might have taken her, with her close-cropped hair and slender body, to be a page, outrageously attired to accompany his mistress to a most improper costume party.

While these thoughts were going through Susan's head, Lady Caroline walked up to Lord and Lady Wibberly and inquired in a ringing voice, "Where is Lord Byron?"

"How—how very nice to see you, Lady Caroline," said Lady Wibberly, rallying a little. "How is your dear mama?"

Lord Wibberly, who had been observing his latest guest with slack-jawed wonder, received an admonitory pinch from his wife. "Glad to see you, my dear," he muttered feebly. "On your way to a masquerade, I take it?"

Lady Caroline gave him an assessing look, shrugged, and returned her attention to her hostess. "Lady Bessborough is quite well, ma'am," she said shortly. "Will you be so good as to tell me whether Byron is here?"

"Yes, he is, Lady Caroline, but—"

"Thank you." Her eyes swept the room. "Yes, I see that he is. You need not trouble to point him out."

"Lady Caroline, let me get your maid," said Lady Wibberly beseechingly, for she had more than a vague premonition that a Scene was about to transpire in her ballroom. "Do you not think that Mr. Lamb—"

"Oh, that is not necessary," said Lady Caroline gaily. "I am quite unattended."

"Wibberly," said her ladyship in a desperate undertone when Lady Caroline had departed in the direction of Byron and Miss Winston, "where is Desmond?"

"Haven't seen him this half hour or so. Very likely took himself off. Not a one for balls, Desmond," he concluded.

"Nonsense! He would not have done so on this occasion. Do you go and find him at once, and tell him his presence is needed urgently!"

Lord Wibberly, obedient to his orders, went off in search of his brother-in-law. Susan, meanwhile, stood transfixed in wonder as Lady Caroline bore down on her with determination.

"Courage, *mon enfant,*" murmured Byron in her ear. "Good evening, Little Mania," he said calmly, addressing her ladyship. "What a surprise to see you here."

"I grew tired of waiting," said Lady Caroline, fixing him with a penetrating stare.

"Oh, did we have an appointment?" he inquired in a tone of cynical amusement. "I thought I had specifically informed you that I was engaged this evening."

"I can see that you are," said Lady Caroline, directing her gaze at Susan in a manner that made the hair stand up on her neck. "But I feel sure there must be some mistake. We are always invited everywhere together."

"Since you evidence such enthusiasm for attending this event, allow me to present Miss Winston, in whose honor it is," he told her. "Miss Winston, this is Lady Caroline Lamb. She is, as you will have gathered, an original. I am only sorry that your husband, or better yet, your mother-in-law, is not present to see this, Caro."

Lady Lamb's glace flicked her with amused disdain. "Byron, what are you about? She is the merest child."

Susan was rather tired of being treated as if she had the sentience of a potted plant and said with some asperity. "I am delighted to make your acquaintance too, ma'am."

Lady Lamb laughed. "Do not cross swords with me, my child. You are quite out of your depth, you know. He may lead you a pretty dance, but he is only using you to make a fool out of me!"

"It is not necessary to use anyone in order to accomplish that," said Byron.

"Lady Caroline," interjected Susan, anxious to clarify her own role in this drama, "I fear you are under some misapprehension—"

"I am in possession of all the information I require, Miss Winston. I suggest you stay out of this."

"Leave the girl alone, Caro," said Lord Byron. "She has nothing to do with it. Do you plan on telling us why you have come to Wibberly House in the guise of a harem slave?"

She laughed giddily. "I have come to claim you as my master," she said.

Susan's eyes widened at this. "I fear I have shocked poor Miss Winston," said Lady Caroline, not sounding in the least regretful. "Dear me!"

"You have shocked a great many more people than that," said Lord Byron. "Every eye in the room is upon you. Is that what you want?"

She shrugged irritably, like a child. "You know that convention has always meant very little to me," she told him.

"Apparently not," he said with a brittle laugh. "Whatever next? Shall you kidnap me?"

"I am tired," she said, her voice suddenly smaller. "I begin to feel ill."

"Indeed, madam, the cure is close at hand. Shall I summon your carriage, or did you come in a sedan chair?"

"Come with me," said Lady Caroline plaintively, "or I shan't go."

Susan could not but feel that Byron was baiting his misguided worshiper and did not appear to be in a hurry to bring the interview to a close. In fact, she had the sense that he was rather enjoying it, and she felt more sorry for Lady Caroline than her behavior would seem to merit. If she had thought she could have done so without arousing attention, she would have slipped away and left them to torment each other on their own.

"I am pledged to take Miss Winston into supper," said Byron, who was no such thing.

"You are mistaken," said a deep voice at Susan's elbow before she could draw a breath to protest, "that honor is mine."

Susan let out the breath again with audible relief. Lord Everly gave her a swift smile and then bent graciously over Lady Caroline's hand. "You are looking quite fetching this evening, Caroline," he said with a glimmer of amusement. "Do you never tire of being outrageous?"

She laughed. "You of all people should understand, Everly. Life at home is so dreadfully dull!"

"Is it?" he asked in an interested tone. "From what I had heard I should have thought you have done a great deal to enliven it this past year."

"Yes, but William is so incredibly *patient*."

"Ha! I understand perfectly," said Lord Everly sympathetically.

She bestowed her most glittering smile on him. "I thought you might. It is hard to behave when one is constantly being forgiven, and with such charity too!"

"Most difficult," his lordship agreed. "Shall you join us for supper?"

She eyed Susan narrowly and said nothing.

"I shall naturally be taking in my ward. I assume you have met Miss Winston?"

"Byron introduced us," she said woodenly.

"Then you will have heard that this party is in her honor. Do you remember your come-out, Caroline? I seem to recall that you were the toast of London."

"I suppose so. It all seems such a long time ago."

"Not so long, I think, that you do not remember how important it is to put one's foot right at the beginning," he suggested.

She gave him an assessing look. "Are you appealing to my better nature? I don't have one, you know!"

"I am merely inviting you to supper," he stated calmly.

Lady Caroline looked at Susan again. "Such a bore to be eighteen!"

Lord Everly laid a restraining hand on Miss Winston's shoulder, and she kept silent.

"I am very tired," said Lady Caroline with a yawn.

"Then perhaps you would prefer to return home," he suggested. "George . . . ?"

Lord Byron, who had been watching this exchange with an expression of amusement, stopped smiling. "I knew it should fall to me to effect a rescue."

"That result, I think, is not unjust," suggested Lord Everly.

"Oh, very well," he said with a shrug. "Come, Caro, I will take you home."

"I hope you are not angry with me," she said to him.

"If I thought it would deter you from such an exhibition as this I would say that I am furious," he said in a mocking tone, "but I fear it would have just the opposite effect."

"Very true," she said cheerfully. "Shall we go then?"

"In a moment." He turned to Susan. "I hope you can forgive me! I had not intended—well, never mind. If you will permit me, Lord Everly, I should like to call on Miss Winston again soon."

Lady Caroline's eyes widened at this.

"I am quite sure you would," said Lord Everly somewhat enigmatically. "But for the moment, I am sure you will agree that time is of the essence."

"You need not worry, Everly," said Lady Caroline, jingling her bracelet, "I have set London about its ears enough for one evening. I wonder if I should say goodbye to your sister. I have the feeling she will be excessively gratified by my departure."

"Do so!" said Everly promptly with a smile. "I promise you Almeria is up to every rig and row!"

"You have always been kind, Desmond," said Lady Caroline seriously. "One day all the pompous bores who have snubbed me will be very sorry!" She swept away across the ballroom, leaving a rather astonished silence in her wake. Lord Byron, directing one of his famous penetrating stares at the company for a moment, soon followed after.

Susan felt as if the wind had been knocked out of her. Her most urgent inclination was to seek solitude in her room, but Everly's hand held a firm grip under her elbow, both supporting and restraining her. "Smile," he said, looking down at her.

She blinked at him. "What?"

"You must appear not to mind," he cautioned her.

"I do mind," she said seriously. "Is she short a sheet, do you think?"

He laughed out loud at this. "Probably not. Just besotted, most likely."

"Well, if that is what it means to be in love, I do not think I should care for it," she confided.

He laughed again. "What? Have you never been in love, Miss Winston?"

"I do not think I can have been, for I never felt the smallest desire to dress up as anyone's slave," she told him.

"But you had not yet met Byron," he said wickedly.

"No," she said thoughtfully, "I had not."

He looked at her with speculation. "And?"

She smiled maliciously and gestured at her sea green ball dress. "As you see, I am still a dead bore."

"You are scarcely that."

"I presume," she said thoughtfully, "that her ladyship's 'affection' is what you were going to warn me about."

"More or less," he admitted.

"Well, I do think you might have done so sooner. Did you think she would come to the party?"

"Good God, no! But with Caroline one never knows."

"Did you . . . could you tell me . . . ?"

"Out with it, my child! What is it you want to know?"

"Did you know Lady Caroline at *her* come-out?"

He chuckled. "Oh yes. Her father was the Earl of Bessborough, Lord Lieutenant of Ireland, and her aunt was the Duchess of Devonshire. It was quite an affair, I promise you."

"And was she the Toast of London, or whatever you said?" she could not help asking.

He regarded her with amusement. "Most certainly, but she was not quite so outrageous. Caro was wild even then, of course, but not, I think, so unhappy. She made a brilliant alliance with the Lambs."

"Yes, it certainly sounds that way," Susan said dryly.

He laughed appreciatively. "Brat! I am relieved to find that you are not going to be prey to a fit of the sulks, at any rate. Shall we go into supper?"

She took the proffered arm. "I never sulk," she said majestically.

Lady Caroline Lamb's uninvited visit to Lord and Lady Wibberly's ball in honor of their protégée, Miss Susan Winston, might have been said to cause little happiness to the host and hostess and their family, although there were some, jealous of Lord Byron's attention to Miss Winston in favor of their own, overlooked progeny, who could not but feel that Miss Winston deserved a bit of a come-down. Nevertheless, there was at least one breast in which the experience excited feelings of unalloyed pleasure. Mr. Cosmo Canby, who had watched Susan's success with trepidation, had feared that she might become even more attractive to Lord Everly as a potential bride, and somehow more acceptable to his relations. He was in no doubt that such an event was under consideration however much his cousins might try to hide it from him; his instinct for self-preservation told him so, and Lady Wibberly's dismay provided confirmation. His previous strategy, hastily considered, had been to puff up Miss Winston in the best possible light, even to the extent of exaggerating her fortune, in the hopes that she might engage the affections of less threatening suitors. That she had aroused the attentions of the notorious Lord Byron Mr. Canby regarded as no help at all, as Byron was unlikely to be attracted for long to an innocent, and was, besides, rather publicly fickle. Mr. Canby, having witnessed with glee the scene in the ballroom, now suspected that Byron's attentions to Miss Winston were merely the best way of provoking Lady Caroline to do outrageous things and thus enhance his reputation. It occurred to him that a secondary strategy for ridding himself of the threat to his inheritance might be to undermine Miss Winston as well, not only to the Wibberlys, who would scarcely be resistant to such a notion, but also to Everly himself. Whatever Everly might have said or done, he was unlikely to ally himself with a girl of blemished reputation, however much he might seem to prefer the company of what could only be generously called experienced females. If Miss Winston, already getting herself talked about in a manner those adhering to strictest decorum would not approve, could be shown to be of unsuitable character in some fashion or other, he did not doubt that the feared union would never take place.

Accordingly, not many days after the ball, when tongues were still wagging over the evening's events, he paid a call on Lady Caroline Lamb.

Lady Caroline, who seldom rose before noon on her most vigorous days, could not remember meeting a Mr. Canby, and only the hastily scrawled message on the back of his card that he was Everly's cousin and desired to see her on a matter of some urgency induced her to admit him to her saloon, and only then after some hesitation. As the wife of a powerful politician, she was used to being importuned by all manner of persons she did not particularly wish to know, and her private affairs were such that unknown persons frequently wished to blackmail her. Since few of her escapades escaped the attention of her husband or, more annoyingly, her mother-in-law, Lady Melbourne, she was not prey to such vulgar schemes and only tolerated the intrusions out of a sort of perverse curiosity to see what the blackmailers had uncovered. However, the intelligence that her caller was Lord Everly's cousin made the idea that he had some idea of extorting money from her ridiculous; had he been in that line, he would have been in a much more advantageous position to do so with Desmond than with her. Although he took a great deal less trouble to cultivate it and seemed more amused than excited by the stories that were told of him, it must be acknowledged Desmond Wyndham was one of few in London with a reputation as shocking as her own.

Mr. Canby was kept cooling his heels for some time in Lady Caroline's blue saloon, but it might have consoled him to know that the striped couch he occupied had played host to a great many of the dashing figures of the day, and not a few of the dandy set, whom he strove to emulate in dress and manner. Though not by nature a patient man, he perceived that being kept waiting was designed to put him in his place, and to show vexation would be to hand his hostess a victory. Thus, when Lady Caroline floated down in a blue watered-silk afternoon dress some three-quarters of an hour after he had sent up his card, he rose to greet her with every appearance of delight and affability.

She extended her fingers to him warily. Her first impression was that she had been mistaken, for he had every appearance of one bent on blackmail, and her experience in these matters rarely misled her. On the other hand, he was Everly's cousin and so, she supposed, must be given the benefit of the doubt. "We have not, I think, been formally introduced," she told him.

In fact he had met her a number of times and had even attended her come-out years before. Swallowing his irritation, he said soothingly, "Indeed we have, m-ma'am, but of course I could not expect you to remember. My cousin Desmond is the dazzling one in the family."

"Yes, I suppose he must be," she said absently. "You mentioned an urgent matter . . . " She gestured toward the sofa again, and he composed himself upon it gratefully so as to display his clothing to greatest advantage. He noted her study of him, and hoped that she noticed that his neckcloth was arranged in a perfect *trône d'amour*.

"First I think I should m-mention that I was, naturally, present at the Wibberly ball a few evenings ago," he began.

She sighed and narrowed her eyes at him. "You are far too late, you know. My husband and his mother are in full possession of all the details."

"Indeed, m-ma'am, I do not know to what you could be referring," he said in a shocked tone.

"Do you not?" she replied in a bored voice. "I felt sure you meant to request some payment in return for your silence, but it is quite useless, I promise you."

"Lady Caroline, I protest! I never had any such intention!" he said, half rising to his feet. "My good n-name, and that of my family—"

"Yes, yes! Well, if I have wronged you I apologize. Then perhaps you will be so good as to tell me why you *have* come."

"May I speak frankly?" he inquired in a conspiratorial tone.

"I do not know," she replied, somewhat disconcertingly. "I find that is often a prelude to disagreeable speech, and I seldom wish to encourage it. You may speak, and I shall stop you when I do not wish to hear any more."

"I think your ladyship will be interested in my speech, but I will leave you to be the judge. It concerns Lord B-Byron and Miss Winston."

She abandoned her languid, half-recumbent pose on the settee and sat up straighter. "Go on."

He suppressed a smile at this early victory. "Well, n-naturally I am on intimate terms with the Wyndham family. You may not know that I am Everly's heir."

"I cannot say I had thought about it one way or the other," she confessed.

He smiled thinly. "You may assume that I only m-mention the m-matter to demonstrate that I stand in such a relation to the family as to validate my information."

"And what, pray, *is* your information?" she asked him.

"Why nothing more nor less, m-ma'am, than the fact that Lord Byron has become very particular in his attentions, and Miss Winston's friends are somewhat concerned."

"Ridiculous!" countered her ladyship with an expression of disdain. "If that is all you came to tell me, you might as well have spared your breath."

He half rose from the sofa. "Indeed, Lady Caroline, in that case I am heartily sorry to have wasted your time."

"I'll admit the girl is quite taking," said Lady Caroline, as if he had not spoken at all, "but she is scarcely more than a child."

Mr. Canby resumed his seat. "If you say so, Lady Caroline," he said mildly.

"I cannot believe that he may be serious," she said, annoyed. "He is only flirting with the girl to annoy me."

"I will allow that you m-must know best," he assured her.

Lady Caroline was beginning to conceive the same antipathy toward her guest as that shared by the members of his family. "If you have evidence to the contrary, Mr. Canby, I suggest you tell me at once," she said through gritted teeth.

"Evidence?" he raised an eyebrow. "A suggestion, m-merely."

"And that is?"

"If you will permit me, Lady Caroline, the girl is—for the moment at least—eminently respectable, with the protection of a socially prominent family. His lordship m-might just consider such a connection the perfect means of establishing himself in the eyes of the world as something more than an adventurer. Can you deny that the established order holds some fascination for his lordship despite the life he has led? By the time the charm of n-novelty palls, it may be far too late."

"Are you suggesting that he might *marry* this chit?" she asked incredulously.

"I do not find the notion quite so incredible as your ladyship," he said smoothly.

"His attachment to me must make any such thing impossible," she protested.

"I must, in all fairness, point out that *you* are already m-married, Lady Caroline."

"What has that to say to anything? Such a union as you suggest would be prohibited by the feelings that we have for each other."

"Perhaps he thinks Lord Everly would stand his patron," said Mr. Canby, shifting away from dangerous ground. "The girl is quite interested in books, you know, and m-might well encourage it. It is only unfortunate that, I believe, Miss Winston has very little fortune of her own."

Lady Caroline showed white teeth. "A bit of information I shall take care to lay before Byron without delay," she told him. "I thank you!"

He inclined his head. "I hope I may be of service to your ladyship in many things," he said unctuously.

She narrowed her eyes at this. "And you are . . . what? Interested in protecting the girl from a rake? An ambassador from Lady Wibberly? You need not tell me that Everly sent you for I would not credit it for a moment!"

"No, my cousin did not send me. Let us just say that I believe you and I might have m-much in common," he suggested.

"I do not find that prospect either likely or entirely agreeable," she told him frankly.

He ignored the snub. "As your ladyship chooses."

"You talk like a servant, Canby," she snapped. "Do get to the point."

"The point, my dear Lady Caroline, is that I believe we are united in wishing ourselves rid of Miss Winston."

"Rid of Miss Winston?" she cried incredulously. "I thought she was Everly's ward!"

"I do not deny that she is under his protection. But I beg leave to inform you that, despite the family's silence on the subject, I believe the same idea I posed with regard to B-Byron—that of reestablishing his reputation in the world by allying himself with a respectable girl too young to have the slightest b-blemish on her character—has also occurred to my cousin."

She stared at him with an open mouth. "Are you saying that Everly is contemplating a marriage with this child as well?"

He shrugged. "I know nothing definite, but there is every sign that the possibility is being seriously explored."

She folded her arms. "And you, as his heir, wish to thrust a spoke in his wheel," she said brutally.

"I do not pretend to possess equal frankness to your ladyship," he said smoothly. "My m-motives may be a matter of speculation, but I shall not confess them."

"Has he by any chance conceived a *tendre* for this chit?" she inquired.

"I think n-not. He appears to find her rather amusing, but otherwise he pays her scant attention."

"I am relieved to hear it. It would go against the grain with me to interfere with any relationship of Everly's if his heart were engaged."

Mr. Canby smiled victoriously. "Then you do see the advantages of our collaboration, Lady Caroline?"

"I see the advantage of ridding myself of a rival, since we are speaking plainly," she told him. "I am not in the least interested in helping you step into Des's shoes."

"N-naturally you are not," he said, accepting this rebuke without apparent dismay. "But in this case you cannot achieve your ends unless I also achieve mine."

"It may suit me well to let you work your mischief, Mr. Canby, but I do not see why I should have a hand in it."

"Because, ma'am, you delight in the outrageous, and what I intend to do is nothing short of that!"

She did not take offense. "How well my reputation has proceeded me. Perhaps you are right. Go on!"

"My plan is twofold," he said with a gleam of excitement. "First I shall attempt to cast doubt on her respectability, since that is the key to her success. For this I need your connections and intervention."

He leaned close and explained what he had in mind. When he had finished, she exploded in mirth. "That is *fiendish!* The poor child! Still, I suppose she will come to no permanent harm."

"Of course not. I am not a m-monster, Lady Caroline."

Lady Caroline struggled for a moment with her composure and ultimately decided her best interest lay in not provoking him, at least for the moment. "You mentioned a twofold plan?" she prompted him.

"Yes, I was coming to that. The second part is to distract my cousin from his intentions—if such exist—with regard to Miss Winston. To present, as it were, a decoy."

"A decoy?" inquired Lady Caroline, confused.

"Is your ladyship acquainted with the Countess d'Abruzzi?"

"Yes, but—"

"I b-believe she lost her husband last year. Would not a visit to London, at the invitation of your ladyship, provide both a solace and a diversion to the b-bereaved young widow?"

"I suppose it might," Lady Caroline said frankly, "but I fail to see how entertaining Clarissa Constable—who was one of the most famous toasts of her own or any other Season—is advantageous to me!"

"Perhaps, Lady Caroline, you will cast your m-mind back over the years and review the list of her principal suitors."

Recognition dawned. "Wasn't she . . . ?

"Precisely," said Mr. Canby, with satisfaction.

Chapter 11

Lord Everly, well aware that tongues would be wagging in light of the events at Miss Winston's ball, began to take pains to shield her reputation. Previously an indifferent guardian, he now judged it best to be seen to exert a benevolent surveillance, and even went so far as to drive her round the park at the hour of "The Grand Strut," and, rather less fashionably, on a trip to view the maze at Hampton Court. Far from finding this a dead bore, he was surprised to find that he was enjoying himself almost as much as Susan, who expressed delight in all the pleasures London had to offer, despite Lady Wibberly's admonishment that such expressions invariably marked one as provincial. Lord Everly had had the forethought to provide himself with the key to the maze, in the anticipation that they would soon grow tired of wandering about in it, but Susan scorned such a provision as unworthy, and insisted on finding her way out by trial and error. Lord Everly had no choice but to follow her down one blind alley after another—since he did not wish to leave her alone, and she would not permit him to lead her out—with the inevitable result that they emerged a great deal of time later—rather hot and exhausted—but in undeniably high spirits.

"I wish we had brought the children," Susan exclaimed when he had led her over to a bench in the shade. "I am sure they have been here many times, but I feel certain they would have enjoyed it!"

He looked at her strangely. "You seem to be quite in charity with Almeria's girls," he said, raising his eyebrows.

"Should I not be?" she asked, surprised. "They are very sweet and most agreeable."

"That is as may be, but you must own that my sister is not! Particularly not to you."

"Oh, that is because she does not want me to marry you, and you can scarcely blame her for that," she said calmly.

"Can I not?" he asked in an interested tone.

"Well, no," she said reasonably. "I have no fortune, my—"

His lips twitched. "Despite my best efforts, I am still what the vulgar would call 'full of juice,'" he told her. "Almeria knows I need not hang out for an heiress."

"Well, but that sort of consideration does not signify with one's relations," she said seriously. "They are always urging one to make a brilliant match, and I am scarcely that."

"You underrate yourself, my child."

She shook her head. "You are very kind to say so, but I do realize that the only reason Lady Wibberly tolerates me is that she is afraid that if she puts your back up too much you will marry me just to spite her, whereas if she does not you may yet think better of the idea."

His mouth dropped. "Do you know that you are the most astonishing child! I thought I knew your sex, but you have surprised me."

"Well, I hope I have not offended you, but I cannot tell you how comfortable it is to be able to speak frankly. Although," she added thoughtfully, "lately I have been wondering whether it is always wise."

He looked at her with amusement. "I hope I haven't done anything to implant such a disastrous notion in your head."

"Well, no," she said seriously, "because I have noticed that you always seem to say exactly what is on your mind."

"What, then?"

"Lady Caroline," she confessed.

"Ah," he said with understanding. "In fairness I should have to say that Caro goes rather farther than plain dealing."

"I perceive that she is a friend of yours, but—"

He laughed. "That is not precisely how I would put it!"

"Would you not?" she asked innocently. "You were very kind to her, however."

"Rid yourself of that notion, Miss Winston! I am neither good-natured nor kind, so do not tax me with it. My relatives—even my mother—will be the first to tell you so."

"Your mother?" she asked, surprised. "Is she living then?"

"Oh yes," he said a trifle bitterly. "She is not . . . well, and does not go into company. She lives at the Dower House at Summerland."

"I should like to meet her," Susan said.

He stared off over the castle grounds and did not reply.

"But not if you didn't wish it, of course," she assured him in a small voice.

He looked at her face again. "It isn't that, my child. It is she who doesn't wish to see me."

"Why not?" she asked, aghast.

"Because she thinks I killed my brother," he said simply. "Does that shock you?"

"Of course it shocks me," she said quietly. "Not because I believe it to be true, but that anyone could think so. It is beyond reason."

"I do not know where you could have acquired such a touching faith—albeit misplaced—in my virtue," he said in a cool tone which did not deceive her. "Besides, you do not know the circumstances."

"No, and you need not tell me."

He smiled sardonically. "It is not so bad as that. He borrowed my horse and crammed it at a fence and broke his neck. My mother never quite forgave me for not stopping him. She never said so, of course. But when she looked at me—" He paused and turned away. After a while he said quietly. "Shortly afterward she had one stroke and then another. She . . . wanders in her wits. I am not sure she even recognizes me, but my presence seems to agitate her, so mostly I keep away."

His manner in relaying this was unruffled, but Susan felt her fingers curl into a fist, her nails digging into her palm. As keenly as if she had suffered it herself did she feel the pain of his rejection. His mother's illness, coupled with his own guilt, had wounded him in a way his other rejection—at the hands of a mercenary woman—never could. When he stepped into his brother's shoes, the fortune, the title, the deference of the world had only served to fuel his sense that he had come by it all undeservedly. No wonder he took such a perverse pleasure in providing the world in general and his family in particular with evidence of his depravity! In the normal way of things, his mother's grief and resentment would have worn themselves out in time, and a rapprochement could have been effected between them. As it was, her illness had frozen their relationship into one that caused him to read in her manner toward him only what gave him fresh pain every time he saw her.

Realizing that pity would be the last thing he would want

from her, she merely said, "Poor soul. No doubt she is very lonely."

He seemed startled at this. "Oh, no! She has many attendants, I promise you."

"Yes, but it would be very uncomfortable to live only in one's own mind, and not be able to communicate with one's family or friends," she told him. "It was so with my father."

"Oh, my dear! I hadn't realized!"

"Fortunately he did not exist such a long time that way, because he was very dignified, you know, and could not have liked being dressed and cosseted like a child." She looked up at him searchingly. "There was nothing, you know, that brought on his stroke. I believe that if one has a tendency to suffer one, there is very little that can be done to prevent it. That, at least, was the opinion of his doctors."

He looked at her, smiling oddly, but his thoughts seem far away. "Perhaps I should visit my mother again," he said after a while. "I have not seen her since I was shot in France."

"Then no doubt she would be very grateful to see that you are whole again," said Susan.

"Would you like to come with me?" he asked suddenly. "It won't be very entertaining for you, I daresay, but—"

"Yes, it would be most shocking if I were to miss a ball or two," cried Susan. "Of course, if you would like me to accompany you, I should very much like to come."

He reached out a finger and touched her cheek. "Thank you, my child. I confess I would be glad of the company. My sister, however, has gone to some lengths to obtain vouchers to Almack's, and we should both be in her black books if we were to leave before she presents you there next week."

"Shall you come with me?" she asked him timidly.

He thought with longing of an evening at his club, and abandoned it with only a trace of regret in favor of flat lemonade, indifferent refreshments, stifling conversation, and the ill-disguised appeal in his young ward's upturned face. "Most certainly," he said with a smile.

In the event, however, neither Miss Winston nor Lady Wibberly found themselves able to attend Almack's the following week. Misfortune, in the form of a rather virulent fever, struck down Miss Louisa, and Dr. Herron was called in to attend her. It was evident that the poor little girl really was quite ill, her head aching dreadfully and her fever causing her to sleep but fretfully, her damp curls tossing on the pillow. The parents were alarmed lest the disease be both highly dangerous and infectious, their firstborn, a fair-haired little boy, having been carried off in his infancy by something similar, and the doctor's assurances to the contrary did little to calm their fears. Miss Eliza was sent away to their country seat at once in the care of her old nurse, who was made miserable by the impossibility of being at the side of both of her beloved charges at the same time. Lady Wibberly would gladly have dispatched Susan as well, but Miss Louisa showed an unaccountable predilection for her company, and indeed seemed to be soothed by her presence. Lady Wibberly, herself all brisk efficiency, felt herself equal to the task of sitting by her daughter, coaxing her to eat and drink, or quietly reading to her till she fell asleep, but she did not relish it, and she could not deny that Miss Winston had a more tranquil demeanor in the sickroom. Lord Wibberly, although the fondest of fond papas, had not spent much time in his children's presence and did not really know what to say to them. Besides, he felt his darling's sufferings so acutely that he found it quite impossible to force her to do anything she might not like, such as swallow her medicine or remain under the covers, and as a result he was not of much use except to pat his wife's hand occasionally in the hope of reassuring her, attentions she tolerated in the interest of marital harmony.

Lord Everly, calling in at the Wibberlys' after a few days' visit to Summerland, was surprised to find the house in turmoil, with Miss Winston installed, apparently at her own request, as general officer of the sickroom. His sister, looking very much more tired and discomposed than when he had taken leave of her only the week before, greeted him in her saloon with the news of his niece's illness, and begged that he would go up as soon as possible. "For you have always been first oars with Louisa, you know," she told him with a smile, "and I am sure it will do her no end of good to see you."

Lord Everly had to smile in return at this description, for although he was fond of his nieces in a general sort of way, he had seen very little of them since their birth. He could not, however, fault his sister's ambition in this regard, and he did not in any event think that this was the time to chide her for it.

"I hope," she added as an afterthought, "that you are not afraid of infection."

He made a derisive sound, which made her say with a rueful

laugh, "Oh, very well, I knew I need not have asked! It is only that Cosmo came to call yesterday, and the haste with which he took his leave after I told him the news quite took my breath away. Shall we go up?"

Lord Everly entered the sickroom to the sound of Miss Winston's voice, apparently embarked upon a lengthy chronicle involving fairies and elves, and other creatures who seemed to delight Miss Louisa. His niece lay back pale and listless against the pillows, but her eyes were bright, and when she caught sight of him they grew even more animated. "Oh, Uncle Desmond!" she said in a pleased voice. "Susan was just telling me the loveliest story."

"You mean Miss Winston," said Lady Wibberly automatically.

"Oh, but she said I might call her Susan," said her daughter hesitantly.

"If you please, ma'am, I should like it very much," Susan said.

"I think it is an excellent suggestion," said his lordship before his sister could protest. He turned to a large bouquet by the bed. "I have come to be one of your admirers, Louisa, but I see I am not the first. Who sent you these beautiful flowers?"

"Oh you will never guess, Uncle Desmond!" said the little girl in an excited voice. "It is famous! They are from *Lord Byron.*"

Lord Everly raised an eyebrow at Miss Winston, who blushed.

"I must say it was very kind of him," said Lady Wibberly. "He called round yesterday to thank us for the ball and to apologize for—for the disturbance—and I had to send down my regrets at not being able to receive him—with the explanation of course. This morning these arrived with a card for Louisa. I cannot like him, but it was so very thoughtful. And Louisa's head has been quite turned."

The patient giggled weakly.

"I am decidedly cast down," said Lord Everly woefully. "I had thought I was 'first oars' with you, and now I find another has usurped my place."

"Oh, Uncle Desmond," protested the child, "you know he likes Susan and not me."

"Oh no!" remonstrated Susan hastily. "I am quite cast into the shade."

"It is time for your medicine," interjected Lady Wibberly sourly.

The child immediately turned querulous. "I don't want it! It tastes bad."

"Well, I have come especially to hold it for you," said Lord Everly, approaching closer to the bedside.

Louisa turned her head fretfully.

"Come, Louisa, do as you are bid," said her mother.

"I won't!"

"I take leave to tell you," said his lordship, raising his brows at his niece, "that you are becoming a dead bore, and I dislike dead bores excessively. Unless you wish us all to go away at once, I suggest you drink down this potion."

"Did I not tell you, my dear," said Susan with a laugh, "that a gentleman's feelings are very sensitive?"

Louisa gave a little choke but opened her mouth reluctantly. Susan raised the little girl to rest against her shoulder while Lord Everly, giving her no chance to change her mind, tilted the contents of the glass down her throat ruthlessly. As he did his hand met Susan's on the glass and their eyes met for an instant.

"I think we should let her sleep now," said Lady Wibberly.

The child pulled at Susan's arm. "You promised you would finished the end of the story!"

Susan laid her gently down again. "Well, it is a very long story, and I do not think we can finish it all today. But I am sure you will sleep better if I tell you what happened to the fairy prince, will you not?"

"Oh yes," Louisa agreed drowsily.

"All right then, but no more talking. If you interrupt me I am likely to lose my place and forget what comes next."

"And what did he find under the toadstool?" inquired the little girl.

Susan told her, and Lord Everly and his sister tiptoed out of the room as Miss Louisa's eyelids dropped, and Susan's voice began to sink into the very quietest of her dreams.

"I must own," said Lady Wibberly to his lordship when they had returned to the saloon, "that while I cannot approve of Miss Winston's allowing Louisa such familiarities—after all, she is practically a stranger among us!—she is very good with her. She can coax her into eating and taking her medicine with a great deal less fuss than anyone else provokes."

Lord Everly, who had noticed that Susan was looking a trifle pulled down, suspected that his sister was imposing on her. "Who is sitting up with the child at night?" he inquired.

Lady Wibberly looked guilty. "Well, Miss Winston *would* offer, and you know it is impossible for me to sleep during the day, so it is much more convenient for her to do so."

"Have you no servants who will sit with her?" inquired Lord Everly, scowling.

"They are all afraid of infection," said her ladyship frankly. "And you need not look like that, Everly. Miss Winston seemed glad of the chance to 'repay our hospitality' as she put it, and the child minds her, after all. I am sure Louisa will be better in a few days, and then she may resume her amusements."

"Very well, Almeria; the situation is quite plain to me—"

"Yes, I'm afraid there is no one else."

"—I shall move in at once, and take turns sitting with the child myself."

"That is not necessary," she protested, taken aback.

"I beg leave to differ," he said curtly. "Send one of your servants with a message to Marston to send round some things. I am going up now to relieve Miss Winston."

"Desmond, this is foolish beyond permission," she told him, but she spoke to thin air.

Reentering the sickroom a few minutes later, he was not surprised to find both his niece and Susan fast asleep, the one against her pillow and the other in the depths of the chair. He touched Miss Winston's shoulder gently and she started awake. He laid a finger over his lips and beckoned her to come into the hall.

"I am sorry," she said when she had left the room. "I must have drifted off." She smiled. "And just at the good part of the story, too."

"My poor child, you look exhausted. I have come to relieve you, so go and get some sleep."

"I am a little tired," she admitted.

"I'm afraid my sister has been abusing your kindness," he told her.

"Oh, you must not think so!" she protested. "We have arranged everything very satisfactorily. I am very glad to see you, but if you are going to talk in that manner I daresay I shall be wishing you at Jericho!"

"But you have your own life," he insisted. "I did not bring you to London so that you could spend the Season in the sickroom!"

"How charming it would be for me to demand that her ladyship entertain me when her daughter lies ill in her bed! Don't be silly, Lord Everly."

"Do you not think that, like Louisa, we might be on a first-name basis? I am Desmond, you know!"

"I know," she said quietly.

"Well?"

"I will try . . . Desmond."

"Excellent. Now off to your bed with you, my child. I will see you in the morning!"

Between Lord Everly's efforts and those of Miss Winston, Miss Louisa was very soon seen to be gaining ground, and while she remained somewhat thin and tired, her color returned, and her spirits became more lively. It was a new experience for Lord Everly to spend all of his waking hours in the sickroom, and since his arrival therein was the signal for Susan to retire to her own bed, he held very little conversation with her, and those few in which they did engage were chiefly concerned with the welfare of their patient.

Lady Wibberly, somewhat taken aback by this previously hidden aspect to her brother's character, was inclined to believe, now that Louisa was manifestly recovering, that the illness had been the most fortunate thing in the world. "For I am sure I have never seen him take the least interest in either of the girls before," she told Lord Wibberly as they were enjoying a comfortable coze before retiring to bed, "despite my best efforts to bring them to his attention. I cannot but hope that he has begun to feel a sense of responsibility at last."

"Ha!" was her spouse's enigmatic response.

"If it is so," she continued, ignoring this unsatisfactory contribution, "I am heartily glad of it, because, although I hope I am as fond of my brother as the next person, I have never made any secret of my belief that he rarely thinks of anything but his own pleasures. Indeed, his wealth has been so great that he can indulge every idle whim, and he has become quite spoilt. I should not be at all surprised if he were bored as well."

"Could be Miss Winston's influence," suggested his lordship.

"Oh no, I cannot think so. Despite the arrangement between them, he does not single her out, you know! It must be that he has decided to settle down at last, and mend his reputation. If that is the case, he will scarcely have need for our houseguest, and I daresay he will find a suitable husband for her."

"Being cautious," contributed her spouse.

"Yes, and it must be for the first time. But a man top over tail in love would not be *cautious*, surely? Indeed, I must believe that he now regrets, in all probability, his earlier rashness. I only hope it is not too late!"

"Doesn't know his own mind," persisted Lord Wibberly.

"Oh, Wibberly, of course he does not!" she responded impatiently. "That is why we must take care to make it up for him!"

"Tell you what, my dear, you'd do better to send that poet fellow packing. Haunts the house night and day."

"He does no such thing!" protested her ladyship, who, although she could not in justice say she altogether approved of Lord Byron, was highly enjoying the enhancement of her reputation as a *tonnish* hostess his frequent presence in her house had provided. "He has merely called a few times to determine how Louisa does, and—"

"Ha!" ejaculated his lordship again.

"And to call on Miss Winston, of course," she concluded. "I will grant that I do not *quite* see the attraction, since his tastes have been for rather more sophisticated companions, but his preference is quite marked. I do not believe, however, that his intentions can be serious. He is far too unstable, and, to my mind, he is undoubtedly pulling a hoax on society."

"Saw Lady Caroline outside the house the other day," he told her. "Looked as mad as fire, too."

"Do you mean she passed you in the street?" inquired her ladyship.

He shook his head. "Not at all. Standing about on the sidewalk, looking up at the windows. I tell you, it gave me a queer turn."

Lady Wibberly gave a delicate shudder. "I cannot believe that any woman of such a family could be so lost to propriety as to follow a man down the streets of town! You must be mistaken!"

"Know what I saw, Almeria! It was not gone four o'clock. Broad daylight, you know."

"Well, if you noticed her, very likely someone else did as well. I cannot like it, but as long as she did not make a scene, I suppose we must be grateful. How tongues are wagging about her!"

"Can't quite like the fellow for allowing it. Must have encouraged her."

"I know what you mean," conceded her ladyship. "However Byron's notice has done *us* a great deal of good socially, and I mean to benefit by it. No doubt he will move on soon, but I want people to remember that he came to this house!"

"But what about the girl, Almeria?" he inquired, savoring the last of a glass of excellent cognac.

"I don't know what you mean," replied her ladyship mendaciously.

"Getting herself talked about, too. Not her fault, but there it is."

"Well, I must say that Miss Winston, whatever else she may be, does not seem like the sort of girl to dress up as a harem slave and build willow cabins in public, thank goodness. I don't think we need fear *that*, at least."

"Might get her heart broken," said Lord Wibberly. "Could, if she thinks the fellow wants to marry her, and Everly doesn't come through."

"I am sure," said her ladyship with some asperity, "that she is far too sensible to consider herself any sort of matrimonial prize whatsoever. If she can only be brought to set her sights a little lower than Byron or Everly, I do not see why her heart must enter into it at all!"

"I'm sure you know best, m'dear," said her husband.

Chapter 12

Lady Wibberly was sufficiently mollified by her daughter's return, for the most part, to health and spirits to enable her to contemplate a renewal of the postponed assault on Almack's with relative tranquillity. Accordingly, she agreed to escort Miss Winston there on the following Wednesday. To her surprise, Lord Everly also agreed to make one of the party, although he was generally known to prefer less tame amusements.

Susan was attired for her entry into the Marriage Mart in a white crepe ball dress with velvet ribbons, and even the most exacting critic could not complain that she looked provincial, or anything other than decidedly à la mode. Lady Wibberly felt that she was insufficiently impressed by the magnanimity of the Ladies' Committee in issuing her vouchers to attend, but she could not deny that her charge's taste, on this occasion at least, was unimpeachable. When Susan went to the sickroom to take leave of Miss Louisa before they set out, her ladyship found herself in the greatest of charity with her, and could even view the prospect of a nearer connection, while still undesirable, without undue dismay.

Lord Everly, suitably dressed in the knee breeches, long tails, and white neckcloth that were de rigueur for Almack's, had a rather bemused air of cynical resignation Susan recognized immediately. She would have preferred, just this once, unqualified admiration, but she was nonetheless grateful that he was to accompany her. Lady Wibberly had implanted in her head the dire consequences of committing a social solecism within the Sacred Portals, but there were so many strictures that she was unable to keep them all in mind and lived in a state of the liveliest dread that she would violate one unknowingly.

Entering Almack's (having passed Cerberus, in the celebrated form of Mr. Willis guarding the front door) on the arm of Lord Everly, Susan was at first at some pains to discern precisely what it was that all the fuss was about. The rooms, while spacious, were much less splendid than the private ballrooms she had already encountered in England and in Europe, and the furnishings might be called functional rather than elegant. However, the line of carriages outside the door was testament to the magnetic power of exclusivity, and Susan was prepared to suspend her critical evaluation until further investigation.

Several of the Patronesses were already present when they were admitted. One of them, Lady Jersey, glided over to Lord Everly with an expression of undisguised glee. "Oh famous!" she cried, laughing up at him. "We have captured you at last. I knew you must admit we reign supreme, however much you have shunned us these many years."

Lord Everly laughed. "I admit nothing, Sally," he said, kissing her hand. "I am merely here to accompany my ward. I take it you have met Miss Winston?"

Lady Jersey's eyes flashed mischievously. "Oh yes. I am so glad you have come, and you, too, Lady Wibberly. Miss Winston, there is someone here who particularly wants to make your acquaintance. Emily," she said, beckoning to an attractive woman who stood nearby, "*this* is Byron's Miss Winston. Miss Winston, may I present Lady Cowper."

Susan, who had not studied the family trees of the Patronesses with sufficient care, could not understand Lady Cowper's sudden, intense scrutiny. "Ma'am," she said, dropping a curtsy.

Lord Everly folded his arms. "*Wicked*, Sally," he whispered to Lady Jersey.

Lady Cowper smiled. "I perceive that Lord Byron has been hoaxing my sister-in-law," she remarked to the world in general. "This is no more than an innocent child."

"Lady Caroline is married to Lady Cowper's brother," confided Lord Everly in an amused tone.

How lovely for you, thought Susan. "Indeed, ma'am?" she said.

"You do not flinch," said Lady Cowper approvingly.

"I have no need," responded Susan promptly.

Lady Cowper considered this boldness and decided she did not condemn it. In fact, though she had expected blushes and a head hung down, she rather approved the girl's style. "I'm glad to hear it," said her ladyship. "Caro is a trifle out of the ordinary, you know. I am glad to hear that she has not put you out of countenance."

Susan smiled at this description of Caroline Lamb as a sort of benevolent eccentric but said nothing.

"What a sweet child," Lady Cowper remarked to Lady Jersey when Susan and her party had passed on to the other hostesses. "I cannot think why Cosmo Canby described her as coming, when her manners are really quite excellent."

"Cosmo Canby is a toad," replied Lady Jersey without hesitation.

"Yes, but a well-connected toad," said Lady Cowper. "However, she seems to be a girl of uncommon sense for her age, and not at all nonplussed by Caroline's antics."

"Emily, *I* am nonplussed by Caroline's antics."

"Caroline is a burden to us all," admitted Lady Cowper sourly. "Even my mother cannot bring her to a sense of her want of conduct, and her infatuation with this poet has made the family a laughingstock!"

"Cannot William do something?" asked Lady Jersey curiously.

"My brother has tried everything in his power to first please and then curb his wife, but I fear his patience is exhausted," Lady Cowper confessed. "He feels that to acknowledge Caro's . . . shall we say . . . problems is to give them credibility in the eyes of the world, and so he affects to ignore the fact that anything is wrong."

"Well, perhaps that is wisest, if he cannot control her," said Lady Jersey sympathetically.

"No doubt, but it cannot continue. My mother is urging him to have her locked up as a Bedlamite!"

"Emily, you cannot mean it," replied Lady Jersey, shocked.

"I have said too much," said Lady Cowper in a quiet voice. "You will oblige me, Sally, by not mentioning this to anyone. We are talked about enough these days as it is."

"Certainly, Emily, certainly," said Lady Jersey sincerely. Emily Cowper knew far too many details of Lady Jersey's past, both recent and distant, which might make embarrassing revelations, and thus she was assured of her silence.

"As for the girl," said Lady Cowper, returning to her original subject, "I am inclined to grant her the benefit of the doubt, whatever Cosmo Canby says. I do not plan to take her up, precisely, but if anyone should ask me I shall say she appears to be a well-brought-up girl."

"Well, let us see," said Lady Jersey. "One should never be too precipitate in showing approval, or one will quickly lose one's position as the Ultimate Arbiter."

"Very true," concurred Lady Cowper.

Despite his characterization at the hands of at least one of the Patronesses as a rather unattractive member of the amphibian family, Mr. Canby was a regular at Almack's. As an aspirant to the dizzy heights of social recognition, he could not afford to stay away, and his connection to the Wyndhams made him, if not a welcome guest, at least an acceptable one. Besides, his sartorial achievements required an audience, and Almack's provided the most *tonnish* audience in the English-speaking world.

His appearance on this particular evening, however, had a more calculated purpose in mind than displaying his finery, and he observed with satisfaction the arrival of Lord Everly, Lady Wibberly, and Miss Winston. Everly's presence required a careful stratagem, but he knew his cousin well and was convinced that he would soon grow bored and take himself off to the card room, leaving the field clear for Mr. Canby to execute his plans.

Miss Winston's reaction upon seeing Lord Everly's cousin's arrival in the rooms was reflective of anything but satisfaction, and came a great deal closer to dismay. He bowed to her from across the room, and she returned his greeting, but to her great relief, he made no effort to approach her. Indeed, after the minuet she did not see him again, and presently she stopped worrying about what mischief he might be making and started enjoying her surroundings. Now that she had passed the first hurdle with the Patronesses, she was feeling more confident, and enjoyed the attentions of a number of Pinks of the Ton. Everly stood up with her for a quadrille, and she confided, with a sparkle in her eyes, that perhaps Almack's was not so dull as she had anticipated.

He laughed. "Well, if you are pleased, then enjoy yourself, brat, with my blessing!"

She eyed him speculatively. "Did you used to come here, before—?" She stopped uncertainly.

"Before I turned my back on Society, you mean?" he said with an amused smile.

"Yes, I was going to say that," she admitted. "I beg your pardon!"

"Well if one is to be precise about it, Society turned its back on *me*," he said without the slightest trace of remorse. "And yes, I did come here after my come-out. One does, that's all. But I cannot say that even then I did not find it just a touch insipid."

"Oh, well, I suspect it must be different for gentlemen," Susan said seriously.

"No doubt," he said, maintaining his gravity. "Now I have danced with you twice, and we will set tongues to wagging if we stand up together again. Should you object very much if I spend the rest of the evening at cards? If I remain in this room Cosmo is certain to approach me with his latest request for pecuniary relief, and I confess the prospect fills me with the liveliest dread."

She giggled. "Does it? I do not blame you! Shall I bid you good night, then?"

"Certainly not," he said with mock severity. "I intend to see you home."

Miss Winston's hand was solicited for several more dances before the fiddles at length struck up a waltz. Obediently, she remained along the sidelines, because Lady Wibberly had instructed her that one must never waltz in public without first obtaining the express permission of one of the Patronesses. Susan was a trifle vague as to what form precisely such permission would take, but as she was sure in any event that she did not have it, she was constrained from joining in. She looked with longing at more fortunate females whirling about the room, and their pitying glances in her direction did little to abate her restlessness or improve her mood. Considering a strategic retreat, she began to look round for Lady Wibberly, but she saw her engaged in conversation with Mr. Canby and did not like to go over.

She was startled to find herself suddenly confronted with the formidable personage of Sir Barnaby Pilbeam, who had been variously described to her as a man milliner by Lord Wibberly and as a regular Golden Ball by his more practical wife. Sir Barnaby was the happy possessor of some sixty thousand pounds, and so his age, which must have been upward of forty, and his eccentric appearance, which all too obviously necessitated the wearing of a corset, did not render him so ineligible as might otherwise have been supposed. His only passion, besides his attire, was for gambling, and it was generally believed that his constitution was such that he could never refuse a bet, no matter how small the stakes.

Susan had not been formally introduced to this paragon, although he had certainly been pointed out to her, and so she was rather surprised when he solicited the honor of leading her onto the floor. When she demurred, he said bracingly, "Come, my dear. Can't have you sitting here looking peaked when the other gels are out dancing. Take a turn around the floor with me! Just the thing for the megrims!"

His face was rather flushed, and quite honestly, he looked as if the effort might be too much for him. Susan suppressed a giggle at the thought of his expiring on the dance floor, and protested that of all things she would naturally prefer to dance with him, but the Patronesses had not yet granted her permission to waltz.

"Well, I don't know about that," he persisted. "Who was it told me to ask you to dance, then?" He nodded in the direction of Lady Sefton, who was surveying the dancers with benign approval.

"Is *that* how permission is granted?" inquired Susan. "I didn't know."

"Never know till the first time, right, my dear?" he said archly. "I promise you, you'll come to no harm in my arms."

Susan glanced in appeal at Lady Wibberly, but her chaperone was still engaged with Mr. Canby. She wondered fleetingly what they could find to discuss at such length, but as she had little taste for parading her ignorance in front of Mr. Canby in particular, she did not interrupt them.

Sir Barnaby was waiting with outstretched hand. He looked so absurd, trying to hide his enormous bulk and increasing age behind what he apparently considered a fashionable appearance, that she felt sorry for him. After all, how much harm could there be in dancing with him just once, as long as Lady Sefton apparently approved?

She took his hand. He smiled at her and turned to lead her into the waltz. She heard a distinct *creak*. The smile slipped a little. "Injured my back," he said stiffly.

"How—how very distressing for you, sir," she said faintly. "Should you rather sit down?"

"No!" he said sharply. "That is, movement. That's the ticket. Just the thing for a bad back."

She was so absorbed in the logistics of moving around the floor with him that it was some moments before she noticed

Lady Wibberly frantically motioning from the sidelines. Mr. Canby stood beside her, the expression on his face enigmatic. They were both regarding her intensely, and Lady Wibberly seemed agitated and pale.

She paused, almost causing a collision with Sir Barnaby's mammoth stomach. "I beg your pardon," she said to his waistcoat.

"My fault," he said magnanimously. "I say," he said, following the direction of her gaze, "does Almeria Wibberly have a nervous disorder?"

"Certainly not!" she told him. "Why do you ask?"

"Keeps jerking her head at us."

"Yes, I see. I believe she wants to talk to me."

"I expect it is just the excitement," said Sir Barnaby, continuing to push her around the floor.

"Please, sir," said Susan, desperate to extricate herself. "I believe I should go over to her at once!"

He seemed to consider this. "Do you think so? Music hasn't stopped yet," he added reasonably.

"Yes, if you please. I fear she may be ill."

Indeed, Lady Wibberly did look rather stricken when they approached her. Mr. Canby was fanning her resolutely, and she seemed as if she might, with the least provocation, slip into a swoon.

"What is it, ma'am?" cried Susan in a concerned voice. "Are you ill?"

Lady Wibberly opened her mouth, considered Sir Barnaby Pilbeam, recalled with some effort the sixty thousand pounds, and shut it again. After a moment she said faintly, "Yes, I am feeling a trifle hot. Perhaps, Sir Barnaby, if you would be so good as to procure for me a glass of lemonade?"

Susan, briefly wondering why Mr. Canby did not perform this office for his cousin in lieu of a virtual stranger, nevertheless volunteered to perform it herself.

"No, no," protested Lady Wibberly. "That is, I should be glad if you stayed by me awhile."

Sir Barnaby bowed majestically and went off on his errand, parting the company before him as he went. Susan, who had begun to be really concerned about her ladyship, said urgently, "Should you not like to sit down, Lady Wibberly? There is a vacant chair beside the wall."

"What I should like," said her ladyship with sudden ferocity, "is to sink through the floor! How came you," she added in a hiss, "to waltz with Sir Barnaby Pilbeam?"

"Is there something wrong with him?" asked Susan, confused.

"Not with him, no!" replied Lady Wibberly in an exasperated tone. *"But you did not have the permission of the Patronesses!"*

Susan cast a stricken glance in the direction of this august bunch, and saw that, indeed, Lady Jersey was gazing at her with glacial hauteur. Princess Esterhazy, who was standing next to Lady Jersey, saw her looking and ostentatiously turned her back. Lady Wibberly gave a little moan.

"But—" was all Susan could think of to say.

"Perhaps M-miss Winston did not realize the prohibition against waltzing without permission," suggested Mr. Canby in a kindly tone.

"I feel quite sure I did not neglect to mention it," said Lady Wibberly frostily. "And now I shall not be surprised if she has completely ruined her chances. After all my efforts!"

"Indeed ma'am, I did know," admitted Susan. "But Sir Barnaby said—that is"—she hesitated, remembering his words—"he didn't *say* precisely, but he certainly implied—that the Patronesses had given him permission to ask me to dance."

"I am afraid that is not how it is done, my dear," said Mr. Canby in the same benevolent voice. "One is always p-presented with an eligible partner by one of the Patronesses. In p-person," he added with a little smile.

"Oh," said Susan, blushing hotly.

"No doubt Sir Barnaby thought that you had already secured permission," he said smoothly. "He knows the r-rules as well as anyone."

"But he said—well, it does not matter now." She put her chin up. "Is it so very bad?"

Lady Wibberly grimaced. "I shall, of course, endeavor to explain. But it can be fatal—*fatal*—to set a foot wrong so early in the game. Now you shall have to correct a bad first impression, and coupled with Lady Caroline's antics, tongues are sure to start wagging." She sighed. "If I had not promised Des . . . " She seemed to recollect what she was saying and turned sharply to Mr. Canby. "Cosmo, try if you can to get Everly to accompany us home. I believe we will have a long wait for the carriage, and I do not think we should remain any longer than necessary."

"Should I apologize, ma'am?" inquired Susan meekly.

"Yes, but not now. You will write a very pretty note to Lady Jersey, after I have told her that you only disobeyed the rules in error, and not out of some forward notion of *flaunting* yourself," she said with a shudder.

"Does it not seem rather—" Susan ventured.

"Rather *what*?"

"Rather a tempest in a teapot," she continued bravely. "How can it be so very important after all whether one waltzes with or without permission?"

Lady Wibberly pressed her hands to her temples. "Miss Winston, if you are going to be one of *us*," she said stiffly, "I must implore—no, I must *insist*—that you rid yourself of such radical notions at once!"

Mr. Canby, en route to the card room in search of his cousin, happened to pass Sir Barnaby coming in the opposite direction with a glass of lemonade. Sir Barnaby paused and said in a hearty voice, "Didn't think I could pull the thing off, did you Canby? I'll wager you never expected to have to pay up so soon!"

"I confess I underrated you," replied Mr. Canby. "I shall of course send round my f-forfeit at once, but I think you will agree this is neither the t-time nor the place. And if you could lower your voice a b-bit, we should not let everyone in the world in on our b-bet."

"Thing is," said Sir Barnaby with a touch of unhappiness, "wasn't quite the way you said it would be. Nice gel, that. *You* said she needed taking down a peg or two."

"I assure you," said Mr. Canby smoothly. "Besides, no permanent harm will come to her because you hoaxed her into w-waltzing with you without permission. By next w-week it will all have blown over."

"Suppose so," said Sir Barnaby dubiously. "Must be going. Your cousin needs her lemonade."

"By all m-means," said Mr. Canby with a smile.

"So what have you been up to, brat?" said Lord Everly with a smile when he had sauntered over to her in response to his cousin's representations. "Can't I leave you alone for even a minute?"

"Apparently not," she said frankly, "I have made a muddle of things. I did warn you that it would be quite useless to try to bring me out in Society, and now it turns out I was right!"

"I can't believe the situation is nearly so desperate as that," he said, maintaining admirable gravity. "What have you done, spilled lemonade on Sally's dress?"

"Worse," she said with a gleam in her eye. "I waltzed without permission!"

He threw back his head and laughed. "Dreadful," he agreed.

"Well, your sister certainly thinks so," said Susan, relieved at his reaction. She filled him in on the particulars, which caused him to laugh once more.

"Barnaby Pilbeam!" he said, wiping his eyes. "I wish I had seen it! The man milliner!"

"That's just what Lord Wibberly says," she confided. "But Lady Wibberly—" She stopped.

"What? Tell me."

"He has sixty thousand pounds a year," said Susan innocently.

"Ha! Almeria would find a rhinoceros a *suitable parti* if he had such a sum. I hope you are not of a similar turn of mind?" he said, teasing her.

"No, I am not very fond of large animals," she told him.

"Vixen! I am, however, relieved to see that you are not quite so distraught at the evening's events as my sister."

"No, but I should be," said Susan seriously. "Lady Wibberly says it is fatal to make a misstep at this stage, and that is just what I have done. Now I shall never appear to be respectable, and no doubt they will not let me come again!"

"Should you mind that?" he said, putting his hand under her chin.

Not if you don't, she thought suddenly. She looked at her feet. "I would not like to disappoint Lady Wibberly after all her trouble," she said at length.

"Ah," he said, misunderstanding her sudden embarrassment. "Then we will do what we must to make amends. Do you think it will help if I grovel at Sally's feet?"

Her smile peeped. "If I am not mistaken, your sister has already suggested groveling. But I am to do it in writing, after she has done so in person." She sighed. "It is a great deal of trouble to go to."

"That is what Lord Wellington said," he told her with a

reminiscent smile. "Did you know they turned him away, too?"

Her eyes grew round. "*Lord Wellington* was turned away?"

"Yes, because he was not wearing knee breeches. He is somewhat absentminded, you know, and he said he just forgot. Nevertheless, he was not admitted!"

What did he do?"

"He laughed, and beat a hasty retreat, as we must do! My sister seems to have collected herself. Are you ready, brat?"

"Yes, I—" Something about the story made her pause. "Lord Wellington told you this? In person?" she asked him.

His face assumed an inscrutable expression. "Yes, but never mind! Shall we go . . . ? Good God!"

He had broken off to look in the direction of the door, where a party of very late arrivals had just been admitted. Among them was one of the most stunning women Susan had ever seen, angelically fair and attired in the most elegant and expensive of fashions. Though she must have been nearly thirty years old, her beauty was scarcely diminished and carefully preserved. Lord Everly was staring at her with an enigmatic expression she could not read, but she thought she saw a shadow of pain flicker across his face. "Who is that?" she asked him.

He did not answer her, but Mr. Canby, who had come up to stand beside her, did. "That," he whispered in her ear, like the devil himself, "is the C-Countess d' Abruzzi."

The name did not mean anything to her. "The Countess d' Abruzzi?"

He smiled. "Why, yes. When our Desmond was in love with her, she was Clarissa Constable. I wonder what she can be doing here?"

Chapter 13

Susan would never discover whether Lord Everly, swept up in a tide of emotion, would have gone inexorably to the countess's side, because as soon as *she* caught sight of *him,* she made her way across the floor to where they were standing, her eyes shining in delight and surprise, her mouth curved into a lovely smile. "Desmond," she said, stretching out her hands to him.

He bowed. "Clarissa, is it indeed you? I am quite astonished."

She gave a silvery laugh. "Have I changed so much?"

He raised an eyebrow. "You know perfectly well that you have not."

She conferred upon him a look of melting sweetness. "Thank you! I must own that at this moment it seems only yesterday that we all met in these very rooms." She studied him with a little frown. "Well, *you* have changed a great deal, my friend. You look considerably more worldly than the young man I knew, and a trifle cynical as well. I hope the years have been kind to you."

Her tone was as intimate as a caress, and Susan, watching this bravura performance, would not have been surprised to hear him confess that she had wrecked his hopes and heart, and that all since had been done in defiance of her power over him. Instead, he shrugged. "Kind enough, I suppose."

"One heard that you were on the Continent a great deal," she told him, letting him know, Susan realized, that she had managed to keep tabs on him, "but you never came to see us."

"No," he said shortly. "Is the count with you in London?"

She put a hand to her heart. "Oh, dear . . . I thought surely you must have heard. . . . I have been a widow these two years and more."

Susan thought she had seldom seen anyone look less bereaved, and then chided herself for her lack of charity. "My condolences, Clarissa," Lord Everly said calmly.

The countess lowered her eyes. "It was quite sudden, but we are better now. My little boy—Federigo—is three, and he is very sensitive, so I did not like to leave him, but Mr. Lamb and Lady Caroline persuaded me that it might do him good. His nurse indulges him so!"

"I did not know you were on such terms with the Lambs," said Lord Everly dryly.

"Oh, Caroline has been everything that is kind!" she said gaily. "She is a mother, too, you know, and understands perfectly. She heard of my bereavement some time back, and determined that I must come to visit. And here I am!" She seemed to notice the others for the first time, and offered her delicately tinted cheek to Lady Wibberly, who had come up beside them. "Oh, my dear Lady Wibberly, what must you think of me? I was so overcome by seeing Desmond again that I quite forgot my manners. How do you do?"

Lady Wibberly addressed her with a cautious reserve. "Very well, I thank you. May I present Miss Winston? She is visiting us for the Season."

The countess favored Susan with a brief, assessing glance, followed by the most dazzling of smiles. "What a lovely child you are," she said in her melodious voice. "And how delightful it must be to be in one's first Season," she added, making Susan feel as if she had just emerged from leading strings. "How long ago it all seems," she said with a sigh.

Susan curtsied, keeping her tongue between her teeth.

"Mr. Canby, I believe you know," offered Lady Wibberly.

"Why yes, we are old friends," she said, taking his hand.

"Oh ha ha! Yes indeed!" ejaculated Mr. Canby. "It is most d-delightful to see you again, Countess."

"Oh, you must all call me Clarissa, as you used to, or I shall feel quite strange. I mean to reestablish all my old friendships, you know."

Susan was afraid to look at Lord Everly to see how he received this news.

"I hope I may call on your ladyship," the countess added.

"Yes, of course. We should be delighted," said Lady Wibberly.

The countess fixed Susan with another of her benevolent smiles. "And I look forward to furthering my acquaintance with you, Miss Winston. Dear me, I thought I had met all of your relations, Desmond."

Lord Everly looked amused at this blatant fishing for information. "Miss Winston is my ward, Clarissa."

An expression of consternation flickered over her countenance so rapidly Susan was not sure she had really seen it. It was replaced almost immediately by a look of the greatest delight. "Miss Winston . . . Oh yes! I believe I've heard Lady Caroline mention your name."

"I don't doubt it," said Lord Everly in a sarcastic tone. "You will excuse us, I know, but we were just on the point of departing. Miss Winston is tired and looking forward to her bed."

"Yes, I know just how it is," said the countess in such a concerned tone of voice that Susan immediately suspected that she had already heard about her faux pas that evening. "I hope we shall meet again very soon." She turned to Lord Everly and offered him her hand.

He took it in his and kissed it. "Goodbye, Clarissa," he said with a queer, twisted smile.

"Good night, Desmond."

The carriage ride home from Almack's to the Wibberlys' town house afforded few if any of the expected pleasures and satisfactions of digesting and elucidating the evening's events in relative comfort and privacy. The ball, which had begun on such a promising note, had encompassed such circumstances as to make the occupants retreat into their individual reflections, so that few words were spoken on any subject. Lord Everly gave Susan's hand a reassuring squeeze, but he occupied himself for the rest of the journey by looking out of the window with an abstracted air, and she did not dare intrude on his thoughts. Indeed, she did not really want to know what they were.

Lady Wibberly's silence was also uncharacteristic, but Susan could only be grateful that her ladyship was apparently too exhausted to give her the tongue lashing she undoubtedly deserved for overturning the rules of Almack's. Lady Wibberly had been at some pains to instruct her in proper behavior, and now all her good work had gone for naught.

Had Susan but known it, what really occupied her ladyship's mind was Clarissa Constable. She wondered what, after so long a time, had brought the countess back into their sphere at the very moment Desmond had made an effort to reestablish himself in the eyes of the world and settle, if not eligibly, at least with respectability. When Clarissa had jilted him in favor of a lover better hosed and shod, Lady Wibberly had repudiated her as mercenary, although, her partiality to her brother aside, she had to confess that her choice had practical benefits, so long as her heart had not been engaged. Indeed, she had been used to think of Clarissa as rather heartless, and not a little selfish. Her appearance this evening, however, gave Lady Wibberly pause. She was too much a woman of the world not to recognize that Clarissa was sending out unmistakable signals of interest in her brother; despite her expressed delight at seeing them all again, her eyes had sought only Desmond. Lady Wibberly began to wonder if she had nursed a *tendre* for him all these years and, now that circumstances had freed her from a marriage that had left her very well able to command the elegancies of life, meant to win him back.

She could not quite decide what she thought about this. It must occur to anyone of a suspicious nature that Desmond, Viscount Everly, was a more attractive marital prospect than Des Wyndham had been, and that the countess, however much she repined nostalgically upon the old days, might not have encouraged him with quite so much enthusiasm had his fortune and consequence not undergone such a fortunate transformation. She sighed and wondered what her brother might be thinking. At one time Desmond had without a doubt been in love with Clarissa Constable; whether his feelings for the Countess d'Abruzzi might be reignited she did not know. He was certainly giving no hints of what he felt to his sister or anyone else as he sat silently staring out the coach window. And *what*, pray, would they do with Miss Winston, should Desmond and Clarissa rekindle their romance? Lady Wibberly supposed she might be sent to relatives somewhere, and was surprised to find this idea cost her a pang. She sighed again, and sat back against the squabs, her head aching. It was all such a muddle.

Susan was in quite as confused and unhappy a state as Lady Wibberly, although for a different reason. The arrival of the Countess d'Abruzzi on the scene, and the look on Lord Everly's face when he had caught sight of her across the room, had caused Susan to experience a moment of self-enlightenment both startling and painful in its intensity. It was a rather uncomfortable discovery, and one she did not feel in the least inclined to confide to anyone else. She looked at Lord Everly, lost in contemplation of some happier past, and imagined his misery. It could not have been any greater than her own.

When she had agreed to consider marrying Lord Everly, she had entered into the arrangement with eyes open, knowing that what he required of her was a respectable home, and an agreement not to interfere with him. As long as she had no feelings for him other than a friendly regard, she thought she could manage to live up to these terms; now that she knew her own mind at last (and she realized that her feelings had been growing steadily for some time), she could not but think it torment to be treated with kind indifference. And if, as she suspected, his heart yearned for another, that would be the cruelest torture of all. Susan had formed a rather more generous view of his lordship's character than that generally held by other members of his family, and she feared that, once he had pledged his word, he would not abandon his plan to marry her however much his heart might be pledged elsewhere. Indeed, his pride might keep him away from the countess, but Susan could not, now that she knew her own heart, accept him on such terms. What this meant for her future she was too tired and unhappy to consider. Following Lady Wibberly's example, she reclined against the carriage seat, closing her eyes, and the rest of the ride back to Mount Street was accomplished in silence and a general air of dissatisfaction.

No such feelings disturbed the ebullience of Mr Canby's nature. The evening's events had fallen out in such a way as might satisfy the most diabolical of schemers, and Mr. Canby took a creator's satisfaction in setting all in motion. Indeed, his only uncertainty at the moment lay in deciding precisely what mode to adopt with the Countess d'Abruzzi, but she solved this for him herself by coming up to him after Lord Everly's party had left and laying her hand prettily on his sleeve. He raised an eyebrow.

"We are old friends, are we not, Mr. Canby?" she said, looking up at him.

He bowed. "I hope your l-ladyship will always c-count me so."

"Oh, pooh! I thought we had settled it that you would call me Clarissa, as you used."

He smiled. "Well, *that* was when I had every expectation of c-claiming you as my c-cousin," he said.

She winced.

"However, if you wish it . . ."

"I do."

"Very well, C-Clarissa. What is it you wish to know?"

She gave him a startled glance and then smiled. "Oh very well. I *did* wish to ask you something. Who is that girl? Caroline has been telling me the most outrageous faradiddles about her and Lord Byron, but I don't believe a word of it. She is not at all the sort of girl for a man of that stripe!"

"Oh, he has b-been paying her some attention," he said silkily. "London is full of talk about it. However, I do not believe that, beyond a certain gratitude that she has actually r-read *Childe Harold*—and she is p-probably the only one among our acquaintance to actually do so—I do not believe he is in earnest. As a m-matter of fact, I imagine that he flirts with her m-mostly to annoy your hostess."

"Yes," she said seriously, "that is what I imagined. Poor Caroline has many admirable qualities, but she has never learned that if one is to keep a man on the string one must allow him some freedom."

"P-perhaps she might be persuaded to take instruction from you," he said blandly.

She looked at him swiftly to see if he was mocking her and then shrugged. "I doubt it. You still have not told me about Miss Winston, my friend. I am quite sure I never heard of her before, and now I find her on most intimate terms with the family. I . . . should like to know more about her."

"So as to prevent her from becoming an even m-more intimate m-member, no doubt."

"You mistake me. I am merely curious," she said with a trace of hauteur.

"M-my apologies, Countess," he said with an ironic bow. "I believe we were at one in wishing to separate her from Everly."

Her eyes widened. "Is that how it stands between them?" she asked him, abandoning pretense.

He shrugged. "I am glad to see that we are speaking without roundaboutation at last. Since you ask me, I m-may tell you that although n-nothing official has been said on the subject, unless something is d-done we may see her installed as Lady Everly before too many months."

"That chit?" she asked incredulously. "She is no more Desmond's style than she is Byron's."

He raised one shoulder eloquently.

"You do not mean to suggest that he is in *love* with her. He had eyes only for me."

He showed white teeth. "I am sure it m-must be as you say," he said in a tone that infuriated her.

"Is he?" she demanded.

"You have d-declared it to be impossible," he said smoothly.

"It *must* be impossible! It cannot be too late, not after so long!"

"I b-believe he does not know his own m-mind," said Mr. Canby at last, taking pity on her. "He is *fond* of her, however, of that we m-may be sure. She is respectable, though without fortune, and he m-means to reestablish himself in the eyes of the world. And, I believe, in the eyes of his m-mother most of all."

"I had understood that her ladyship was dead," said the countess.

He shook his head. "She wanders in her wits, but I believe she might be recalled to herself were he to announce his b-betrothal. And that is p-precisely what we must work to prevent. Once he has committed himself, you know that Des will never cry off."

"And just how do you propose to prevent it?" she demanded.

"Oh ha ha!" he tittered. "I do not *p-propose* to tell you, although I have confided, perhaps unwisely in Lady Caroline. It would be better for you n-not to know, so that your innocent concern will be convincing. You m-must be there to express your most tender regard when M-miss Winston has ruined herself and been sent away in disgrace. Well, I n-need not tell you how to conduct yourself. It is easy to see that you are a woman of considerable experience."

Her eyes narrowed and she studied him intently. "I do not precisely see," she said seriously, "how *you* are to benefit from all this. That is, I do see how it is in your best interest to separate Lord Everly from Miss Winston, or from anyone who threatens your position as his heir. But *I* mean to have him, you know! And that will not serve your purposes at all!"

As a matter of fact, Mr. Canby was forced to acknowledge the truth of this, but providence, in the form of some well-placed bribes, had provided him with the means to separate Lord Everly from the countess as well, should that become necessary. Despite her appearance of virtue, her ladyship had succumbed to a rather continental view of her marriage and had been so careless as to send billet-doux to more than one of her lovers. Some of these having, by dint of a great deal of patience and a rather exorbitant sum, fallen at last into Mr. Canby's willing hands, he was confident that he would be able to rid himself of her presence with considerably less effort than that he was expending to rid himself of Miss Winston. It was not part of his plan, however, to tell her so, and for the moment it suited him to have her allied on his side. He said merely, "You m-mistake me, Clarissa. I have no wish to prevent anything but what we in the family feel to be a m-most improvident m-marriage. Besides, if you were to, shall we say, succeed M-miss Winston, what possible objection could there be to *you*?"

She did not entirely believe him, but she was certain that, in view of Everly's earlier passion for her, she could, without too much difficulty, rekindle his attraction. She had already rehearsed a piteous story of parental pressure and dire financial difficulties to explain away her sudden elopement with the count when she and Desmond had been on the brink of betrothal, and though she could see by the look in his eyes that he was wary, she did not doubt she could bring him round in the end. Mr. Canby she might use to serve her own ends, but it was clearly necessary, at least until she was safely wed, to treat him with a degree of caution. She gave him a frank smile. "I am so glad you feel that way, and that we understand each other so well."

He smiled in return. "Oh ha ha! Very well, I should say." He bowed. "And n-now I must take my leave of you and call on a lady."

"At this hour?" she asked, surprised.

"I believe it is her f-favorite for receiving visitors."

She frowned and then remembered to smile. "And who is this lady, pray?"

"You might have heard of her as the Venus Mendicant," he told her.

She choked. "Good God! Is she not . . ."

"A high flyer, yes! One of the loveliest of the F-fashionable Impures. At one time she was under the protection of my esteemed cousin Desmond." He smiled ironically. "I am glad to see that your female d-delicacy does not lend you into pretending you do not recognize the name."

She ignored the jibe. "Whatever can you want with such a person?"

He raised an eyebrow. "N-nothing in the ordinary way, I assure you. Wait . . . let me see . . . but seven more days, and you will be privy to the secret of my visit. In fact, if I am successful, all of London will be in the know!"

Chapter 14

London was soon abuzz with the news that the gay young widow, the Countess d'Abruzzi, had returned after an absence of many years. As the guest of the Lambs she was received everywhere, and presently there was scarcely a fashionable party or outing at which she did not make up one of the number. It was noted that she and Lady Caroline made a very pretty combination, which showed to the advantage of each. Lady Caroline's saucy piquancy offset the countess's angelic fairness, and soon they were everywhere called "spice and nice" behind their backs.

Susan, whose feelings made her rather acutely sensitive to the countess's presence, began to notice her everywhere they went. At the theater, she was one of a *tonnish* party in the box next to theirs. If Lord Everly took her driving in the park, they invariably encountered her there with friends, perched elegantly on top of a high-top phaeton or riding her own beautiful mount. Susan also discovered, with irritation, that it was only those occasions in which his lordship was likely to be present that compelled her presence; she supposed that the spies Lady Caroline had set on their house had divulged their routines and habits to her guests as well. As Lord Everly treated his former love with a sort of ironic formality, Susan could not easily discern the true nature of his feelings. He said little and played his cards very close to his vest, which afforded as little satisfaction to the countess as to herself. The only positive aspect of the situation was that Byron, having made his point to Lady Caroline, had reduced the number of his calls, so that they were no longer in danger of encountering *that* lady with such frequency as heretofore.

One place where Susan need not fear meeting either of them was Almack's. The Ladies Committee was considering her case, but until it rendered a verdict it was suggested—in the kindest of terms by Lady Sefton—that Miss Winston might re-

main at home on Wednesday nights. Lady Wibberly insisted
that nothing significant could be inferred from this injunction;
the Patronesses might just as easily take her up again after ad-
ministering the necessary warning, but Susan nonetheless felt
the sting of ostracism and discovered, with some chagrin, precisely how much she had come to enjoy acceptance. Lady
Wibberly's attempt at soothing her was abstracted, and Susan
had the sense that her mind was elsewhere. They all seemed to
be waiting, as if a storm were about to break.

One afternoon when Lord Everly had called upon his sister
and the three of them were sitting in the yellow saloon planning the proposed outing to the Dower House at Summerland,
Jervis brought up a card. One glance sufficed to make it obvious that he was big with news, but her ladyship, with scarcely
a look at him, reached for the card on the salver. She gasped,
and it slipped from her nerveless fingers. She looked at her
brother, her eyes wide.

"What is it, Almeria?" he inquired, with maddening calm.

"Lord Wellington," she enunciated in dramatic accents.
"Here."

He raised an eyebrow but said blandly. "Do you wish to
keep him cooling his heels downstairs?"

"No, I—Of course not! Show him up at once, Jervis."

Arthur Wellesley, Marquess of Wellington, hero of a dozen
battles and the most famous soldier in Europe outside of
Napoleon (who might be considered out of the running by
virtue of his position as Emperor), entered the Wibberlys' saloon one foot at a time, like ordinary mortals. He smiled at
them all and bowed over her ladyship's hand. "You must forgive me for intruding on you like this," he told them. "Everly,
your butler told me you were here, and since I am summoned
away at once I took the liberty of calling on you here."

"How can I serve you, sir?" asked Desmond.

"You can't, my boy, you can't," Lord Wellington said
kindly. "I wanted to see with my own eyes that you were recovered. You were pretty well dished the last time I saw you."

"You are very kind, sir," said Desmond faintly. "There was
no need to go to such trouble. As you see, I am quite fit. Indeed, I am ready to oblige you on any undertaking whatsoever."

Lady Wibberly was staring at this exchange openmouthed.
She could not comprehend it, and was only glad that her hus-

band was not there to say what would invariably be the wrong thing.

The marquess put his hand on Lord Everly's shoulder. "I know you are, my boy, but the fact is you are too well known. Any one of dozens on the other side know your face, and the next time they'll likely put a bullet through your brain instead of your shoulder!"

Susan cleared her throat. "Lord Everly has been too modest to tell his family exactly how he came to be wounded," she said in a small voice.

Desmond gave her a dark look. "My ward, Miss Winston. Her father, I believe, might have been known to you: General John Winston."

Lord Wellington surveyed her with pleasure. "Indeed he was, ma'am, indeed he was. I am more sorry than I can say that we have lost him!" He put a finger under her chin. "So you are John's little girl! I have not seen you since you were a babe." He smiled. "You spit up on my dress uniform, if I remember, and had to be taken away!"

Susan laughed. "I am very sorry, sir. I must say, it was very brave of you to pick me up!"

He winked at her. "Oh, no! I am the greatest coward where children are concerned. I am quite sure you must have been thrust upon me."

"Very likely," replied Susan "But you were saying about Lord Everly's wound . . . ?"

"I do not recall that I was saying anything in particular," he replied, amused. "If Everly does not wish me to divulge the details, I shall certainly not do so." He turned toward Lord Everly. "That does not mean, however, that I do not intend to see that you are awarded a medal for your service to your country."

"A medal?" gasped Lady Wibberly.

"Yes, ma'am," said the marquess soberly. "For the very highest degree of selfless bravery and sacrifice. I am not at liberty to relate what occurred, and not just because of your brother's modesty! There are compelling reasons why these matters must remain secret, at least until we are sure of victory. But please accept my assurances that I am very much in Everly's debt."

"I am more honored than I can say, sir," said Lord Everly quietly. "Whatever I have done, it did not deserve so large a reward as this."

"Nonsense, my boy," said Wellington heartily. He stood. "And now I regret I must take my leave of you. I am so glad to have found you here."

"You must call again when you are next in London," offered Lady Wibberly hopefully.

"Perhaps I will. Everly, we shall meet again soon! Lady Wibberly, Miss Winston, your servant!" He exited the saloon, noticeably affecting even the awe-inspiring gentility of Jervis, who unbent so far as to comment, when he showed him out the door, that he spoke for all the servants in wishing his lordship every success in Europe.

The mood abovestairs was scarcely less confounded.

"Why didn't you *tell* us?" Lady Wibberly demanded of her brother. "I had no idea!"

"It was a strictly private affair," responded Lord Everly. "Besides, it was better that you not know, any of you."

I knew, thought Susan, but she said nothing.

"But you let us all think you had been shot in some vulgar duel," said Lady Wibberly in shocked tones. "When you might have been a *hero*."

"Almeria, you should know by now that I am not particularly interested in the world's opinion of my actions or affairs," he said in an amused tone of voice.

"Perhaps not, but what about your family?" she demanded.

"My family was free to think what it chose," he pointed out.

"You may say that we should have guessed," said his sister, rejecting the implied rebuke, "but you were at some pains to mislead us. It is quite abominable. Well, I shall take care everyone is in possession of the true story as soon as may be."

"That you will not!" responded Lord Everly. "You will say nothing to anyone!"

"Not even to Clarissa?"

"Most particularly not to Clarissa," he said firmly.

Lady Wibberly sighed. "Very well, if you insist. But if you think the word will not get out that Arthur Wellesley has called to see you, I fear you are likely to be disappointed!"

Lady Wibberly, the possessor of a great deal of worldly wisdom, was delighted to discover that she was not mistaken. The news of Lord Wellington's visit to Mount Street circulated with the same rapidity as the story of Byron's attentions to Miss Winston. The precise details of the visit remaining somewhat fuzzy, invention was given free rein, and a range of astonishing tales began to spread. Lord Everly had thrown himself in front of a bullet meant for the marquess. He had seduced the Empress to learn the closest military secrets, and had injured himself jumping from the window of her bedroom. He had been left for dead in the Pyrenees and had traversed hundreds of miles on foot to deliver documents to British headquarters. Young boys started to stare at him worshipfully on the streets, and girls sighed into their pillows. From being the Wicked Viscount, he now became positively lionized, and those who had condemned his rake-hell ways now found that they had known he was a gentleman of spirit and bravery all along.

Lord Everly was not amused. "Hypocrite!" he muttered to Susan, upon receiving the salute of one of the dandy set as they walked in the park two days later, her hand tucked under his arm. "He used to cut my acquaintance."

"Anyone would think you would prefer to be thought a monster of depravity or some such thing," said Susan calmly.

His eyes gleamed underneath his lids. "Well, perhaps I do," he told her. "I am certainly no hero."

"Lord Wellington seemed to think otherwise," she reminded him.

"Reports were exaggerated," he said succinctly. "I was neither so brave, nor so badly injured as everyone would like to believe."

She looked up at him. "I saw you on that stage," she said quietly.

He seemed startled. "Do you know, I had almost forgotten that! It seems I have known you much longer than a few months." He smiled at her. "Very well, I will concede the injury. I wish you would tell me how it is that you were the only one of my acquaintance who would not believe I got that bullet in an affair of honor?"

Because your guard was down, she thought. "Well, perhaps it is because you did not just at that moment look like the type to seduce another man's wife, or whatever it is men fight over," she told him lightly.

He laughed. "What a lowering thought! I should at least like to be thought capable of it," he said.

"I know you would," she told him. She was silent a few moments, and then brought up the subject that had been in her heart since that night at Almack's. "Sir, has it occurred to you that this has accomplished everything you might hope?" she asked, not looking at him. "You are as respectably reestablished as you could wish to be, and you need not, that is . . . "

"What is it you are trying to say, Susan?" he asked her gently.

She drew in a breath and soldiered resolutely on. "You need not marry, if you should not wish to, and you certainly do not need to marry *me*."

He possessed himself of her hand and lifted it to his lips. "Is that what's been troubling you?"

She felt a lump rise in her throat and could not speak.

"It has occurred to me," he said in a queer tone. "I—"

"Miss Winston! Desmond!" cried a silvery voice, which turned out to belong to the Countess d'Abruzzi, perched atop her phaeton. "How fortunate running into you this way! I do not scruple to tell you that I am quite bored with driving myself, and would love some company. May I join you for a few moments?"

"By all means," said Lord Everly tonelessly.

"Desmond, I shall never forgive you for holding out on me," she said archly. "How came you not to tell me that you were working for Wellington in Europe?"

"As a matter of fact, Clarissa, I had no reason to suppose that my activities would hold the least bit of interest for you," he said dryly.

She laid a hand on his arm. "You know better than that, my friend," she said in a voice that was heavy with intimacy. She looked at Susan. "We must scold him, must we not, Miss Winston? It is quite abominable to keep *his dearest friends* so much in the dark!"

"*My dearest friends*," said Lord Everly meaningfully, "will oblige me by forgetting the entire thing. It is quite finished now."

"Does that mean you will not be returning to Europe?" she asked him.

"For the moment, that is what it means."

She smiled. "Then I fear we will not all meet so frequently, because soon I must go home to my little boy. However, I know he would like to visit England, so perhaps I may return."

Lord Everly appeared to bear this news with equanimity. "I think you will, Clarissa. London is full of tales about the glamorous Countess d'Abruzzi, and you will never lack for gaiety!"

"Oh pooh! As if I care for that!" she responded. "Well, I must not keep the horses waiting any longer. Miss Winston, shall you come back with me? I can drop you off on my way home."

Susan opened her mouth to say no—indeed, the first word she would have uttered during this most unsatisfactory conversation—but Lord Everly cut her short. "Yes, do, my child. I shall see you at the ball tonight."

Susan, who would not give the countess the satisfaction of viewing her disappointment, said with a dazzling smile, "Oh, please! I should appreciate it very much."

Clarissa signed for the groom to stand down and permit Miss Winston to mount up beside her. This having been accomplished, the countess turned to her almost instantly and remarked, "Do you know, I am so glad to have this opportunity of speaking with you, Miss Winston, and of furthering our acquaintance. You are so often with Desmond that I began to believe I would never find you alone."

"Lord Everly has been everything that is kind," replied Susan cautiously.

Clarissa smiled. "How very odd it is to think of Desmond's being *kind!* I do not doubt that he has done all that is proper, but kindness is a trait I do not associate with the reputation he has established for himself over the years."

"I assure you, ma'am."

Clarissa studied her with speculation. "Yes, it is apparent that he holds you in some affection. Have you known him very long?"

"Scarcely a few months. We met in France."

"Ah, I collect your father did him some service there."

Susan said nothing to this. The countess put the horses neatly through the gateway. "You drive very well," she said, hoping to turn the subject.

"Thank you," said Clarissa, showing white teeth. "Desmond taught me when we—well, years ago, at any rate—and the count was a notable whipster as well. I am glad you are not frightened to drive with me."

Susan, who had ridden in or driven far more dangerous vehicles at her father's encampments, merely smiled and said, "No indeed."

The countess laid a hand on her knee. "Will you allow me to speak without reserve?"

Short of jumping down from the carriage she could hardly prevent her from doing so, so she said, "If you like" in a level voice.

"Thank you! I knew you must sympathize with my plight."

Susan said nothing.

"Dear me, this is a trifle awkward after all," said the countess sweetly. "You may be aware, perhaps, that at one time Desmond and I were betrothed."

"Formally?" inquired Susan innocently, though she suspected it had been no such thing.

"Well, not precisely," admitted the countess with some chagrin. "But everything was understood between us. We were so very happy, it all seemed like a dream. And then, something tragic occurred!"

"Tragic?"

"Yes," said the countess in dramatic accents. "Fate intervened to tear us apart."

Susan had to suppress a smile, which she sensed would not be well received at this point. "I am sorry; I seem to have misunderstood. I thought your ladyship decided to marry the Count d'Abruzzi instead."

"Alas, yes! But I was forced into it. My parents would not hear of my marrying Desmond once Giovanni asked permission to pay his addresses. I wept and pleaded, but in the end I was forced to give in!"

"But you were happy with the count," suggested Susan reasonably.

"He spoiled me dreadfully," she said with a reminiscent smile, "and of course we had our darling Federigo." She sighed. "But my heart was never engaged."

"How very difficult for you," said Susan dryly.

"I knew you would understand!" cried Clarissa, touching her knee again. "I knew that if I opened my heart to you, you could not refuse to help me."

"I'm not sure that I do understand, Countess. What is it that you expect me to do?"

Clarissa flicked the horses smartly with her whip. "Why, help me win Desmond back, of course."

"I see," said Susan, staring out over the park.

"I thought you might," replied Clarissa. "You see, Lord Everly was . . . rather hurt when I broke things off with him. His pride may make it difficult for him to acknowledge that he still has feelings for me."

Susan swallowed. "And are you quite sure that he *does* still have such feelings?"

Clarissa gave a satisfied smile. "He has not said so; how

could he? But I believe . . . indeed, I am quite certain . . . that he will soon come to know his own mind! It must be so!"

"In that case, I do not see that your ladyship requires any assistance whatsoever," replied Susan, holding on to her temper.

"Oh, I agree with you there! If I am not very much mistaken, he already believes himself to be in love with me all over again! However, *dear* Miss Winston—forgive me if I intrude on private matters, but you will see that I must speak frankly—I fear that he may feel himself under an obligation to you. It *must* be impossible, because of the differences in your ages and circumstances—but I must know whether he is likely to consider himself engaged to you."

Susan did not have to ask her whom she had been speaking to. "Your ladyship has declared it to be impossible," she said woodenly.

"Oh dear, I fear I have hurt your feelings," said the countess, not sounding in the least remorseful. "My dear, you must see that even if I were not in the picture, you are far too young and innocent to make a suitable wife for Desmond! You are very pretty and charming, but Desmond requires a woman of experience who is sophisticated enough to look the other way from time to time when necessary, not someone who will hang upon his sleeve! He would be stifled to death before the bride-visits had all been paid. I, on the other hand, can reestablish him on the very highest rungs of society, which I believe is what he most desires."

"Your ladyship is very frank," said Susan between gritted teeth. "I do not quite see what it is you wish me to say or do."

"I wish you to tell me whether you are engaged to Lord Everly."

Susan lifted her chin. "I am not," she admitted.

Clarissa let out a breath. "And does he consider himself under any sort of obligation to you?" she inquired as the carriage drew up in front of the Wibberlys' town house.

Susan turned her head to look at the countess. "I have already told you that we are not engaged. I do not choose to answer any more questions with regard to Lord Everly."

"Never mind. You have answered them nonetheless," said the countess less sweetly. "I should like to know if you mean to try to enforce whatever this obligation is, should he wish to marry me instead."

"I would not," she said bleakly.

"That is very wise," commended her ladyship. "And will

you give me an understanding that you will never enter into an engagement with him?"

Susan stared at her. "Of course I will not."

Clarissa shrugged. "It is of no consequence. I meant only to protect you. I fear your heart will be broken, Miss Winston, but that is not my affair."

"No, it is not!" replied Susan, disembarking from the phaeton unassisted, with as much grace as she could manage. "And now I must tell *you* that since you have chosen to insult me in every way possible, I will not suffer your impertinent questions or your condescending manner any longer. I hope, for Lord Everly's sake, that he does not marry you, for I am persuaded you would make him very unhappy, as you did before. However, that is for him to decide. I bid you good day. I hope we may meet again with tolerable civility, but only on the condition that this subject, whatever the outcome, is never renewed between us!"

"Obstinate girl!" cried the countess, unused to being crossed in quite so straightforward a fashion. "Desmond was quite right in saying that your manners are not just what one expects to find in a girl of birth and breeding."

"If he has complained of me to you, I can but wonder at the necessity for this entire conversation," said Susan, stung.

"Do not cross swords with me, Miss Winston," said Clarissa, abandoning even a hint of friendliness in her tone. "When I am Lady Everly, I shall have you banished from Summerland Abbey, whatever your claim on Desmond."

"Your ladyship need have no fears on that score," said Susan. "When you are Lady Everly, I can tell you with every confidence that mine is one foot that shall never cross your threshold! And since, whatever you think of my *birth and breeding,* I do not propose to go on arguing in the street, I am going to go into the house!" She whirled, letting her lilac jaconet muslin skirts swirl around her, and marched up to the door. The countess, her mouth still open on *the last word,* stared after her in frustration.

Chapter 15

Despite her brave words to the Countess d'Abruzzi, Susan was very much afraid that Clarissa might have been right. Her age and her background did make her less than a match for the glamorous, worldly countess, who was very clever at hiding a scheming nature and a calculating heart under an exterior of melting sweetness. On the whole, Susan thought she preferred Lady Caroline Lamb's straightforward mania to the countess's hypocritical friendliness, but she did her enough justice to admit that it would not be difficult to be deceived by it, particularly when allied with all the emotional force of a youthful passion. Clarissa's confidence that Lord Everly had fallen in love with her again was too genuine to be discounted as hopeful imaginings, and as Susan had not been privy to all that had gone on between them since the countess had returned to London, she had to assume that it was probable that the confidence had some basis in fact. Certainly Lord Everly, while apparently regarding Susan in the light of an esteemed younger sister, had never given her any indication that he might be in love with *her*.

Susan did not think that Clarissa would make Lord Everly happy, but if the countess was the woman he wanted she would not be an obstacle in his way. She did not think she was quite up to wishing him joy with a full heart—that would be an agony almost past bearing—but an equal agony would be to be married to him knowing that he was in love with someone else. Like Clarissa, she felt it very likely that he would feel himself honor bound to offer for her in all events because of the representations he had already made to her, and she was determined that she would not allow him to wreck his hope of happiness for the sake of his scruples. She pondered how best to release him without damaging his affection for her, in the very probable event he found his heart engaged elsewhere.

These melancholy thoughts did not put her in a mood for the

ball—the last she would be attending before they went down to Summerland for a few days—to be given by Lady Melbourne and the Lambs in honor of their guest. The prospect of maintaining her equanimity while watching Lord Everly whirl Clarissa around the dance floor, much less of receiving the triumphant looks of the honoree, made her shrink in horror. She had enough confidence in Clarissa's social manners and her own to be assured that they could meet with the appearance, at least, of civility, but she placed no such dependence on the self-restraint of Lady Caroline Lamb. Now that Byron had ceased to pay her so much public attention she could only hope that Lady Caroline's jealousy was assuaged, but one could not be certain that her ladyship would view things in such a rational light. She could only trust that the presence of her mother-in-law and husband would act as a check upon her unpredictable starts and fits.

It occurred to her that the easiest manner of resolving all these difficulties might be to plead a headache, but she hated, with every fiber of her being, to hand her rival such an easy victory. Clarissa would see through her ruse in a moment, discerning within it, correctly, her capitulation. She curled her fingers into a fist and reminded herself that she was a soldier's daughter. She would not let anyone—not Desmond, or his family, or the odious Clarissa d'Abruzzi—see how her heart was breaking.

While Susan was dressing for the ball, engaged in her own internal struggle, Lord and Lady Wibberly were having the sort of conversation common to a great many husbands and wives in the tenth year of their marriage.

"Haven't said I won't go," said Lord Wibberly, placing his boutonniere in his coat with all the enthusiasm of one laying a funereal wreath, "just wish we didn't have to."

"Not go to a ball thrown by Lord and Lady Melbourne and the Lambs?" asked his wife incredulously. "It is by far the most exclusive invitation in town!"

"Going to be deadly dull," remarked his lordship gloomily.

"What is that to say to anything? One does not go to such an event expecting to be entertained. One goes to be seen!" she instructed him.

He sighed. "I suppose so."

She studied him through narrow eyes. "Anyone would suppose you'd prefer to be going to the Cyprians' Ball."

"Dash it all, Almeria, you know I'm not in the petticoat line," he said, coloring.

"I know," she told him.

"Besides," he said defensively, "not a fitting subject for a lady!"

It was her turn to sigh. "You need not censure me, Wibberly. Naturally I would not discuss such a thing with anyone but my husband But men are very much mistaken if they think their wives are not aware of such goings on, however much we may feign ignorance in public. Really, you are quite naïve!"

"I never underestimate you, Almeria," he said fondly.

She smiled. "I thank you! And I do you the credit of believing that you really would prefer a night of cards to parading around the Argyle Rooms with some fancy bit of muslin. I fear it is quite different with Desmond, however."

He nodded. "Daresay it will be the first time he's missed it in years."

"Let us hope he does not contrive to slip out of the Lambs' ball, just when his credit is beginning to stand high again! It is so vexatious that the ball should be on the same night as that sordid party!"

"Caro Lamb probably did it on purpose," suggested Lord Wibberly.

"Oh, dear," said her ladyship, somewhat struck by this idea. "You may be right. It would be just like her. Well, if Desmond has been lured away from just the sort of event he most seems to prefer, I believe we have Clarissa Constable—I mean, the Countess d'Abruzzi— to thank for it."

"Or Miss Winston," said her husband.

She looked at him. "You cannot still be clinging to the notion that he is harboring anything more than brotherly affection for that child? He has taken pains not to single her out, and I believe that if he had not conceived the idiotish notion that she would make a comfortable wife and made certain representations to her he would have long since sent her back to her family!"

Lord Wibberly thought that the care that Lord Everly had taken to shield Miss Winston from gossip was instead an indication of just the reverse, but he did not like to cross his wife in these or other matters without greater cause. He shrugged and said, "Whatever you say, my dear."

"Besides," said her ladyship, "though I cannot quite like the way Clarissa treated him before, I believe she is now heartily sorry. And if she has become wealthy, that is all the better for Des! And you must admit that she is very beautiful and glamorous, just the sort of woman he would prefer."

"Don't like her myself," offered her husband.

"Why not?" asked his wife, surprised.

"Heart like a flint," he said succinctly.

"Nonsense," said Lady Wibberly dismissively.

The Lambs' party gave every promise of being the ordeal Susan had envisioned as she was dressing. The splendor of the rooms and the glittering exclusivity of the affair paid a tribute to the countess's popularity and position that even the most prejudiced observer must find seductive. Susan scarcely dared to contemplate their effect on Lord Everly, who seemed detached and remote, and far from the Desmond Wyndham with whom she stood on such friendly terms. Even the rose pink ball gown, which set off her dark coloring to perfection, could not raise her spirits as she mounted the staircase behind Lord and Lady Wibberly, and her expectation of pleasure in the evening was on a par with that professed earlier by his lordship.

Lady Caroline and Clarissa, standing side by side, deployed the element of surprise and greeted her with such dazzling warmth that she was taken aback, and could barely stammer out a courteous reply. She saw at once that in the face of such social aplomb her youth and inexperience were all the more apparent, so she put up her chin and made a graceful curtsy. Everly, who was just behind her with Mr. Canby, looked at her curiously but said nothing. When she passed on to Lady Melbourne, she felt as if she had cleared the first hurdle, and she stiffened her spine for the next trial.

It was not long in coming. Mr. Canby, with unexpected decisiveness, secured her hand for the first dance, and offered, while they were waiting for the set to begin, to procure them all a glass of champagne.

Lord Everly smiled paternally at Susan and said, "I think Miss Winston would prefer lemonade, Cosmo."

Susan glanced over to where the countess, stunning in a watered silk ball gown of the palest blue, stood sipping her champagne, chatting and laughing with a circle of admirers. She tossed her head. "No, I quite like champagne," she said mendaciously.

Lord Everly raised an eyebrow. "As you please, brat."

"Really, D-Desmond, Miss Winston is not a child," said Mr. Canby, unexpectedly entering the lists on her side. "You treat her as if she were still in l-leading strings!"

"Do I?" inquired his lordship meditatively. "How very kind of you to remind me!"

"Oh ha ha!" tittered Mr. Canby nervously. "I shall return in a m-moment with our champagne."

"None for me, I thank you," said Lord Everly, calling after him. "*Do* I treat you like a child?" he asked Susan when Mr. Canby had left them and Lady Wibberly had turned to engage in conversation with an acquaintance.

She looked up at him. "Yes," she said.

He smiled. "Do you mind?"

"A little," she confessed.

"Well, you are very young, you know! How *would* you like to be treated?"

Like the countess, she thought. "Like a friend," she told him lightly.

His eyes held an arrested look. "No more than that?"

She looked into his eyes, trying to read his expression. She drew a breath to answer him, still uncertain as to how to reply, when Mr. Canby returned. "Miss Winston," he said, handing her a glass of champagne with a flourish.

Lord Everly sketched a bow. "Cosmo, Susan, I see someone I must speak to. I hope I may have the honor of standing up with you later this evening, Miss Winston?" he inquired with amused formality.

She nodded in what she hoped was cool sophistication. Lord Everly grinned and left them.

"Drink your champagne," prompted Mr. Canby. "It is almost t-time for our dance to begin."

She sipped it obediently, disliking the slightly bitter taste it left on her tongue but trying to look as if she had never enjoyed anything so much in her life. She saw, out of the corner of her eye, Lord Everly drifting toward the countess, and took a very big swallow.

"Excellent," said Mr. Canby, "I knew you would l-like it!"

"Thank you," said Susan miserably.

The musicians struck up the dance. "One more sip," encouraged Mr. Canby.

She obeyed, and set the glass thankfully down on the tray. It was already making her feel light-headed, and she did not want to drink any more of it. She leaned almost gratefully on Mr. Canby's arm as he led her onto the floor.

Halfway through the dance, she knew that she would faint if she did not sit down. She felt like a fool.

"I'm afraid I—" she began, putting a hand to her forehead suddenly.

Mr. Canby was all solicitude. "It is very hot. Let me take you to where it is cooler," he said, leading her out the windows and onto the terrace. "Sit here, on this b-bench."

She did, thankfully, but her dizziness did not subside. She tried to focus her gaze on a yew tree beyond the terrace, but the image swam before her eyes. "I'm afraid I shall be sick," she said frankly.

Mr. Canby clucked his tongue. "Oh dear. Shall I get Lady Wibberly? Or Everly, p-perhaps?"

She envisioned the ensuing fuss with distaste and said hastily, "No, please! Only let me rest here a moment and I shall be fine."

"Perhaps Lady Caroline could send her m-maid to you," suggested Mr. Canby.

"No!" cried Susan, horrified. "I am much better now!" To demonstrate this, she rose to her feet, and promptly slid back onto the bench again.

"M-miss Winston, it is clear that you are ill," remonstrated Mr. Canby. "If you wish to slip away unnoticed, I could, if you like, summon your carriage, and deliver a m-message to my cousin."

The room was beginning to swirl around her and close in. "Perhaps that would be best," she said faintly. "I do not want to be sick here!" she added with a shudder.

"No indeed," said Mr. Canby with understanding. "What would the countess say to that?"

Susan thought the countess would most likely infer that she had had too much champagne and would waste no time in spreading this news throughout the *ton*.

He cleared his throat. "If I m-might just suggest one thing . . . "

Susan put a hand to her temple. "Yes?"

"Could you write Desmond a n-note telling him that you are going home because you are ill?"

Susan considered with some dismay the effort this would require in her present state. "Could you not simply tell Lady Wibberly . . . ?"

Mr. Canby hung his head like a schoolboy. "I fear m-my cousin does not altogether trust me," he said sadly.

"Very well," she agreed, too weak to dispute the truth of this. When he had procured pen and paper for her she wrote in a shaky hand: "Dear Lord Everly, I am feeling unwell and have returned home. Please do not worry about me, and convey my apologies to Lord and Lady Wibberly. Yours sincerely, Susan Winston." She thought a moment longer and added, "P.S. Mr. Canby has been very kind."

She permitted Mr. Canby to lead her along the terrace, bypassing the roomful of guests, and down to the front door. The porter at the door received Miss Winston's name with recognition. "Your coach is already here, miss," he said. He nodded to a waiting coachman, sitting muffled and silent in the darkness, and Mr. Canby bundled her into the carriage. "Thank you," she said, sinking back against the cushions. "Tell Lord Everly . . . "

"Don't worry," he told her solicitously, leaning over her to tuck a blanket around her legs, "I'll take care of everything."

Sometime later Lady Wibberly, who had been enjoying a comfortable coze with one of her oldest friends on the subject of the relative merits of the Egyptian motif in decorating as opposed to Greek Revival, noticed that she had not seen her charge in a half hour or more.

"Really," she told her friend confidentially, "it is most tiresome. One never knows what that child will be up to next, and if she gets into trouble, Everly will no doubt lay the blame at my door!"

Her confidante clucked sympathetically and said that it was most unjust of him, particularly when the girl was nothing at all to her whatsoever.

An image, unbidden and unwelcome, of Miss Winston at the sickbed of her daughter sprang up in Lady Wibberly's mind. "Well, yes . . . " she said slowly. "I suppose I must go look for her. Will you excuse me, Amabel?"

Amabel would, so Lady Wibberly made her way around the room in a state of confusion. Miss Winston was nowhere to be found, and no one had seen her since Mr. Canby had led her onto the floor in a dance. She was mulling this piece of information when her brother approached her. "Where is Susan?" he demanded. "She is promised to me for this set, and I have not seen her this half hour and more!"

"Oh dear," cried Lady Wibberly. "That is just what I was

wondering. Drelincourt tells me that Cosmo was the last person to be seen with her, so perhaps he knows."

"If that little weasel has said something to offend her, he will most decidedly predecease me," he told her.

"Now, Desmond, there is no reason to assume—ah, here he is now! Cosmo, have you seen Miss Winston?"

Mr. Canby sidled up to them with a knowing look on his face. "Well, yes, as a m-matter of fact I have," he confided.

"Well?" said Lord Everly with a look that made his cousin shrink back a little.

Mr. Canby swallowed. "She asked me to give you this note. She went home nearly three-quarters of an hour ago."

"Home?" inquired Lady Wibberly.

Mr. Canby bowed. "I assume so. At l-least she said that is what she intended."

"You seem to have taken a great deal of time in informing us," said Lord Everly in a dangerous tone of voice.

"Desmond—" began his sister.

"No, that is quite all r-right," replied Mr. Canby. "N-naturally you are annoyed, but M-miss Winston most particularly desired that I should wait to give it to you, so that you n-need not feel you should come after her."

Lord Everly opened Susan's note and read it. "It says she was feeling ill and went home, just as he suggests," he told his sister. "I wonder what the deuce can have happened?"

"As a m-matter of fact, she appeared to have had too m-much champagne," remarked Mr. Canby.

"Oh dear," said Lady Wibberly.

"And who the devil gave it to her, Cosmo?" thundered Lord Everly. "That is what I would like to know!"

"Well, if you m-must know, cousin," said Mr. Canby, "it is really your own fault. You insisted on treating her like a child, and I believe she was d-determined to convince you she was no such thing. Really, I felt quite sorry for her," he said. "You were lucky I was there to look after her," he added in an injured tone.

Lord Everly's hand clenched into a fist, but his sister laid a restraining hand on his arm. "As a matter of fact, that *is* the truth, Desmond. You do treat her as if she were scarcely older than Eliza and Louisa. If she has had too much champagne, the best thing we can do is leave her alone. I feel very sure she will feel most chagrined in the morning and will have learned her lesson."

Lord Everly looked thoughtful. "Very well, Almeria, if that is what you think." He surveyed his heir with a certain measure of chagrin. "Cosmo, it seems I owe you an apology. She does say in her note that you were very kind. I am grateful to you for looking after her."

Mr. Canby showed white teeth. "Oh n-not at all, Everly. N-not at all!"

Miss Winston, meanwhile, was in a decidedly wretched state. Her vision was still clouded, and her wits were obscured by a sort of fog. She was not so naïve as to believe that such disastrous effects could be caused by drinking a half glass of champagne and was inclined to think that she was coming down with influenza or something equally serious. Whatever it was, she wanted nothing so much as to get home to her bed and her solitude, so that she need not continue to make such supreme efforts at remaining vertical.

Her eyes were closed for the duration of the carriage ride, and it was with relief that she felt the carriage pull up before her door and the coachman descend from his perch. She opened her eyes a little, but her head was still throbbing.

"Here we are, miss," said a strange voice.

She looked up at the coachman, slightly puzzled, because she had thought that John, Lord and Lady Wibberly's usual man, had driven her. However, it was of no consequence. She swayed on her feet, and the man supported her across the threshold with his arm. She tried to will herself not to faint, an act which took all her concentration. Thus it was that she did not notice until she had entered the room that she was not in her own house.

She gasped and looked around her. She was standing in an extremely beautiful entrance hall, the sides painted in fresco in *trompe l'oeil* Grecian columns, and lit with a lamp of antique design. Ahead of her lay elegant folding doors covered in crimson, and beyond that she could see a grand staircase, up which a number of persons were proceeding. She was most definitely *not* in the Wibberlys' town house, and in fact had no idea where she might be. She turned back to inform the coachman, but he had utterly vanished, along with the carriage itself. *Oh no,* she thought. She had never felt so foolish in her life.

A wave of dizziness swept over her again, and she determined that, whatever happened, she must find a way to get home at once. She looked round for a footman or some attendant but found no one other than a beautifully dressed page, a child of about six who informed her that these were the Argyle Rooms—which did not enlighten her a great deal—and that the rest of the party might be found upstairs. As he seemed unwilling to believe that she might not wish to join the others she sighed and determined to make her way up the staircase. Surely someone among the guests would help her.

At first Susan was so involved in the effort of arriving at the head of this grand staircase, lined with green cloth, over which lay a beautiful morode carpet bordered with *a-la-grec*, that she had little leisure for observing the guests. Several of these passed her on the stairs, however, and she noticed that most of the men were elegantly attired in evening dress and were wearing dominoes. The women, while largely unmasked, wore dresses rather more revealing than was commonly seen in polite ballrooms, though their throats sparkled with diamonds or, in the case of one stunning beauty, sapphires as big as bird's eggs. To Susan's untrained eyes, it looked as if more than one had dampened her petticoat, so tenaciously did their skirts cling to their forms. When she reached the top of the stairs she found herself in an elegant lounge, designed and painted to look like an Athenian temple. A man, old enough to be her father, looked at her through his mask in a manner she could not quite like and pinched her cheek.

"Please, sir," she said coldly.

He giggled and leaned over her bosom. "Oh delightful! Yes, most delightful!"

Susan stepped back in horror. "Sir, you are not behaving as a gentleman," she told him.

This admonition, which, in her admittedly limited experience, had never yet failed to appeal to man of birth and breeding, appeared to have no effect on him whatsoever. Susan perceived from his glittering eye that he was odiously castaway, but she considered that no excuse.

Her tormentor made a lunge at her and she backed into a wall, almost upsetting a vase on a side table. She reached out to catch it, and wondered if by chance she were trapped in some particularly monstrous nightmare.

"That is enough, Sir Harold," drawled a melodious voice behind her. "Go find another bird for your dovecote."

"How did you know who I was?" he asked, pouting.

"I know who everyone is," said the woman with assurance. "Except you, perhaps," she inquired of Susan.

Susan found herself looking at a woman who could only be called of a certain age, though her face was painted and her blond hair tinted to retain at least the patina of youth. Her figure was magnificent, revealed beneath a diaphanous satin gown cut so low a chance sigh might very well reveal All. Her eyes were intelligent, but rather cynical. She wore a parure of emeralds round her neck which would not have shamed the Queen herself.

Susan sketched a curtsy. "I am Miss Winston, ma'am. If you please, I—"

"You are very young," said the woman, lifting a brow at her.

Susan did not understand what that had to say to anything. "I am feeling faint, ma'am," she tried to explain, "and I would like to go home."

The woman's eyes narrowed. "Are you increasing?"

Susan's mouth fell open. "Of course not!" she replied, shocked.

The woman shrugged. "It sometimes happens with amateurs." She studied Susan with speculation. "I daresay all it is is that you have lost your nerve. Perhaps you should go home then and wait till you are older. Write me a note, and I shall see that you are invited next year." She gave a little laugh at Susan's look of confusion. "You know who I am, of course?"

"No, I—"

An expression of annoyance clouded her features. "I am Barbara Tremayne."

This did not, as Miss Tremayne apparently expected, prove enlightening to Miss Winston. "They call me the Venus Mendicant," she explained.

Susan's eyes grew round. "The Venue Mendicant? But that is a . . . that is to say, I—"

Miss Tremayne's expression changed from annoyance to amusement. "Miss Winston, do you have any idea where you are?"

"The page told me . . . the Argyle Rooms," she said faintly.

"Indeed they are. And tonight is the Cyprians' Ball. Surely, young as you are, you have heard of *that*?"

Susan shook her head to clear it. Her wits were beginning to return, but she still could not understand how she came to find herself in such a situation. "I am new in town, ma'am," she offered by way of explanation.

"The greenest of the green," observed Miss Tremayne with

a bitter little laugh. "My dear innocent, if that is what you are, the Cyprians' Ball is an entertainment we ladies of . . . experience . . . hold for our protectors. Now do you understand?"

"Yes," said Susan calmly. "I understand."

"Good. Well, you do not blush and bridle, at least. Will you sit down?"

Susan sank onto one of the embroidered sofas gratefully.

"Now perhaps you will tell me how you came to be here," said Miss Tremayne. "We do occasionally entertain *tonnish* guests at the ball, you know, especially matrons who like to experience a frisson of danger. But they come in masks, and, I promise you, they do not give their real names!"

"I fear I have intruded on you by mistake," said Susan, explaining how she had left the party and the carriage had inexplicably carried her to this door. "It sounds preposterous, I know. I do not know how to explain it, but I fear I must have gotten into the wrong carriage."

Miss Tremayne put her lips together. "Were you at the ball at the Lambs'?"

Susan nodded.

"I see," said the woman, staring off across the room at the revelers. Susan followed her eye and then quickly looked away again. "Do you know, I had quite forgotten," Miss Tremayne said, as if to herself. "I suppose a bargain is a bargain but . . . " She looked forthrightly at Susan. "I fear you have been the victim of a rather cruel hoax. You must know that it will quite ruin you to be seen here, especially if your only explanation is so preposterous. Hmmm. I believe I have honored my part of the agreement, so let us see how we are to get you out of here without anyone else finding out. Did you give anyone your name?"

"Only you," said Susan, in the dark as to the import of this speech.

"Excellent! For a start, you must come away from so public a room. There is a small chamber off the hall; wait there and rest till I send for you. Will you trust me?"

Susan nodded.

"Good girl! If we are very lucky, all may yet come right again."

Chapter 16

Lord Everly, despite his rather selfish reputation, did not like to spoil his sister's pleasure, but he was finding the Lambs' ball rather flat. Indeed, he very quickly joined his brother-in-law in the card room, to the consternation of more than one female guest. He knew that Clarissa was expecting him to ask her to dance, and he supposed she would view his refusal to do so as an attempt to spite her, but in reality he did not feel like dancing with anyone. His luck was out at cards, too, and Mr. Canby, who had made up one of the number at the table, won a sizable sum off of him, something he very rarely allowed to occur. He signed irritably and wondered why it should suddenly be so difficult to find pleasure in his usual indulgences.

He was preparing to arise from his chair and take leave of his hostess, whatever his sister might say about such an early departure, when a footman brought him a note on a tray.

"There is a young person outside," said the servant in a voice heavy with disapproval, "who insisted that this be delivered to you, my lord. A *very* young person."

Lord Everly opened the note lazily and scanned its contents. He sat up straighter in his chair. "Cousin, a word with you in private please," he said to Mr. Canby. "Gentlemen, you'll excuse us."

"What is it, Everly?" inquired Mr. Canby when his lordship had propelled him out the door and into the cool night air. "Has something happened to one of the f-family?"

"Cosmo, did you or did you not tell me that you sent Miss Winston home in her carriage because she was ill?" said his lordship, laying hold of his arm.

"Naturally I did," replied Mr. Canby in a wounded tone. "That is what happened. Is something am-miss?"

"Apparently," said Lord Everly grimly, handing him the note.

Mr. Canby held it up to the torchlight. "I cannot read it. The light is too dim."

"Then I will tell you what it says, cousin," remarked Lord Everly in a deliberate tone those who knew him best had learned to respect. "It says that Miss Winston is, even as we speak, attending the Cyprians' Ball."

"What?" squeaked Mr. Canby. "This is quite p-preposterous. Someone is hoaxing you."

"I think not," replied his lordship. "Judging by the footman's reaction, I should guess that one of the Mendicant's pages brought the note. I have not seen such a look of disapproval since my brother and I broke a window throwing rocks at the chapel wall!"

"But why should M-miss Winston wish to do a thing l-like that. It will r-ruin her!" suggested Mr. Canby helpfully.

"That is precisely what I wish to find out. Now, so there is no misunderstanding, let us review what has occurred. She became ill, she gave you a note, you summoned her carriage, you put her in it, and as far as you know she went home. Do I have that correct?"

"Yes . . . No! Now that I recall, there was something strange . . ."

"Do you plan to tell me what it was?" demanded Lord Everly in a menacing tone.

"Now I have it!" cried Mr. Canby. "The carriage was already waiting when we went outside. I was so concerned about M-miss Winston, I did not think to wonder how it came to be there before it was summoned."

Lord Everly signaled the servant who called for the carriages. "Has Lord and Lady Wibberly's carriage returned?" he inquired.

"Returned, my lord?" inquired the man.

"Yes, I believe it was summoned earlier this evening."

The servant shook his head. "Oh no, sir. Begging your lordship's pardon, but it has not been sent for since it dropped off Lord and Lady Wibberly and the young lady."

"I see." He turned toward Mr. Canby. *"Well?"*

"I am s-sure I thought it was her carriage," said Mr. Canby peevishly. "She got in it, d-didn't she? I was trying to help her and I was n-not paying much attention to anything else!"

Lord Everly watched him through narrowed eyes. "Are you telling me the truth, Cosmo?"

"Why should I l-lie?" said Mr. Canby, brushing an invisible

piece of lint off of his coat. "Ask this man if you don't believe me."

His lordship turned an inquiring eye to the porter, who said hastily, "It's as the gentleman says. He came down with the young lady, and the carriage was already here. The coachman said he had been told to wait for her, so I didn't see the harm. Really, my lord, how was I to know?" the man asked plaintively.

"You weren't," replied his lordship shortly. "Thank you. Now would you bring my carriage round at once, if you please!"

"Really, Everly, has it occurred to you that the child was d-deceiving us all?" said Mr. Canby when the porter had left. "Perhaps it was p-pre-arranged. Perhaps she was m-meeting someone. I am sure it was in all innocence," he added hastily, seeing the expression on Lord Everly's face, "b-but you know she has b-been anxious to show you she is grown up, and it may be she thought this was the way. Surely she cannot have the least idea what the Cyprians' Ball is all about."

"That much, at least, I will grant you," said Lord Everly grimly. "Please convey my apologies to Almeria."

"What are you going to d-do?" asked Mr. Canby.

"I am going to go to the Cyprians' Ball," he replied. "It certainly won't be the first time."

"Shall I come with you?"

"Certainly not. The fewer people involved in this the better. And take care you keep your tongue between your teeth!"

"Naturally," said Mr. Canby smoothly. "But you know, I did think we m-might have been overheard by Chuffy Clitheroe when you told me the n-news. And you know what a gossip he is."

"Damnation!" cried Lord Everly. "Well, it is too late now!"

"What shall I tell Cousin Almeria?"

"Anything but the truth!" he said, jumping into his carriage as it was brought up to the door.

"You may r-rely on me," said Mr. Canby.

"Where did Desmond hurry off to?" inquired the Countess d'Abruzzi when Mr. Canby had reentered the ballroom a minute or two later.

Mr. Canby, who still had possession of the note, laid it thoughtfully on the table in front of him. "He received this n-note," he told her carefully. "I fear I am not at liberty to d-divulge what it says. D-dear me, I seem to have r-run out of champagne. May I p-procure a glass for you as well, Countess?"

She gave him a dazzling smile. "Thank you. I should adore it."

He bowed and turned away, and she lifted the paper from the table. When she had made herself mistress of its contents, she exclaimed, "You devil!" Lady Caroline, who had an unerring instinct for Events, approached her demanding an explanation. When she had heard it, she went off into peals of laughter.

Mr. Canby, returning, handed them each a glass of champagne. "Oh, d-dear," he said calmly. "I fear you have d-discovered what ought to have been kept p-private. How very c-careless of me."

"This is your doing, is it not, Cosmo?" inquired the countess.

"My d-dear Clarissa, you might very well think so, but I couldn't p-possibly comment," said Mr. Canby with a smile.

"But what is to be done?" inquired Lady Caroline excitedly. "Ah, I have it! We must attempt a rescue! We shall don masks and dominoes, and go to the Cyprians' Ball. I wonder I should not have thought of it before!"

"A r-rescue, Lady Lamb, or a scene?" asked Mr. Canby.

She shrugged. "It does not matter."

"Should you object if we asked Chuffy Clitheroe to j-join us?" asked Mr. Canby with admirable foresight.

"He is odiously foxed," said Lady Caroline. "And an idiot as well."

"All the better. I should like to convince him that the rescue m-mission is his own idea. I shall attempt to dissuade him, of course, but I shall be overborne."

"What do you think, Clarissa?" asked Lady Caroline.

The countess looked out the window, her lips curved in an enigmatic smile. "I think it is an excellent scheme," she said calmly.

Despite the embarrassment of finding herself in such circumstances, Susan was inclined to believe that the Saloon Theater, of which she had had a glimpse on her way to seclusion, was the most beautiful room she had ever seen. The pictures from the Odyssey, the antique chandeliers, the boxes decorated in bronze and gold presented a dazzling scheme she would have liked to have examined at more leisure. Her hostess informed her with a smile that more respectable entertainments were frequently held there, which led her into a brief flight of fantasy in which she attended some glittering event on Lord Everly's arm. The thought of Lord Everly brought her up short, however; she wondered how she could ever explain tonight's events in a way that he—and the Wibberlys—might find acceptable. The truth was so absurd that she could not blame them if they did not believe her. In any event, what mattered most was not to bring any further embarrassment upon the family by publicizing her presence at the most disreputable event of the Season. Short of appearing openly in a brothel, it would be hard to imagine anything more definitively ruinous.

In spite of the impropriety of such thoughts, Susan could not help feeling more than a little curious about the Cyprians' party, and not nearly so censorious as she ought. It was true that the standards of behavior were not what one had come to expect in the drawing rooms of the *ton*, but neither were they so very far from the antics of Lady Caroline and her set. The Venus Mendicant, rather than showing herself to be a monster of depravity, had been rather kind, and in other circumstances Susan thought they might even have been, if not friends, at least on the most civil of terms. Men, who did not live under the strictures which limited the lives of women, had been enjoying such friendships for years.

Her head was aching, and she was still longing for her bed, but the swooning feeling had subsided and she no longer felt as if she could not keep her feet. She supposed it might have been the champagne after all, since the effect seemed to be wearing off. Her mind was functioning better, as well, because she remembered that she had not asked Miss Tremayne what arrangements she should make to return home with as little notice as possible. She vaguely recalled that Miss Tremayne had told her to rest, and not to worry, but surely she should be calling a hackney, or even walking home. The thought of walking about the streets of London at night unattended did not unduly frighten her, particularly when set beside the certain evil that would attend her if anyone recognized her here, a likelihood that would increase with every passing minute she remained. She got to her feet, swaying just a little, and stepped out into the hall. She did not see anyone, so she ventured further, into the Turkish room with blue carpets she seemed to remember from earlier in the evening. "Miss Tremayne," she called softly.

"Hardly," said a voice behind her.

She whirled, and had to support herself with one hand on the back of the chair. "Oh, no."

"Do you know, I find myself in perfect agreement with your sentiments," said Lord Everly in a tone of voice she had never heard him use before. "Do you care to tell me how you came to be at the Cyprians' Ball?"

A thousand explanations passed through Susan's mind and were rejected. "I am not quite sure," she said simply.

"Perhaps I can help you," he continued in the same tone of voice. "Someone—Lord Byron perhaps?—suggested to you that this might be the sort of outré behavior that would enable you to cut a figure in Society that would rival Caroline Lamb's."

"Of course not," she said, stung by this explanation. "I have no desire whatsoever to emulate Lady Caroline!"

He raised an eyebrow. "Indeed? Or the Countess d' Abruzzi?"

She flushed. "That is unfair, and cruel as well."

"What am I to believe, when you have demonstrated such ill judgment as to show yourself at such an affair as this? I did not want to believe that you had come here of your own free will, but what else am I to think when I hear you addressing a well-known woman of the town by name? When you have no explanation to offer? If you wanted to prove that the conventions mean nothing to you, you have certainly succeeded."

"This from *you*, my lord?" she asked quietly.

He winced. "*Touché.* I am well served, am I not? I had thought to start over again, but—"

"You seem to believe the worst of me," she said in a tight voice.

"What choice do I have? You have not provided an alternative."

"You could listen," she told him. "Surely you of all people are aware that appearance and reality may be quite different."

"I—" began Lord Everly, taken aback.

At this moment, Miss Tremayne entered the room, her bosom heaving. It was a fascinating phenomenon, and at any other time Susan would have been amused by the look on his lordship's face. "Hello, Barbara," he said quietly.

"Everly, Miss Winston, I am very sorry! I tried to have them turned away but—"

"But what, Barbara?" prompted his lordship.

But he needed no explanation. A party of revelers wearing masks and dominoes burst in on them. A familiar voice cried, "There they are!" and with a sinking heart his lordship recognized Chuffy Clitheroe. "We've come to rescue Miss Winston!" cried Mr. Clitheroe, with what he apparently felt was a swashbuckling manner. He swayed, and a hand reached out to steady him.

Susan watched, stricken, while a figure in an apple green domino and mask stepped forward. It did not take very much imagination to recognize Caroline Lamb.

"I quite admire you, Miss Winston," said Lady Caroline. "Even I could not have been so foolish as this!"

"You all seem to be under some misapprehension," said Lord Everly. "Miss Winston does not need rescuing."

"Then let's stay and have a dance!" cried someone among the party, who was obviously very well to pass.

Lord Everly had eyes only for a small figure whose fair curls could be seen even behind her mask. "What are you doing here, Clarissa?" he asked.

"I have come to lend you my support," said the countess. "And to offer Miss Winston my help if she should need it." She lowered her voice. "I'm afraid Chuffy overheard you talking to Mr. Canby," she said. "Your cousin and I tried to persuade Chuffy not to come, but you know what he is. Once he gets hold of an idea . . . We thought it best to accompany him, or the scene would have been far worse, I promise you." She paused and laid a hand on his arm. "You must forgive her, Desmond. I am quite sure she did not mean to cause any harm by coming here."

Susan gritted her teeth. "My being here, *if it is any concern of yours*, is the result of an accident."

Lord Everly frowned. "Ungenerous, Susan. The countess is just trying to help."

"Naturally you arrived by accident," said Clarissa in the tone one might use to address a rabid dog, "and we have come to take you home. Such company is not fit for a young girl," she added with a delicate shudder.

"That's rich," said Barbara Tremayne with a scornful laugh. "I daresay this company is a great deal more fit than some I could name!"

"That's enough, Barbara," said Lord Everly.

"But—"

"I really should n-not, if I w-were you," whispered a figure in a black domino in Miss Tremayne's ear. She thought of the very large sum she had been promised for embarrassing a certain Miss Winston and held her tongue.

"I must be getting back to my guests, Lord Everly," said Miss Tremayne, summoning her dignity. "I am sure you will want to remove your ward from the pollution of my presence without further delay."

Someone of the watching figures sniggered, and Susan stepped forward, extending her hand to the Venus Mendicant. A general gasp went up, which she ignored. "I have imposed on you most dreadfully, ma'am," she said sincerely, "and you have been very kind. I am very grateful to you, and hope we may meet again."

Miss Tremayne smiled. "You are a lady, Miss Winston. I wish you luck! I fear you may need it after tonight." She gave Lord Everly an assessing glance. "I know you do not like to receive advice, my friend, but I fear you are on the verge of making a very serious mistake. I hope you will not!"

Susan partook of breakfast in bed some hours later. She was too young to be deprived of sleep by a recollection of the night's adventures, but she had awakened with a clouded mind, and it had taken her some moments to remember why she should be feeling in such low spirits.

At length she remembered, and shivered a little under the blankets. The memory of the previous evening's parting with Lady Caroline and the Countess d'Abruzzi—the one openly exultant and the other tenderly solicitous, gently chiding her for recognizing the Venus Mendicant in so public a fashion, all the while excusing her with the most patronizing protestations of her youth and inexperience—especially rankled. Of the two, Susan preferred by far the open hostility of Lady Caroline; it galled her that Everly might be deceived into believing that the countess really did wish her well instead of assiduously working to undermine her in his eyes. In *that* however, it appeared that very little assistance was required. She had handed her rival a triumph on a plate, and at the same time succeeded in making Lord Everly exceedingly angry. His stony silence as he escorted her to her door confirmed that. Thank heavens he had not come into the carriage with her! She did not think she could have borne it if she had told him the truth and he had still rejected her explanation.

She realized, upon reflection, that she had been the victim of either a cruel hoax or a rather bizarre set of accidental events, but in either case it would not matter. By now she was experienced enough in London ways to know that all over town polite society would be digesting the story of her appearance at the Cyprians' Ball with their breakfasts. The truth of what had occurred was irrelevant; it was the gossip that mattered. Suddenly she pushed away the tray with resolution, rising to her feet. She must leave London as soon as might be conveniently arranged. She could not but feel that her continuing presence in the household would be a burden, if not a provocation, to its members, and removing herself until the tempest subsided (if not longer) must be the most effective way of requiting their kindness to her. She did not want to think of the future beyond that. She sat down at her desk and penned a note to her Aunt Harrington and Cousin William in Yorkshire, and when she had dressed, she went out to post it herself.

Lord Everly, owing to a lengthy and somewhat unsatisfactory appointment at his tailor's in Bond Street, found himself rather later than he had anticipated in calling at his sister's. He could not say that he was looking forward to enduring Almeria's animadversions on the dire consequences—long predicted—of nurturing a viper in one's bosom, but there was little chance that she would not have heard the news of the previous evening's events. If she had not, she must be the only sentient being in Greater London still in ignorance, and his sister was rarely behindhand with gossip. He could only hope that she would be out, and that he might have the chance to speak with Miss Winston alone.

Lord Everly found himself in a state of some indecision. His own feelings toward the girl he had almost casually selected to be his bride had pitchforked him into a nagging uncertainty, a state of affairs to which he was largely a stranger. He had been very angry the night before because he had been embarrassed and disappointed; his cousin Cosmo's explanation—that Susan had wanted to draw a bustle in Society—had seemed the only rational one for her behavior. Clarissa, too, had seemed to concur. In ordinary circumstances Lord Everly might have suspected his cousin of having a hand in it, but Susan herself had exonerated him in her note. The porter, too, had confirmed his innocence. Still, he could not quite square his cousin's explanation with what he knew of Susan's character, or with—he was forced to admit it—what his feelings had become. He found himself strongly attracted to her in a way far different from what he had envisioned when he had first proposed that she become his wife, and certainly not at all typical of his usual flirtations. He liked her composure, her compassion, and the fact that she had refused to cut the Venus Mendicant when she had every compelling reason to do so. He thought he had never seen such bravery in the face of social opprobrium. In fact, he could not rid himself of the suspicion that he had somehow wronged her, and he recalled with chagrin that she had taxed him with not listening. *Surely you of all people are aware that appearance and reality may be quite different,* she had said to him.

He knew he must tread cautiously. Their bargain had been made under very different circumstances from the ones he would now propose, and he could not be sure she reciprocated his feelings. Above all, she must remain free to choose, and since he could not see into her heart he did not want to begin something he would be unable to finish with honor. Much depended on their upcoming interview.

Thus involved in this complicated and peculiarly unsatisfying line of speculation, he almost collided with Lord Byron on his sister's doorstep. The encounter did not improve his affability, because he supposed that if anyone had planted the idea of attending the Cyprians' Ball in Miss Winston's mind, it was very likely his lordship. Still, he said with reasonable geniality, "Good afternoon, George. Are you calling on my sister?"

Byron grinned at him. "On Miss Winston, actually. I've come to offer her my congratulations."

Before Lord Everly could reply to this, the footman opened the door to them, greeting them with the intelligence that Lord Wibberly had retired to his club and her ladyship had not yet risen from her bed.

Lord Everly, consulting his timepiece, raised an eyebrow. "And Miss Winston?"

"Miss went out a few minutes ago, sir," said the man. "She did not say when she would return."

"Will you come in in any case, George? I am sure my sister will lend us the use of her saloon for a few minutes."

"Yes," said Byron with a shrug. "As a matter of fact I have

come to take my leave of your ward, and I do not know when I may return."

When Jervis had brought in refreshments and left them alone, Lord Everly inquired politely, "You were saying, George?"

Byron smiled impishly. "I had hoped to see Miss Winston in person. I particularly wanted to tell her how much I approve of her thumbing her nose at the Dragonesses by showing up at the Cyprians' Ball! I'm sure there is an epic in it somewhere!"

Lord Everly was forced to smile in return. "You did not, just by chance, happen to suggest to her that such an action would meet with approval?"

"Alas, no! I wish I had thought of it. Although," he added thoughtfully, "even then I might not have made the suggestion. You think my character deplorable, I know, but toward Miss Winston I harbor only the purest of intentions and feelings. I would not help her to ruin, even to poke a finger in Caro's eye."

"Admirable," said Lord Everly dryly.

Byron laughed. "Perhaps I was not *quite* so noble with regard to your ward," he admitted. "I did pay rather a lot of attention to her, mostly to show Caro that I might. However, I do not think she nourished a *tendre* for me as a result!"

"Much you would care if she did."

"Well, perhaps you are right," acknowledged the poet. "But I promise you, she took no harm from it. Quite the reverse, in fact."

"We should no doubt debate the issue at some other time," suggested Lord Everly. "You indicated, did you not, that you had come to take your leave of us?"

"Yes. I have—shall we say—begun to find the situation in London a bit intolerable, in more ways that you might guess," said Byron gloomily.

Lord Everly, who was privy to the rumors of Byron's financial difficulties, as well as his troubled relationship with Lady Caroline, rather thought he could, but said nothing. "Do you go to Newstead, then?" he inquired politely. Newstead Abbey was the Byron ancestral home in Yorkshire, and the logical place to go if he was rusticating.

Byron gave him a thin smile. "My home, you mean? I fear it will not be so for very long!"

Lord Everly was somewhat taken aback. Putting one's inheritance on the block was an extreme action, taken only in the most desperate of circumstances. "I'm sorry, George," he said quietly. "I had no idea things were anywhere near so bad as that."

"I am quite done up," the poet said simply.

"Do you go abroad then?"

Byron shrugged. "In time, perhaps. But first I mean to try my luck in *Durham*." He pronounced the name of the town as if it had been as remote as Timbuktu.

"Durham?" inquired Lord Everly politely.

"Are you acquainted with Miss Annabella Milbanke? I am escorting her to her home there."

"I believe I have not had the honor," said Lord Everly.

"She is Lady Melbourne's niece."

"And Lady Caroline's cousin?" inquired his lordship incredulously. "You do live dangerously, George!"

Byron showed white teeth. "As yet, Caro knows nothing whatsoever about my interest in Miss Milbanke, and I hope it remains that way, at least until I have the chance to fix my interest with the girl. She is very worthy, you know."

"You mean she is very rich," suggested Lord Everly languidly.

"Well, yes, that, too! But you know, it was Lady Melbourne who put it all in perspective for me. She says that love affairs should not interfere with more serious things such as getting on with one's career and advancing one's social status."

"She should know," said Lord Everly. Lady Melbourne herself was a veteran of numerous liaisons.

"That is just what I thought. And Miss Milbanke is everything that is virtuous. She is a prodigy in mathematics, and at seventeen she wrote a critical commentary of Bacon's *De Augmentis Scientiarum*!"

"She sounds like a dead bore," suggested Lord Everly.

Byron, far from being offended, laughed. "I confess I should like her more if she were less perfect. However, if she is willing to assume the task of redeeming my character, all may yet be well."

Lord Everly did not give voice to his doubts on this subject.

At this star-crossed point in the conversation, Susan returned from posting her letter and walked past the saloon on her way to her room. Lord Byron's comment had caught her attention, and she would not have been human if she had not lingered for a moment outside the door.

"Do you know, Everly, she is just the sort of girl you should marry if you are bent on reestablishing yourself. You are even better known for avoiding the parson's mousetrap than I am, but it might be just the thing for you. Perhaps if I do not succeed . . . "

"I thank you, no! The advantages of such a match have already occurred to me, but since we are speaking frankly I must tell you that I can think of no surer route to unhappiness than to enter into marriage—however noble the reasons or however great the debt—where there is no affection!" said Lord Everly vehemently. "Nevertheless, you are welcome to your pursuit of her, if that is what you wish. My affections, in point of fact, are already engaged elsewhere."

"Are they?" inquired Lord Byron. "I thought they might be. The countess is a bewitching woman, to be sure."

Susan, her hand over her mouth, ran soundless back down the stairs again and out into the street. She had already dismissed her maid, but she could not face going into the house again until she was positive Lord Everly was clear of it. She had heard enough to know that the death knell had been sounded for any hopes she might have entertained of his returning her regard, and she would not marry him when his heart was pledged to somebody else. Indeed, he seemed to hope that Lord Byron would relieve him of his *debt,* as if she would ever have considered such a thing. If she could have, she would have fled to her Aunt Harrington's house at once. As it was, she meant to delay her departure by no more than the time necessary to find adequate transportation—a mail coach if need be!

Lord Byron and Lord Everly, meanwhile, remained in ignorance of the devastating effect of their conversation on its inadvertent eavesdropper. "Clarissa is in many ways an estimable woman," agreed Lord Everly, "but I can think of nothing I should less desire than to become leg-shackled to her."

"*Not* the countess?" inquired Lord Byron, raising an eyebrow.

"Most decidedly not."

"Then who . . . ? Forgive me, Everly! It is none of my affair."

"No, it is not," said his lordship pleasantly.

Byron smiled. "I hope that I may soon wish you joy. Goodbye, Everly! I fear I cannot wait any longer. I hope you will present my apologies to your sister and Miss Winston.

"I shall convey your deepest regrets," Lord Everly assured him. "Shall I wish you luck with your heiress, George?"

"Indeed you should! If she should refuse me . . . Well, you know my nature, Everly! When I am desperate, I am quite capable of anything. It is as well, perhaps, that I did not meet Miss Winston after all!"

He said it lightly, but with an undertone of seriousness Lord Everly did not overlook. "Then I shall take care to keep her out of your sight until you are safely wed," he told him in much the same tone. "Goodbye, Byron!"

Chapter 17

In the event, Lord Everly's attempts to protect Miss Winston were destined for immediate failure. No sooner had Lord Byron left the house than he turned the corner of the block and almost collided with her, pacing to and fro out of sight of the house in, if she had but known it, much the same fashion as Lady Caroline had adopted for her surveillance.

"Miss Winston!" said Lord Byron with a delighted smile. "How very unconventional of you to be out alone! I am so pleased to have encountered you, for I have just called at Lady Wibberly's to make my farewells."

Susan was so mortified by the conversation she had overheard that at first she could scarcely answer him, but then she recollected that at least *Byron* had been her champion. However little favor his attentions might ultimately find in her eyes, the memory reanimated her gratitude, and she said warmly that she was sure London would be very dull without him. "As a matter of fact," she told him seriously, "I shall be leaving very shortly myself."

"Indeed? I have just come from Lord Everly, and he made no mention of it."

"He does not know it yet," said Susan ingenuously.

"Really?" inquired his lordship, not at all loath to thrust a spoke into this particular wheel, for reasons that did not reflect particularly well on his character. "How *shortly* are you planning to leave?"

"As soon as I may acquire a ticket on the post chaise," Susan told him. "After the events of last night, I cannot stay here any longer. To do so would be an intolerable imposition on Lord and Lady Wibberly."

"My dear, one thing I have learned about Society is that it is always better to face it down. There is no such thing as an immutable disaster."

"Perhaps you are right," Susan told him, "but there are other reasons as well."

"Hmmm?" said his lordship, momentarily distracted by a glimpse of, he feared, a most unwelcome and profoundly inconvenient figure regarding him intently from around the corner. Wouldn't Caro ever give up? "Forgive me," he told Miss Winston. "Where will you go?"

"To relatives in Yorkshire."

Byron suddenly saw how Miss Winston should serve his needs most admirably, though he doubted she would agree if he explained it to her. Really, it was most fortunate encountering her like this, just when he needed to distract Caro from his imminent departure with Miss Milbanke! "I may be able to assist you," he told her gravely, striving to hide his glee at concocting such a delicious plan. "*I* am going with a party of friends to, well, north of Yorkshire, and we would be only too happy to convey you to your relatives. A young friend and her chaperone will be traveling in my coach, so you see it will be quite proper for you. The only thing is, we must set off at once!"

"Oh that would be most kind!" said Susan, grateful and pleased that, so far from importuning her with unwelcome attention, he was taking care to observe the proprieties. "If you do not think your friends would mind."

"They will be pleased to learn that someone among my acquaintance is as respectable and pretty-behaved as yourself," said Byron truthfully. "Can you be ready in an hour?"

"If I hurry!" She was overjoyed at the prospect that she might make her escape without having to face Lord Everly again. "I'm afraid I . . . that is, would you mind very much if I met you somewhere? There are reasons why it would be better for you not to call on me."

Byron, who had every intention of enacting an apparent elopement under Lady Caroline's observation, agreed gravely to this stricture. "I shall be happy to oblige. It would not do, however, for you to be seen climbing into a carriage with me with all your bandboxes in broad daylight, so let us say I shall be waiting for you in the alley there, just behind the house. We shall then go on to Highgate, where we shall meet the rest of our party. Will that be quite convenient?"

Susan would have felt more comfortable if the rest of the party were made up before he picked her up, but she did not think Byron was so lost to principle as to force an abduction upon her against her will, especially in view of the fact that, much to her relief, he was exhibiting no loverlike tendencies whatsoever. In fact, he might have been her older brother, so solicitous did he seem for her comfort and reputation. "Yes, thank you," she said at last.

He smiled and picked up her hand and kissed it. *Are you watching, Caro?* he wondered. "Until an hour, then."

Miss Winston was relieved to discover that Lord Everly had quit the house a few minutes before she reentered it, so that she was free to make her preparations for departure without first enduring the ordeal of a final interview with him. She was being a coward, but she did not think she could face him without revealing her feelings, and that she was determined not to do. Let them part as friends, as they had begun. She threw a few of her most urgent necessities into a portmanteau—she would ask Lady Wibberly to send the rest on to her when she was settled—and sat down at the desk to compose two notes of farewell.

These epistles cost her a great deal of toil and struggle, crossing out lines and ripping up several pages before she had achieved reasonably satisfactory results. The letter to Lord and Lady Wibberly begged pardon for the embarrassment of the previous evening's events and any other actions she had taken which might not reflect to their credit, assured them of her gratitude for their kindness in taking her in, and professed a profound disinclination for London society which necessitated her immediate removal from it. She did not think they would question her motives or feel any emotion connected with her departure, other than relief.

The note to Lord Everly was more difficult. Her pride was hurt and her heart was sore, but still she did not want to explain her leaving in terms that might wound him. Finally she decided to say that she had received an invitation to visit her stepmother, and that she had decided she would prefer not to live in England after all. She was sure that he would understand from this that she was exercising the option he had given her to withdraw from their agreement. She knew that if she told him the truth about where she was going pity might inspire him to do that which affection did not. If he came after her, she was not sure she would have the strength to resist him, however much her head urged it, so she must make sure he did not know she was returning to her Aunt Harrington and the life he had determined to rescue her from. How much better for her if she had never succumbed to the temptation to leave there! It would be a kinder fate to be buried in the solitude of Fenwood Hall than to live in such misery.

By the time she had finished writing there were scarcely a few minutes left until it was time to meet Lord Byron. She folded up the letters, sealed them, and set them on the table. Then she took a last look around, shook herself mentally, and picked up her portmanteau. She dropped it from her window into the bushes below, and made her way down the stairs, past the footman, and out the front door.

A half hour later, Miss Louisa and Miss Eliza, returning from their brief restorative sojourn in the country to the delights of London, knocked at the door of Susan's room. Their mother had received them in her bedchamber with the news that she had a splitting headache and would not think of getting up that day, so they must go with their governess and remain very very quiet. This worthy woman, who had entertained her charges for the entire journey back to town and was looking forward to a respite, however brief, told them patiently that they must go to the library and secure a book to read, and that tomorrow's lesson would be an examination over the content of their reading. They were not in the mood for such employment, but the habit of obedience was such as to make them go off to the library at once, and dutifully make their selections. With these in hand, they hit upon the excellent scheme of finding Susan, in the hope that she might regale them with one of her stories, the delights of which would, presumably, exceed those of Allardyce's *Sermons for Young Ladies*.

Susan's door was slightly ajar, and it opened under Eliza's touch like the entrance to Aladdin's cave. "Miss Winston?" she called softly.

The room was empty not only of its occupant but of most of her possessions as well. "Where is she?" asked Louisa.

"I don't know. Mama didn't say anything about her leaving, so—"

They both noticed the notes on the desk at the same time. "Mine!" shouted Louisa.

"I saw them first," protested Eliza, attempting to wrest the papers from her sister's grasp.

The paper ripped under the stress, leaving a large corner of one of the letters to fall to the floor.

The culprits looked at it in dismay. "Maybe we can paste it back together," said Eliza dubiously.

"It's your fault," insisted Louisa. "If you hadn't tried to grab it away—" She sighed. "Now we're going to get into trouble."

"We shouldn't read it anyway," said Eliza. "They might be private."

They both looked down at the sealed missives. "One is addressed to Mama and Papa," said Eliza, "and the other is to Uncle Desmond!"

"What does it mean?" asked Louisa.

"It means she's left, stupid! Why else would she write the notes?"

"I don't want her to leave. I liked her," gulped Louisa. "Why did she?"

Eliza lifted up a corner of the letter to look.

"Girls! Why are you in Miss Winston's room?" demanded their governess, from the doorway. "What are you doing looking at her things?"

Eliza whirled and put the letters behind her back, stuffing them between the covers of one of the books. "Nothing," she said, sticking out her chin.

"She's—" began Louisa. Eliza trod on her foot. "Ouch!"

"She's gone out, but she said we could borrow her sealing wax," said Eliza innocently. "Only we couldn't find it."

"Well, you may use mine. Come away from here at once. Your father is home and wishes to see you in the drawing room, so hurry along!"

"Papa!" cried Louisa, delighted.

Seduced by this felicitous turn of events, they followed the governess out the door, forgetting their books on the desk table. Sometime later, the afternoon maid, tidying up the room, noticed two books from the master's library out of their proper places and returned them to the shelves. Since she could not read, she placed them in the first two vacant slots she could find and promptly forgot them.

Owing to the disruption of the household's usual schedule, it was some time before Miss Winston's absence was noted by her host and hostess. Lady Wibberly found herself unequal to the task of rising from her bed to face the calls of solicitous friends who, learning that she had sponsored a young lady apparently lost to shame into Society, made haste to offer their sympathy. She was even less eager to confront the iniquitous Miss Winston herself, although she supposed it must be done some time or other, and she found it altogether more comfortable to take her supper on a tray in her room. His lordship availed himself of the opportunity to dine with his daughters in the nursery, and so he, too, was unaware of Miss Winston's absence. Miss Eliza and Miss Louisa had almost forgotten the afternoon's incident in the excitement of their return to the routine of domestic life, and since no one thought to ask them anything as to their older friend's whereabouts, the subject did not arise. The servants certainly knew that Miss Winston was not in the house, but they were also aware that she had somehow incurred her ladyship's severe displeasure and thought she might have been sent away with dispatch. In all events, it was the next morning before Lady Wibberly, fortified by a good night's sleep and the resolution that the problem of Miss Winston must be attended to *at once,* summoned the culprit to an audience and received the intelligence that her guest had quit the house the day before and had not returned.

Lord Everly, less fortunate than his sister, did not enjoy the restorative benefits of a night of rest. On the contrary, he had tossed and turned on his mattress for the better part of several hours, reliving in his mind's eye the events of the night of the Lambs' ball. These were not conducive to reposeful sleep, and the more he thought about it now that his anger had had a chance to cool the more he perceived that he had not done justice to Miss Winston at all. He was chagrined that he had not waited for her return to his sister's house the day before, but Byron's visit had further annoyed him, and he had spent the evening at his club, drinking deep and losing a great deal of money at cards. These were activities in which he had not engaged for some time, and he was surprised to find that he had, on the whole, lost his taste for them. In fact the only possible action which he did not hold in dislike at the moment was to rush to Miss Winston's side and beg her forgiveness, and only the inconveniently early hour prevented him from doing so. This feeling of restlessness was acute enough to make him blue-deviled and distinctly out of sorts, so that he even spoke brusquely to Marston, an event rare enough to cause the latter's brows to rise and Lord Everly to apologize for his ill nature.

He was engaged in moodily pushing some eggs and venison sausage around his plate when his butler, with an air of scarcely suppressed curiosity, brought in three cream-colored envelopes on a tray.

Lord Everly did not generally receive missives at such an early hour and at any event was not in the mood to be distracted. "Couldn't these wait, Ingraham?" he inquired.

"Begging your lordship's pardon, but I was to tell you it was urgent," the butler offered apologetically.

Lord Everly eyed the tray with distaste. "Which one?"

"*All* of them, sir," intoned the man dramatically.

Lord Everly sighed and picked up the top envelope. "Very well," he said.

The letter it contained was well scented and poorly spelled, written in a hasty scrawl, and unsigned. "My lord," it read, "you should know that Miss Winston's presence at the Siprean's Ball was the falt of Another, who shall not be namcd. This persin payed the Lady of the House to embares Miss Winston. Beleeve me, I am A Frend."

Lord Everly raised an eyebrow. "Who brought this, Ingraham?"

"A little boy, sir," said the butler, his frigid tones indicating his disapproval of this species. "Will there be any reply?"

Lord Everly was staring out the window, lost in thought. "Now I wonder who . . . I'm sorry, Ingraham. What did you say?"

"Will there be any reply, my lord?"

"No, no reply." He sighed again. "I suppose I had better look at the others."

The second letter was from the Countess d'Abruzzi asking him to call round as soon as possible on a important matter of the utmost urgency regarding Miss Winston. "What the devil!" he exclaimed, throwing aside his napkin and getting to his feet. "Ingraham, I am going out." He ripped open the third letter, glancing at it hastily. It was from his sister, and it, too, demanded his immediate presence. It would have to wait. He thrust all three missives inside his waistcoat.

"Will your lordship be dining in today?" inquired Ingraham in a colorless tone.

"I do not know," replied his lordship.

"I trust it is not bad news," said the butler, fishing.

"No, merely something of a mystery," replied Lord Everly

curtly. "Have my curricle brought round at once. I am going to pay a call on the Countess d'Abruzzi."

Ingraham, who had been privy to his master's early *tendre* for Clarissa Constable, did not hold that lady in high esteem. "Very good, sir," he said in a wooden tone that was no less eloquent for being understated.

Lord Everly looked at him. "Ingraham, do I permit you too much license?"

The butler coughed. "Almost certainly, sir."

"Good. I thought I must have done. Don't take advantage of it, will you?"

"Never, sir," said Ingraham with a rare chuckle.

The Countess d'Abruzzi was in a state of considerable agitation. Lady Caroline had apprised her of the apparent elopement of Lord Byron and Miss Susan Winston, fortuitously witnessed by herself as she happened to be passing the Wibberlys' house in Mount Street. Clarissa was undeceived by this, because she knew that Byron's waning enthusiasm for her friend's companionship had inspired Caroline to have him watched again, and furthermore, she could not, despite her dislike for Miss Winston, believe that she would be so foolish as to place herself under the protection of a man who did not intend marriage. If Miss Winston had had a fortune she would have been more inclined to believe the tale, because Byron was undeniably charming when he wanted to be and the girl was naive and young enough to think she might be able to change him. Miss Winston had no fortune, however, and Byron would never marry without one; besides, she was virtually certain that the girl had set her cap for Everly. Caroline was nonetheless adamant about what she had seen, and her unhappiness and jealously were tangibly real. Clarissa began to nourish the tiny hope that the story might be true; perhaps, after the delicious scene at the Cyprians' Ball, Desmond had told the chit that his heart would never be hers and she had bolted.

If there was any truth to the story, not a breath of the scandal had yet reached her ears. She wondered how best to use the information to her advantage to draw Desmond closer to her still. She was pondering this weighty matter when Lady Caroline descended the grand staircase dressed in traveling clothes, laying a finger to her lips.

Clarissa started. "Caroline, where are you going?"

Lady Caroline looked triumphant. "I have told William and the Dragon that I will be visiting friends in Hertfordshire a few days. They are convinced I need to get away to *regain my balance*, as my mother-in-law so charmingly put it, so it was really quite simple."

Clarissa shook her head. "Caroline, you are *not* by chance entertaining the idea of going after Lord Byron, are you? It would cause no end of scandal, and it could end by Mr. Lamb's sending you away for good."

"I wish he would divorce me," Caroline said, her eyes unnaturally bright. "I do not care what he thinks or does. And I will not let *that girl* get away with stealing Byron out from under my very nose."

Clarissa stared at her openmouthed. "But—" she began.

Lady Caroline raised a hand to stop her. "If you wish to preserve our friendship, you will not prevent me," she said. "I presume I may count on your silence?"

Clarissa nodded, defeated. "Of course."

"Good!" cried Caroline, embracing her. "I knew I might trust you! You will have returned to Italy before I return, so I'll bid you farewell now. My husband and I hope you will visit us again soon," she said formally and with an earnest look that led Clarissa to believe that she must be disordered in her mind.

"Thank you," she said faintly, accepting the outstretched fingers,.

Once Caroline had departed, she was in a quandary as to what to do. It did not at all suit her purposes for the runaway couple to be tracked down and brought back, at least until Miss Winston's ruin had been accomplished. Clarissa's glee at this unlooked-for triumph—so much better than she had ever expected, even after the embarrassment of the ball—was checked only by the realization that she must be extremely circumspect in her public behavior and find a way to break the news to Lord Everly as gently, as sorrowfully, and as late as possible. She could not, however, wait so late that, on the off chance that Lady Caroline's recovery mission might be attended with success, the offending couple were apprehended before a scandal had time to develop. Clarissa agonized as to the appropriate moment and method of her revelation, and finally sent the urgent missive that now sent Lord Everly hurrying toward her door.

*   *   *

Lord Everly was shown into the Lambs' exquisite morning room without delay. The countess was wearing a watered silk dress of the palest lilac which enhanced her interesting air of pensive melancholy. She rose to greet him, a sad little smile on her beautiful face. "Ah, my friend, I knew you would come quickly," she said with a gentle sigh.

"Naturally you did, since you mentioned that the matter was urgent and involved Miss Winston," said the viscount, bending over her hand with a grim smile. "However, I believe I know what it is you wish to tell me, and I shall be very grateful if you put me in possession of the facts immediately."

Clarissa was taken aback. "You do?"

He withdrew the perfumed note from his waistcoat. "Perhaps you received one of these this morning as I did. She does not sign it, but I believe it comes from Barbara Tremayne."

Clarissa shuddered. "Why should you think that woman would write to *me*? *I* have nothing to do with such persons as that."

Lord Everly's expression hardened. "She writes to clear Miss Winston's name. Forgive me, Clarissa, but if that is not what you wished to see me about, what *is* it that you have to tell me?"

"Clear her name?" persisted the countess.

"The writer implies that Miss Winston was set up, that her appearance at that unfortunate event was through no fault of her own. Naturally, I intend to get to the bottom of it."

Clarissa did not like the direction the conversation was taking and decided to regain control. "I am very glad to hear it," she said, sounding not the least big overjoyed. She fetched up a languishing sigh. "Unhappy girl! If only she could have waited, all might yet have been well."

"What are you talking about, Clarissa?" inquired Lord Everly in a dangerous tone.

"Oh, it is as I feared," said the countess. "You have not yet heard the news."

"What news?" he asked through gritted teeth.

"You must prepare yourself, my friend, for I fear you will not like it." She glanced down at her lap. "I'm afraid that Miss Winston has eloped with Byron."

He laughed aloud, not at all the reaction she had expected. "Nonsense!" he told her. "Who told you such a ridiculous Banbury tale?"

"Of course you would not wish to believe . . . But I assure you it is quite true. Miss Winston was seen climbing into his carriage with her portmanteau, in broad daylight."

"Seen by whom?"

Clarissa looked at her lap again. "Lady Caroline."

"Ha! Has she been spying again? No doubt she saw them converse in the street and imagined all the rest. You know what she is."

"I know what she is," said Clarissa, "but she is quite certain as to what she saw."

"I see," he said, taking out a pinch of snuff from an enameled box with a practiced motion. "And why have you sent for me to impart this information?"

"Because I did not wish for you to hear it first as common gossip!" she cried. "You know how London is! First the ball, and now this. The poor child is quite ruined, and I know that you have assumed a kind of responsibility for her."

He gave her a searching look. "You really do believe this story?"

She nodded. "I hope I am wrong. Perhaps you have seen Miss Winston quite recently?"

He felt the first frisson of doubt, which he banished instantly. "No, I—Really, Clarissa, it is quite absurd. She has no fortune, and Byron could not marry without one."

Clarissa blushed. "That is what I *fear* as well."

An image, unbidden and unwelcome, of Byron telling him that if Miss Milbanke did not smile upon his suit he might do something desperate, sprang to mind. *It is perhaps just as well I did not meet Miss Winston,* Byron had said. Everly shook his head to clear it. In all events, Miss Winston—Susan—would never have run away with Byron when she might . . . Surely she could not have been so upset about her appearance at the Ball and his angry words that she would . . . "

He got to his feet. "I should go," he said brusquely.

She rose as well and laid a hand on his arm. "Perhaps it is all for the best, Desmond," she said, gazing up into his eyes.

His own narrowed. "What the devil do you mean by that?"

"You must surely see that this event—however unfortunate—has the effect of releasing you from whatever sense of misplaced obligation you might feel toward the unhappy girl."

He removed her hand gently from his arm. "You don't seem

to realize that I do not wish to be released from my obligation," he told her.

"You are a fool, Desmond," cried Clarissa, stung. "She is not worthy of you."

"You are wrong, Clarissa," he said in a kind voice that set her teeth on edge. "It is the other way around."

"And I suppose you intend to make her your wife?" she asked bitterly.

He did not reply.

"You will say it is none of my business," she told him.

"I have no wish to be rude," he said simply.

"But what about me?" she cried, forgetting all her resolution in a moment of panic. The interview was not going as she intended.

"I'm afraid I don't follow you," he said with the same bland calm she found so irritating.

"You loved me once. You wanted to marry *me*."

He bowed.

"I see what it is. You are trying to pay me back because I could not marry you when you asked me. You need not do so, Desmond. I married the count against my will, but my sentiments for you remained unchanged."

He looked at her with an expression that was disturbingly assessing. "You compel me, Clarissa, to say what a gentleman should not. I am afraid that your sentiments are not of a great deal of interest to me. You see, my wife would have to love *me* more than my title and my fortune."

"And does *she* love you for yourself?" she could not forbear asking.

"I do not know whether she loves me at all," he said frankly. "But I intend to find out without delay."

"You are most likely to find her with her paramour," she said bitterly. "Remember what you have lost when you become the laughingstock of London."

"We have each of us gone too far," said Lord Everly coldly. "My best wishes for your future happiness, Clarissa. I do not think we should meet again."

"I—"

Lord Everly was not to hear her reply to this because at this moment the Lambs' butler entered the room with the news that Mr. Cosmo Canby had called to see the Countess d'Abruzzi.

A spasm of panic crossed her face. "Tell Mr. Canby I am not at home," she said hurriedly.

Lord Everly had not missed her reaction and regarded her curiously. "Oh no, Clarissa, do not deny him on my account. I had no idea you stood on such terms with my cousin."

Clarissa could not imagine anyone she would less rather see at this moment, but she could not think of an adequate excuse for refusing to admit him in the face of Lord Everly's comment. "Well, if you wish it, Desmond," she said coolly. "Tell Mr. Canby that his cousin is here as well," she instructed the butler.

Lord Everly laid a hand on her wrist. "I prefer that my presence be a surprise," he said levelly.

The butler looked from one to the other. The Countess d'Abruzzi was only a guest in the house, and not a very popular one at that. "Very good, my lord," he said to the viscount. "I'll show him up directly."

Lord Everly stepped to the side of the room where he would not be visible from the door. His expression was enigmatic.

Clarissa hid her balled fists in her skirts and said nervously, "I cannot think why Mr. Canby should be calling on me. I have scarcely spoken to him these many years."

"No doubt we shall soon find out," said his lordship, regarding the countess with such a steady gaze that she put a hand to her throat and blushed.

"Mr. Canby, madam," intoned the butler.

Mr. Canby entered the room under full sail. "C-Clarissa," he cried in a bantering tone, "I have c-come to receive your felicitations! D-did I not say I would rid us of—"

Clarissa choked.

Chapter 18

Of what, Cosmo?" inquired Lord Everly politely, stepping forward into his cousin's view.

Mr. Canby gave a little gasp. "Oh ha ha! I did not see you there, cousin. I b-believed the countess to b-be alone."

"Evidently," said his lordship in the same pleasant tone. "You were saying?"

"Oh it is n-nothing," replied Mr. Canby. "Only a silly b-bet I have with the countess. But it will keep for another time. I am sure you will both be wishing me at Jericho," he added with a fatuous smile. "I have no wish to interrupt your t-tête-à-t-tête."

"On the contrary, Cosmo, your presence is quite . . . enlightening," protested Lord Everly. "I had not realized, for example, that you stood on such terms with the countess."

"Desmond—" began Clarissa.

"Not now, my dear. My cousin was just about to tell us of what undesirable—shall I say object?—he has succeeded in ridding you."

"Really, Everly, you are making a lot of fuss about n-nothing. In fact, you have put whatever I was going to say quite out of m-my head," replied Mr. Canby.

"I suppose you have also forgotten the matter for which you were just now soliciting felicitations?" inquired Lord Everly.

Mr. Canby ran a finger under his neckcloth. "As a m-matter of fact, I have."

"Then permit me to refresh your memory. Does it, by chance, have anything to do with Miss Winston's finding herself at the Cyprians' Ball the other night?"

Mr. Canby did his best to give his cousin an affronted look. "Certainly n-not."

"You always were a poor liar, Cosmo, even when you were a little boy," said his lordship, one hand idly playing with his quizzing glass. "I am not yet in full possession of the facts about that evening, but I do not intend to rest until I have found out how Miss Winston came to be there."

"I am at a 1-loss to understand you, Everly," said Mr. Canby, seeming to shrink back into his chair.

"Are you? Then let me make my meaning even clearer. If you had anything to do with the despicable incident, I recommend—in fact, I feel I must insist—that you consider a rather lengthy visit somewhere far from London and Summerland Abbey. If you do not, you will almost certainly predecease me," said Lord Everly. He turned his gaze on the countess, whose countenance was rather pale.

She lifted an imploring hand toward him, then let it fall. "You are making a very great mistake," she said.

"Yes, I have done so already," he confessed. "I should have known better than to trust even a little in your friendship, Clarissa."

"I m-must be going," said Mr. Canby in a hoarse voice, rising to his feet.

"Yes, indeed you must, Cosmo," said Lord Everly. "I do not know how much longer I shall be able to answer for myself if you remain in this room."

Mr. Canby bowed himself out of the room and exited hastily.

"Desmond—" said the countess, when he had gone.

"There is nothing left to say between us, Clarissa," said Lord Everly coldly.

"I think there is," she told him. "Your cousin is a worm, and his motive in wanting to separate you from that girl is an obvious one. But can you not credit your friends with a sincere interest in keeping you from making a very grave error?" she asked beseechingly.

He was silent.

"You are determined then to believe the worst," she said bitterly. "I am heartily sorry for you, because I believe that you are shortly to discover that you have been deceived in your beloved Miss Winston's character!"

He walked to the door, opened it, and closed it gently behind him. "Goodbye, Clarissa," he said softly and made his way down the stairs.

Lord Everly had every intention of making his feelings clear to Miss Winston without further delay. His sister's summons, urgently expressed, coincided rather nicely with this scheme and sent him hurrying toward the Wibberlys' house in Mount Street. The matter of the Cyprians' Ball was still pending, but he did not doubt that he could persuade the Venus Mendicant to part with the truth. The truth would not expunge the incident from the memory and tongues of Society, of course, but in time it would all be forgotten. They would shortly go down to Summerland, and if Susan agreed they could be quietly wed there. The thought lightened his heart in a way he had not felt in a very long time.

He suffered a check, however, when Jervis informed him, with a discreet little cough, that Miss Winston had disappeared, and the household was in turmoil.

He took the steps up the to drawing room two at a time, without waiting to be announced. Lady Wibberly was reclining against the back of the sofa, her eyes half closed, a restorative next to her on the table. As he had rarely known her to have recourse to a vinaigrette, cordial, or other means of reviving her dampened spirits, he thought she must be sadly out of frame. His brother-in-law, seated on a chair by the fire, saw him first and jumped to his feet. "Desmond! By God, I'm glad you've come."

His sister fixed him with a look of reproach. "You certainly took your time in getting here."

"I am here now, Almeria," he said grimly. "What the devil did Jervis mean by saying Miss Winston had *disappeared*?"

"Precisely what he said, I should imagine," remarked Lady Wibberly wearily. "Her room is empty and her portmanteau is missing. The entire household is in turmoil. Eliza and Louisa are quite upset."

"Good God," said Lord Everly. "How long has she been missing?"

Lady Wibberly's glance shifted to her husband. "Since yesterday, I fear," she said at last.

"*What?*" roared Lord Everly. "Why did you not send for me before this? Did she tell no one where she was going? Did she leave no note?"

Lady Wibberly looked at her feet with uncharacteristic embarrassment.

"Tell him, Almeria," prompted her husband.

"I was . . . indisposed yesterday. I did not leave my room." She did not meet his eyes.

"I am well aware of the reason for your indisposition, Almeria," her brother told her. "Go on."

"Eliza and Louisa went to Miss Winston's room sometime late yesterday. They discovered then that she had left. They said . . . "

"Yes?"

She sighed. "They said there were two notes in her room. One was for Wibberly and me. The other was addressed to you." She hesitated.

The import of this speech was not lost on Lord Everly. "They *said* there were two notes? What happened to them?"

"The girls had some sort of a tussle trying to read 'em," said their father apologetically. "Seems one of them ripped. Little minxes knew they hadn't behaved as they ought, so they didn't say anything more about it until today." He stopped, apparently feeling no further explanation was necessary.

Lord Everly raised an eyebrow. "I promise you, I am attempting to be patient," he said in a tone which belied his words. "The—ahem!—notes, Tom?"

"Disappeared," said his brother-in-law gloomily.

"Like Miss Winston," said Lady Wibberly succinctly.

"Things seem to go missing from this house with somewhat alarming regularity," remarked Lord Everly.

"Just what I thought," agreed Lord Wibberly.

"You'll forgive the suggestion, Almeria," said Lord Everly blandly, 'but you don't think perhaps they might have, ah, concealed the evidence?"

She started to look affronted and then thought better of it. "I own I am seriously displeased by their behavior, but I believe they are telling the truth. They remember leaving the notes in Miss Winston's room, although the details, I'm afraid, are rather vague." She sighed. "They are very upset by Miss Winston's sudden departure. They were rather fond of her. Of course they know nothing whatsoever of her reasons for leaving."

Lord Everly's eyes narrowed. "And what *are* her reasons for leaving, Almeria?"

She lifted her chin. "You need not look like that. Whatever your feelings for her, you must admit that she behaved very stupidly by going to that . . . that *place* and exposing herself—and us!—to humiliation. I understand—though I cannot credit it—that she even parted in a friendly and public manner from a notorious woman of easy virtue! Is it any wonder that she was ashamed to face us afterward?"

"Can't have known what she was about," said Lord Wibberly magnanimously. "Just a girl. Just out of the school-room."

"Thank you, Tom," said Lord Everly, acknowledging his gesture. He turned to his sister. "As a matter of fact, she acted in such a generous and courageous fashion that even the Queen herself could not have faulted her behavior," he declared with sudden certainty. "If I had not been misled—no, the devil of it is I *knew* what she is, and still I acted like a fool! The truth is that there is every reason to believe that Cosmo somehow tricked her into appearing there."

"You cannot mean it!" cried Lady Wibberly. "Even *he* would not stoop so low—" She stopped, remembering that her cousin had offered to assist her in ridding herself of her unwanted guest. The thought shamed her and she colored. "Well, perhaps he would," she admitted. She raised her eyes to her brother's face. "I am so sorry, Desmond," she said.

"Always said the fellow was a loose fish," contributed her husband. "But what's to be done now?"

"Will you try to find her, Des?" inquired Lady Wibberly after several seconds of silence had slipped by. Her brother was looking unusually grim, even under the circumstances.

Lord Everly brushed a piece of imaginary lint off of his coat. "As a matter of fact, Clarissa has just spent the last hour trying to convince me that she has eloped with Byron. I didn't believe it, but now . . . "

"Stuff!" ejaculated Lord Wibberly. "Fellow's not the marrying kind!"

"Wibberly!" cried his wife in a horrified tone.

"That thought had also occurred to me," said Lord Everly, very white about the mouth. "Clarissa, I fear, was privy to our cousin's plot, if not a party to it, but she insists that Lady Caroline saw Susan getting in Byron's carriage with a portmanteau."

"When?" asked Lady Wibberly in a hushed voice.

"Late yesterday."

Lady Wibberly bowed her head in sorrow at her brother's pain. "Then it is too late. She is quite ruined." She lifted her head. "And if she *has* married him she is almost more to be pitied. I am so desperately sorry, Desmond. Perhaps if I had been kinder to her, more accepting of . . . of her future role in this family . . . she would not have been driven to throwing herself on that man's protection,."

"We will not quarrel for the greater share of the blame,

Almeria," said her brother. "She tried to tell me, but I wouldn't listen. In fact, my entire dealings with her have been at fault, from the time I approached her about becoming my wife. I assumed too much. I prevailed upon her to accept terms which must, as I shrink to recall, give disgust to a girl of sensibility. I said we need not interfere with each other," he told them. "I said it would be a marriage of convenience. It is no wonder if she has taken me in dislike and fled from the whole idea of our marriage."

"Taken you in dislike?" asked Lord Wibberly incredulously. "Whatever put a maggoty notion like that in your head? Gel's head over heels in love with you!"

"You are the best of good fellows, Tom," said Lord Everly with a wan smile, "but—"

"Oh, it's quite true," interrupted Lady Wibberly in authoritative accents. "You may take it from *me*. You know it *must* have been obvious if even Tom noticed it. At least you have been spared thinking . . . well, it is not at all like Clarissa. However, I am afraid there is nothing to be done. If she has eloped with Byron, it is far too late now for you to even consider . . . " She gave him a concerned glance. "Desmond?"

Lord Everly, who had been somewhat vacantly staring out the window, found his attention arrested. "What did you say?" he asked his sister,.

"That it is far too late for anything to be done."

"No. Before that."

Lady Wibberly considered. "That is not like Clarissa?" she suggested.

"Yes," he told her. "I mean, no, it is not." Lord Everly was granted an instant of illumination which put an end to his indecision. He had wasted so many years of his life—had become cynical, bored, and largely idle—because Clarissa had spurned him for a titled fortune, and because his mother had blamed him—wrongly, and in a moment of weakness—for his brother's death. The polite world had cast him as Childe Harold, and he had taken a perverse pleasure in giving evidence of his depravity. The stirrings of conscience and a sense of his own uselessness had led him into dangerous action under Wellington, but he had taken pains that no one should believe him capable of such feats. He had relished Society's opprobrium, knowing it to be mercenary and hypocritical, but somewhere along the way he had permitted his scorn to misdirect his life.

Now fate, or luck, or the inner promptings of his long-neglected heart had given him a second chance with Susan, and he had come very close to casting that away as well. He only hoped it was not too late to find her—in whatever circumstances!—and convince her of his regard. He would not believe that she had eloped with Byron, whatever Caroline Lamb might have seen. Perhaps she had fallen in with Byron's plan to escort Miss Milbanke to Durham, or perhaps—and here his fists clenched—the poet had abducted her in a mood of desperation! He was certainly capable of it, and had hinted as much. If it were so, not all his fame or the world's adulation could save him.. . . . Whatever the truth of it was, Susan was undeniably gone, and Lord Everly would not rest until he had discovered where she was. He got to his feet.

"Where are you going?" asked Lady Wibberly, alarmed by his expression.

The possibilities raced through his mind. The Spanish stepmother . . . Gretna Green . . . Durham . . . the mausoleum in Yorkshire . . . "North," he said decisively. "I'm going north!"

"Good boy," said Lord Wibberly with approval.

Chapter 19

Miss Winston, meanwhile, in happy ignorance of the forces that were shortly to converge upon her, was nonetheless in a rather distracted state. In one hand she carried a basin of mustard bath, in the other, a warm blanket from her own bed and a very dilapidated copy of Aristotle's *De Anima*, which gave off, despite her best efforts to clean it, a rather moldy smell. She paused before the guest room door, considering which objects she should put down on the dusty carpet in order to raise her hand to knock. Finding none of the prospects appealing, she compromised by calling faintly, "Miss Milbanke! Betty! I have brought the mustard bath."

The door was presently opened by the maid, in whose hands reposed a bowl of gruel. The maid curtsied, which caused a little of the contents to spill over onto the rug, an event Susan decided to ignore for the moment. She stepped into the room and addressed its other occupant, a fair-haired girl with intelligent blue eyes and a grave manner who was, at present, reclining on the bed of Fenwood Hall's best guest room, suffering from a hideous cold.

"How are you feeling?" inquired Susan with concern. Miss Milbanke looked feverish, and she was shivering with a chill. "I've brought you another blanket as well." She put down her parcels and went to draw the curtains across the windows, where a cold draft was leaking in around the frames.

Miss Milbanke attempted a feeble smile. "You are very good." She spotted the book Susan had set down beside her and the smile grew warmer. "And the Aristotle, too, I see. How very kind of you to get it for me."

"I'm afraid it is not in very good condition," replied Susan apologetically. "Fenwood Hall's library is sadly neglected, I fear."

Miss Milbanke nodded serenely. "It is of no consequence.

Presently I shall quite lose myself in the words, and forget all about anything else. It is always so."

"Would you not prefer something less . . . difficult?" asked Susan in surprise. "I should think that given your illness, it would make your head ache!"

Miss Milbanke regarded her blankly. "Difficult?"

Susan smiled. "For me, at least. You are very learned, Miss Milbanke."

Miss Milbanke coughed but said benignly, "I have been fortunate in my teachers."

Susan found her guest rather unnerving. When Byron had said he was escorting a party of friends to Durham, she had not realized that Miss Milbanke was Lady Melbourne's niece. More unsettling than her rank and fortune were her piety—which Susan applauded in principle but could not help but feel would be made more appealing by a certain leavening, at least in ordinary conversation—and her learning, which was of a ponderous sort designed to kill even the best-intentioned efforts at communication. Miss Milbanke's gravity of manner must have made the Archbishop of Canterbury seem given over to frivolity and riotous living.

"Where is Byron?" inquired this paragon, interrupting Susan's train of thought. "Is he composing a poem? He promised me that he would, without further delay." She sighed. "He is very gifted, you know, but a trifle undisciplined. He looks to his friends to inspire him to do that which he knows already in his heart and mind that he must."

Susan knew for certain that Lord Byron was out riding, for she had seen him herself on his way to the stables. Since Miss Milbanke's illness had forced their party to break their journey with an unexpected stay of some days at Fenwood Hall, the poet's attendance upon the sickroom had been somewhat erratic, at best. His attentions mainly took the form of floral tributes culled from the Hall's faded and overgrown knot garden, and little notes sent up on Miss Milbanke's tray which caused her to smile slightly, folding them and preserving them in a wooden box she kept beside her bedside. If his absence from the sickroom itself troubled her, she gave no hint of it and merely indicated that she was glad to see that he was getting on with his writing. It was apparent to Susan that such behavior might not be considered devoted in one who hoped to call himself, in time, Miss Milbanke's husband, but his inamorata seemed to find his genius reason enough to excuse him from the common civilities.

Susan found herself torn between irritation and amusement at Byron's behavior, and was surprised that so learned a person as Miss Milbanke could be taken in by him. She herself had been acutely embarrassed by his behavior toward Cousin William and her great aunt. It was apparent that he misunderstood her position here completely, and, so far from regarding himself and his party as a nuisance—in light of the rundown condition, shorthandedness, and scant accommodations at the Hall—seemed rather to act as if he were conferring the greatest of favors on all of them by his presence.

Cousin William, willing enough to receive her once more into his house as the caretaker for his mother, was less welcoming toward the party she brought with her, for whom suitable bedchambers must be arranged, and who, it developed, expected considerably more lavish entertainment than the house customarily afforded. The daily diminishment of his larders and his wine cellar gave Lord Harrington little cause for enjoyment, despite Miss Winston's assurances that his guests were not only respectable, but persons of some fame. As he did not hold much with poetry himself, these arguments did little to soften his resistance, and he grew steadily more peevish as the days progressed. Susan watched Miss Milbanke hopefully for signs of recovery, and did all she could to hasten that desirable event. Her only consolation in the accelerating tensions the situation afforded was that there was no time to dwell, as she otherwise might have done, on the unhappy events that had brought her here in the first place.

A knock on the door cut short these reflections. The butler, wheezing from the exertion of climbing the stairs and navigating the hall, stood propped against the door frame, his hand to his heart.

"What is it, Fribble?" she inquired, worried lest she might have two patients on her hands. "You should not have come yourself."

"There is no one else, miss," intoned this personage lugubriously, when his heart had settled in his chest again. "The master sent me to remind you that it is time for her ladyship's afternoon airing," he said.

Susan was chagrined that her tardiness had forced him into what was clearly, for him, an unnatural degree of exercise.

"Do go, Miss Winston," said Miss Milbanke generously. "I shall be quite all right alone with my book."

And your personal maid, thought Susan, and then chided herself for lack of charity. Betty gave herself airs and would not wait upon any but Miss Milbanke, despite the woefully apparent inability of the Hall's staff to rise to the occasion of Visitors.

"Thank you," she said dryly. "I shall be back in an hour or so to see if you need anything further."

Miss Milbanke, her aquiline nose already buried in the Aristotle, did not reply.

Lady Harrington's daily "outing" had thus far consisted of an hour spent in a chair overlooking the same prospect where Lord Everly had first asked Susan to become his wife. She said very little and often appeared to be dozing, so that Susan could not be sure how much she really comprehended of what was going on about her. As before, Susan sometimes had the unsettling feeling that some of her great aunt's "senility" was feigned out of mischief, but that was merely a suspicion. In all events she was grateful that Lady Harrington's presence for an hour was so undemanding, as it was almost the only leisure that she had for contemplation. Unfortunately, just at the moment there was almost no subject she could turn her thoughts to which did not occasion her some pain, so she attempted to read a novel instead.

Despite her resolution to keep herself so occupied she had no time to dwell on what, for lack of a less fanciful expression, could only be termed her broken heart, her visit to this particular spot could not help awakening her feelings and memories, as well as exciting certain resolutions about her future. It seemed such a long time ago that Lord Everly had smiled at her, and called her his friend. *That is not such a small thing, and very much more comfortable than scenes and tears and all the other accompaniments of an affair of passion, I promise you,* he had told her. How ironic that, in the end, both of them had preferred passion to friendship after all! The only problem was, Lord Everly's passion had not been for her. . . .

Her one consolation was that she was free once more to make her own life, even in the straitened circumstances in which she now lived. At least she would not have to move in Society, with its topsy-turvy values and ideals, where courtesans were more honorable than countesses, and the greatest military hero of the age could not enter a party because his attire was deemed inappropriate! Here, at least, she would not be ruined because she had dared to waltz without permission or had taken the wrong carriage home. Society reserved its ostracism for those who broke its pettiest of rules; those who broke them in a spectacular and self-centered fashion, like Lord Byron and Lady Caroline Lamb, were just as likely to become the Rage. Susan had always suspected she was unsuited for such a life, and now she was sure of it. Whatever befell her here in Yorkshire, General Winston's daughter would make the best of it, and on her own terms!

She put down the book she had been attempting, without success, to read, and found Lord Byron regarding her with amusement. "Shall I put you in a poem?" he said, with a lurking smile.

She laughed. "I hope not!"

"Man's love is of man's life a thing apart, 'Tis woman's whole existence. . . ."

Her cheeks colored and then she smiled. "That's romantic nonsense," she told him. "It's no such thing."

"What, a cynic so young, Miss Winston?" He gave a mock sigh and seated himself on the grass before her. "Have you become jaded in the ways of love already?"

"I thought you had gone riding," she told him, ignoring the taunt.

He grinned mischievously. "I did, but the poem overtook me," he said in such a flippant tone that she could not tell whether he was serious or not.

"Miss Milbanke said you would be working," said Susan, turning the subject.

He sighed. "Sometimes Annabella does get it right. How is the Princess of Parallelograms today?"

"For shame, my lord! You should not speak of her that way," chided Susan, suppressing a smile.

Byron sucked a blade of grass thoughtfully. "My intentions are quite honorable, you know."

"All the more reason."

"Perhaps. I know she is too good for me, but I find her interest in improving me utterly irresistible. You will forgive me, I know, if—just occasionally—I find the burden of so much *worthiness* a trifle difficult to bear without resorting to an unbecoming levity."

Susan, who had often been accused the same thing, could not help laughing.

"You see?" he challenged her.

"She is a little better, I think," said Susan, ignoring him, "though still quite afflicted. I left her reading Aristotle."

"Good God," Byron said, but Susan could hear the unmistakable note of pride his voice held.

"I am sure that a visit from you would do much toward elevating her spirits," suggested Susan.

"That is a far from subtle hint that I have been neglecting my duty," said Byron. "Alas, it is true. I am not at my best in the sickroom. Indeed—"

"I see somebody," interrupted Lady Harrington in a singsong voice. Her words startled them, as they had almost forgotten her presence. Susan glanced out over the distant view and saw that there was, indeed, a carriage coming up the road. She heard Byron's quick intake of breath and got to her feet. "I wonder who . . . ?" she started to say.

"I see somebody," said her great aunt again, casting off her blanket and rubbing her hands together in childish glee.

Susan picked it up again and tucked it around her, for despite the nearness of summer the air had a slight chill. "Indeed, ma'am, there is a carriage coming up the drive. Would you like to go in?"

Her great aunt unmistakably shook her head. Susan watched the carriage drive past the front of the house and pull up at the end of the path on which she stood. A figure alighted. Her eyes widened and she turned around in search of Byron.

He had disappeared.

Furious at this desertion in her hour of need, she squared her shoulders and stepped forward to greet the new arrival, leaving Lady Harrington behind in her chair. She did not know what was about to be said, but she did not want to expose the old lady to any unnecessary unpleasantness.

The figure accelerated toward her. "Where is he?"

Susan sighed. "Good afternoon, Lady Caroline."

Lady Caroline looked at her assessingly. "I followed you from London, you know, but I lost the trail. I have been to Gretna Green," she said triumphantly, "but you were not there! It is only with the greatest of difficulty that I learned where you were."

"No, of course I was not there," said Susan, attempting to keep her temper.

"Then you are not married?" inquired Lady Caroline in an exultant tone.

"I am not," said Susan steadily, "but—"

"Where is he? Where is Lord Byron?" interrupted Lady Caroline in frozen accents. "You need not stoop to dissemble. You cannot deny, surely, that he is here. I fancy you did not expect to see *me* in such a place as this, but it will avail you nothing to try to hide him."

Despite her irritation, Susan almost giggled at the absurd theatricality of this scene. "Lady Caroline, I am not *hiding* anyone," she began with a smile.

Two spots of color appeared in Lady Caroline's cheeks. "Miss Winston, this levity will not serve. Are you lost to every scruple of female delicacy? You may think to trap him but he will not marry you *now*," she added, with a flourish worthy of the stage.

Susan struggled to control her rising sense of hysteria. Despite the ugliness of the accusation, it was too ridiculous to merit her anger. Besides, the thought of Lady Caroline accusing her of indelicacy threatened to send her off into the giggles again. She collected herself. "Lady Caroline, you are laboring under a misapprehension," she said in a soothing voice. "I do not know how you came by the impression that—"

"I saw you. I saw you climb into the carriage with *him*. Do you deny it?"

"No, but—"

"Aha!" Her eyes shifted beyond Susan to where Lady Harrington stirred in her chair. "Who is that person?" she demanded. "I must know who that person is."

Susan sighed. "That is my great aunt, Lady Harrington," she told Lady Caroline. "This is her house."

Lady Caroline strode forward decisively, apparently affected by this information in some purposeful fashion. She planted herself in front of chair and said firmly, "How do you do, ma'am? You will forgive me dispensing with the civilities, I am sure. I make my appeal directly to you, ma'am, since Miss Winston refuses to tell me what I wish to know."

"My great aunt—" Susan began to explain.

Lady Caroline cut her off. "Where *is* Byron, Lady Harrington? I have come all the way from London just to see him. If he sends me away I shall go, but I must at least see him."

Lady Harrington cackled.

"You refuse me?" said Lady Caroline dramatically. "I shall die if I do not, I promise you."

"Saucebox," said Lady Harrington with devastating clarity. "Are you dicked in the nob?"

Lady Caroline took a step backward. "I fear I may be," she said in an interested tone, "but I do not care."

"I saw something nasty in the barn," confided Lady Harrington. "Perhaps he is in there."

"Oh no, Aunt Harrington," said Susan, recalling the gist of this speech from her previous visit. "Lady Caroline—" she called, but her ladyship had already walked off in search of this promising structure. Her great aunt cackled again.

Susan felt a giddy sense that events were spinning out of control. What would Lady Caroline do when she found out about Miss Milbanke? At least it might have the effect of ridding the house of her unwanted visitors, so perhaps she should encourage the discovery! She took an indecisive step in the direction of the house when Byron stepped out of a copse of trees and walked over to her.

"Is she gone?" he whispered.

"For the moment," she said, rounding on him with something akin to disgust. A soldier's daughter, she knew cowardice when she saw it. "I'm afraid she has gone off to look for you! Why did you leave me to face her all alone?"

Lord Byron ignored this inconvenient question. "Does she know about Annabella yet?"

"Not yet. But it may be only a matter of moments before she finds out."

"Listen to me, Miss Winston, Susan! She must not be allowed to learn of my intentions. Miss Milbanke is on the point of agreeing to our betrothal, and Caro must not be permitted to spoil it. You must find her at once, and tell her I have departed for Newstead Abbey this very morning. That will keep her occupied for a few days at least, and give Annabella time to recover enough to resume our journey to Durham. You must do this for me, Miss Winston!" He grabbed her hand and kissed it. "I am a desperate man!"

Susan attempted to wrest her hand away without success. "If I had an ounce of compassion for Miss Milbanke I would make her privy to what has gone on here today," she protested. "I do not believe I should *help* you at all!"

Byron laughed madly and fell to his knees. "I shall make you yield to my entreaty," he said, his eyes glittering. "Dearest, kindest, most generous Susan, will you not—" He broke off suddenly. "Damnation!" he cried.

Susan's eyes followed the direction of his gaze. For the second time in the space of half an hour, her heart turned over in her mouth.

Across the lawn, looking at her with an expression she hoped never to see again in her life, was Lord Everly.

Chapter 20

L ord Everly felt his last hope shrivel in his heart, leaving dry dust in its stead. Every instinct told him to run, to admit he had been a fool (again!) and fly without delay from the scene of his humiliation. Byron's laugh as he bent over Susan's hand, his falling to his knees, could only mean one thing. He turned on his heel.

Susan's voice stopped him. He stood suspended for a moment and then turned around again. He was being a coward. If she had chosen Byron, for whatever reason, he *owed* it to her at least to make sure that the poet behaved honorably toward her. He schooled his face into an expression of bored indifference and walked across the lawn to where they were standing.

"Now we *are* in the basket," muttered Byron as he approached. "Why did you call him back? We shall never keep the truth from Caro now!"

"Don't you ever think of anything but yourself?" hissed Susan furiously. Just at the moment, she found his utter selfishness maddening.

Byron grinned. "No," he confessed. He shrugged. "Welcome, Everly. What brings you here?"

"The well-being of my ward, of course," drawled Lord Everly in a bored tone. He could not bring himself to look at Susan directly, so he continued to address Lord Byron. "I take it I may offer you my congratulations?"

"Why, thank you," asked Byron, surprised that Lord Everly took such an interest in his relations with Miss Milbanke. "It is not quite settled between us yet, but I have every hope of bringing it off before long."

Susan stood baffled and hurt by his refusal to even speak to her or meet her eyes. Her heart had leapt at the sight of him and her guess at what his presence must mean, but now he was confounding her with his apparent indifference. Her heart twisted. If she did not do something soon, she would lose him forever without a struggle. "Lord Everly!"

His eyes slid to hers, and she read the pain there. She reached out a hand to him.

He half turned from her. "Your pardon, ma'am. I have not yet wished you joy."

"Wished me . . . ?" Comprehension dawned. "Oh *no*." Relief flooded her and she laughed, almost giddily. "Desmond, for heaven's sake! You are as bad as Lady Caroline!"

Byron grinned. "I feel I shall shortly be in the way. Now, I wonder where I can hide?" he said, turning round. "I have it! I shall take your great aunt for a stroll in the woods, Miss Winston. Little Mania will never look for me there. Everly, your servant. Miss Winston, do your possible, for pity's sake, or I am lost." He walked over to where Lady Harrington sat regarding him with a mischievous gleam in her eye.

"Scapegrace," she told him.

"Indeed, ma'am." He extended his arm to her, helping her to stand. "You have never fooled me, you know," he told her.

"Humph!" she said, taking his arm.

Susan watched in amazement. "She went with him," she said wonderingly.

Lord Everly wheeled her around to face him. "What the devil is going on here?" he said in unloverlike accents.

Susan was not deceived. "Oh, Desmond," she said, by way of explanation, and he caught her up in his arms, kissing her ruthlessly.

She was agreeably surprised to discover that the experience was every bit as pleasant as she had imagined it might be, and that he did not act at all like a man who was assuming a disagreeable burden while his heart was pledged to another. She wanted to ask him about Clarissa, but she was in no hurry. Some time passed before the conversation resumed.

"You are not, I take it, betrothed to Byron," he inquired at length, with a shaky laugh.

"Of course not. He is here with Miss Milbanke, who has a cold." She paused "I tried to explain in my note that I . . . "

"Do not tell me! I have been a fool! In any case, it was mislaid, so I never read it."

Susan let out a relieved breath. "I am glad you didn't. You

are not betrothed to the countess?" she asked in a teasing voice she would have thought impossible only an hour ago.

He responded in a way that was quite a bit more satisfactory than words. "Clarissa need not trouble either of us again," he said presently. "Nor Cosmo, at least for a very long time." He sketched for her what he had learned about the incident at the Cyprians' Ball, which now seemed a long way away and quite unimportant.

"Well, I am sorry since he is your cousin, Desmond, but I fear he is the most odious bounder alive. I think he drugged me! I hope I may never lay eyes on him again."

"That is an opinion shared by all of his relatives," remarked Lord Everly. "At least we will not have to have him at the wedding."

"The wedding?" inquired Susan, suddenly shy.

He lifted her chin with his fingers. There was an expression in his eyes that brought the color rushing to her cheeks. "Yes, if you can forgive me for not knowing my own mind soon enough to tell you that I love you with all my heart. I think I must have ever since I first saw you with that ridiculous owl."

The mention of Minnie intruded into her reverie and reminded her of the barn, which in turn reminded her of the presence of Lady Caroline, still, presumably, roaming the house and grounds in search of Byron. She held him off a little, her hands against his chest. "I forgot to tell you that Lady Caroline is here," she said.

He looked at her with undisguised horror. "Good God!"

"She . . . she followed Byron here. She thinks I am hiding him from her! He wants me to tell her that he has left for Newstead Abbey. Oh, Desmond, she doesn't know that Miss Milbanke is staying here! I do not know what she may do when she learns the truth, but from what I have seen this afternoon I would not put a great deal past her," she told him.

"I do not intend to wait to find out," he said grimly. "We are leaving here at once!"

She laughed. "You cannot mean it! I couldn't leave Cousin William to cope with having all these dreadful people here tonight. Especially when it is mostly my fault!"

"I am of the opinion that Lord Harrington richly deserves whatever difficulties may come his way," said his lordship vehemently, tugging on her hand. "Besides, can you really envision sitting down to dinner with such an ill-assorted group? It doesn't bear thinking of."

"Well—" began Susan, tempted. "Oh dear, I fear it is already too late."

Indeed, Lady Caroline was coming toward them across the lawn, her spirits visibly drooping. She moved slowly and her eyes were cast down. She raised a hand to her brow dramatically. "I have had a sign," she intoned in thrilling accents. "My death is not far off."

Susan stared at her openmouthed. "I—I beg your pardon?" she said politely.

"It is unmistakable, I'm afraid," said Lady Caroline sadly. "I saw it."

"Saw what, Caroline?" asked Lord Everly, amused and exasperated.

"The messenger. It flew at me out of the darkness and circled my head. And then"—she disclosed in an awed whisper—"it *shrieked* like a banshee."

"I collect the Malaga eagle has made another timely appearance," said Lord Everly to Miss Winston with admirable gravity.

"It was *not* an eagle," insisted Lady Caroline hysterically. "I cannot think why you would say such a thing. It was meant as a sign for me, I tell you."

"Lady Caroline—" began Susan.

Lord Everly laid a restraining hand on her arm. "I think you have had a bad shock, Caroline. No doubt you would feel less . . . pessimistic were you to retire and rest."

"You are naturally anxious to be rid of me," said her ladyship. She studied Lord Everly as if seeing him for the first time. "What are *you* doing here, Desmond?"

He raised an eyebrow. "Not that it is any of your concern, Caroline, but I have come to marry Miss Winston."

Lady Caroline stiffened. "Does *everyone* want to marry her?"

"I am only prepared to speak for myself," said Lord Everly, his eyes gleaming with amusement.

Lady Caroline turned an assessing gaze on Susan. "Are you going to marry him?"

"I . . . " She looked up at Lord Everly. "Yes."

He squeezed her hand. "As a matter of fact, we were in the process of settling the issue when you approached, Caro," hinted Lord Everly.

Lady Caroline ignored him. "What about Byron?" she demanded of Susan.

"I assure your ladyship that I have never had the least desire to marry Lord Byron, nor he me," Susan told her.

Lady Caroline sighed. "And do you promise me that you do not, at this moment, know where he is?"

Lord Everly squeezed her hand so hard she almost winced. Susan considered, squared it with her conscience by means of an extremely literal interpretation of the truth, and answered. "I do not at this moment know where he is," she said.

"Did he not escort you here some days ago?" Lady Caroline persisted.

"Yes, he did."

Lady Caroline's eyes narrowed with displeasure. "Perhaps he is at Newstead, then, after all. I take my leave of you, Miss Winston. I consider that you are gravely at fault in this. I am seriously upset."

"I see," said Susan dryly. "Perhaps, then, I can relieve your mind of one of its concerns."

Lady Caroline regarded her with dislike. "Yes?"

"The . . . ah . . . messenger in the barn."

Lord Everly gave a little cough.

"It was not a harbinger of death," said Susan.

"Was it not?" asked Lady Caroline, sounding almost disappointed. "What was it then?"

Susan lowered her voice. "Well, I can't say for sure, of course, but I think it might have been Great Uncle Matthew."

Lord Everly appeared to have been severely afflicted with respiratory difficulties, which necessitated his turning away.

"Great Uncle Matthew?" inquired Lady Caroline in a suspicious tone.

"Yes, he was excessively bookish and most particularly disliked being interrupted when he was reading. I am told he often took refuge in the barn and would fly out at anyone who disturbed him," Susan said with, as it happened, perfect truth. "He died 10 years ago."

Lady Caroline fixed her with a stony gaze. "I send no compliments to your great aunt, Miss Winston. She deliberately misled me."

"She—she wanders in her mind," Susan told her, hanging on to her gravity with some difficulty.

"Does she?" inquired Lady Caroline in a surprised tone. "She seemed perfectly sane to me."

Susan could not think of anything to reply to this.

Lady Caroline looked at Lord Everly. "I suppose I must wish you happy," she said.

"Caroline, the only thing you must do is go away," he told her. "I hope you do not think me uncivil, but at the moment you are a trifle—let us say—de trop.

Unexpectedly, she smiled. "I am always de trop. I'll be off then."

"Where were we?" inquired Lord Everly of Miss Winston when she had gone. He took her up in his arms and crushed her to his chest. "Here, I think," he said.

She held him off with her hands before he could kiss her again. "Desmond, wait!"

He looked down at her searchingly with a queer, twisted smile. "Second thoughts already, my love?"

"No! I . . . that is, Desmond, are you perfectly sure you want to marry me?"

"Oh, is that all?" he said with a shaky laugh, preparing to clasp her in his arms again.

"I am serious, Desmond!" she protested. "I—I think Almack's is excessively silly."

"Excessively," agreed his lordship, looking into her eyes in a manner that made her feel a little unsteady on her feet.

"And I don't intend to ask permission to waltz or pretend I don't like books or paintings ever again," she confided anxiously.

"You should be as bookish as Great Uncle Matthew, and fly out at me whenever I interrupt you," he said with a smile. "And we shall have Minnie and a whole parliament of owls if you want them! Now are you convinced?"

"There is one thing more," she told him, determined to make him aware of the extent of her rebellion.

"I tremble to hear it," said Lord Everly, looking not at all discomposed.

"I *like* Barbara Tremayne,"she said, producing her most shocking iniquity for his inspection.

He laughed aloud and possessed himself of her hands. "As a matter of fact, so do I," he told her. "Susan, my foolish little love, have I not told you that the conventions of what the bored and idle are pleased to call Polite Society do not interest me in the slightest? I would be perfectly pleased to consign the world to the devil and live in a tent in Arabia, so long as you are there with me! Will that content you?"

"Yes," she said mistily.

"Excellent," he said firmly and kissed her again.

Lord Byron, stumbling on this scene with Lady Harrington on his arm, checked his steps. He smiled.

Lady Harrington sniffed. "Persons in the throes of excessive emotion are quite vulgar," she said. She looked up at Byron. "Take me into the house, young man. I want my tea."

Afterword

George Gordon, Lord Byron, married Annabella Milbanke in 1815. The marriage was not a happy one, and Annabella returned to her father's protection one month after their child, August Ada, was born (1816). Byron left England in 1816, never to return. He died in Missolonghi, Greece, of malaria in 1824. Lady Caroline Lamb revenged herself on the poet by publishing the novel *Glenarvon*, in which the central character, a murderer and seducer much given to melancholy, is a thinly veiled portrait of Byron himself. Annabella and Lady Melbourne also figure prominently in the work in an unflattering light, and her husband's family attempted to suppress publication. Lady Caroline is said to have become permanently deranged after encountering Byron's funeral procession. She died in 1828.